EDWARD JAMES is rather lik
Richard Hakluyt; neither of
fascinated by ships and seafa
blames it on growing up besic
the big ships still came up rive

    After taking a history deg.... at Oxford, Edward initially became a university lecturer in Britain and America teaching social policy, and later a civil servant in what is now the Department of Work and Pensions in London. After a stint at the European Commission in Brussels he moved on to become an independent consultant on social security to governments as diverse as Russia, Kyrghystan and Albania. On retiring to Cheltenham he went back to history as a Review Editor for the Historical Novel Society and to writing about ships and the sea in the Age of Discovery. You can find out more about him, including a selection of his short stories and interviews, on his blog busywords.wordpress.com.

Winner of the Kobo-SilverWood Writing Competition

To celebrate their 2014 Writing & Self-Publishing Open Day, SilverWood Books announced an exciting new writing competition in association with Kobo Writing Life.

The first Open Day Writing Competition welcomed unpublished (or self-published) fiction. First Prize was a paperback and digital publishing deal. The Runner Up received a brand new Kobo Aura H_2O e-reader.

The standard of entries was extremely high and the judges were delighted to discover a high standard of writing and a wide range of compelling stories. SilverWood's Publishing Director Helen Hart says, "It was a challenge to select a winner, however Edward James's manuscript *The Frozen Dream* ultimately triumphed with its intricate blend of action, romance, intrigue, and atmospheric historical detail."

Runner Up was Sarah Channing-Wright with *The Angels of Islington*.

The Frozen Dream

EDWARD JAMES

To Karen

Happy Reading

Edward James

SilverWood

Published in 2015 by SilverWood Books

SilverWood Books Ltd
14 Small Street, Bristol, BS1 1DE, United Kingdom
www.silverwoodbooks.co.uk

ISBN 978-1-78132-426-4 (paperback)
ISBN 978-1-78132-427-1 (ebook)

British Library Cataloguing in Publication Data
A CIP catalogue record for this book is available from
the British Library

Set in Adobe Garamond Pro by SilverWood Books
Printed by Imprint Digital on responsibly sourced paper

Contents

Prologue

It is the middle of the night. The sun has set six weeks ago and will rise in another six.

The three-month winter night in Lapland is seldom completely dark. The never-setting moon silvers the snow of the high fells and the Northern Lights trail curtains of pink and purple flame among the frost-bright stars.

It is darker below the cliffs in the bay. Two graceless ships, almost as broad as they are long, sit upon the land-fast ice in the shadows. The topmasts have been taken down and the sails and spars now form a canopy over the main deck between the fore and stern castles. No lights shine. Nothing stirs. There is no watch on deck, yet the ships are not deserted.

There are no common sailors aboard, although some of their bodies lie stacked on the scree at the foot of the cliff, for the ground has frozen too hard to bury them. Admiral Sir Hugh Willoughby sits in his stateroom at the head of his table and his officers are at their places – all bar one whose chair is upturned and who lies sprawled by the door. The wine is poured but the meal lies unfinished; every man is quite dead. They have perished between courses. Their frozen, uncorrupted corpses await the daylight and the thaw.

When the ships and their ghastly complement are found it will be assumed that the officers have died of cold in some strange, instantaneous fashion while overwintering in the Arctic. The official record will note that they died "twixt cup and lip', a theory nobody dares question. The fate of the men will not be recorded.

And so the Bona Esperanza and the Bona Confidenzia sail out of history, leaving the Edward Bonaventura, which left the Thames with them seven months before, to sail on alone to make its mark on history.

Part 1

1

Whither But Cathay?

The hall was scented with wood smoke and despair.

The Great Hall at Penshurst Place had been built before the days of chimneys and fireplaces. The only warmth to fend off the autumn chill came from an open fire, blazing on a stone slab set in the middle of the hall. The smoke drifted lazily to the roof beams high above, to seep out under the eaves, lifting with it the chatter of rich men and women complaining of hard times. If only they knew real despair, thought Kate.

'Pardon my asking,' said the woman next to Kate, edging closer along the bench and putting her face close to Kate's ear, to be heard above the hubbub, 'but you seem much younger than the other ladies here – and prettier, too, I should add. Do you have money of your own to put into Sir Henry's venture? Are you a widow?'

Kate looked around and counted five women among about thirty men. They all looked older than her, but it was difficult to tell their ages, for they all dressed much the same; good quality cloth in long, loose, old-fashioned styles and sober colours, mostly black (the most expensive dye). City merchants trying to look rich and prudent, thought Kate. She was dressed much the same herself. They reminded her of a flock of crows cawing around a ploughshare.

She was minded not to answer her inquisitive neighbour, but she was lonely for all that Sir John was only inches away on her left, deep in a heated conversation with some other merchants.

Also, she could not afford to offend any of his friends.

'To answer your second question first, my lady, I am indeed a widow. I lost my William four years since, in the year of the sweating sickness. We had been married nine months.' Tears pricked at her eyes and she fought to hold them back. 'As for money, I have none, although I have a trading house in London with twenty servants who look to me for a living.'

'That must have been hard for you, left to manage on your own and you so young.'

'Not so hard. My servants are very able and they do the work. We managed well enough until last year, when everything in England went mad. Now nobody wants to lend money any more, at least not to a small enterprise like mine, and if we can't borrow money how can we pay for the wool to take to our weavers? And then this year the Cloth Fleet didn't sail.' She could feel the tears once again.

'I know, I know. I'm a widow myself. I lost two husbands, although luckily they were both quite rich. My name is Mary, Lady Mary Knollys. And you are?'

'Kate Thomas.'

'I'm in the cloth trade too, Kate. I dare say most of us here are. What cloth do you deal in?'

'Kerseys, from Suffolk.'

'Ah, the heavy, rough stuff. I deal in finer cloth myself. Like you I send it to Antwerp with the Cloth Fleet, or I did until this year. Now it's rotting in a warehouse by the Thames. I blame the German emperor,' she added, warming to her theme. 'He's the king of Spain too, so why did he let Spain fail to honour her debts? You'd think that with all that silver coming from the Indies they wouldn't have any problems, but no, they spend it all before it arrives. Europe is in a worse state than England. Sir Henry is right. We must find somewhere else to sell our cloth! But tell me, if you have no money to invest, why are you here?'

'I came with Sir John.' Kate nodded toward his white-haired

bulk beside her. 'He asked me to ride down through Kent with him and meet his friends.'

'You mean to show off the pretty wench he's found for himself. I know the old devil.' Lady Mary put her mouth closer to Kate's ear. 'Keep with it, Kate! John knows how to make money and you stand to inherit the richest fortune in the city.'

Kate blushed. This was entirely the reason she was here.

'With your looks,' continued Lady Mary, 'you could have the pick of any rich widower in London. But beauty doesn't last. Invest it while you can.'

'I'll do my best,' murmured Kate.

'Have you been to court?' asked Mary. 'Have you seen Princess Elizabeth?'

'I've never been to court.'

'No, of course, you wouldn't have done. Well, the young king's sister is the very image of yourself – the same fair skin and lovely red hair. It's a pity the king isn't so healthy. They say he's very poorly.'

'Did I hear you two ladies talking about the king?' said Sir John, turning towards them. 'Gerald here has a lady friend who serves in the king's bedchamber and he says she tells him that Edward's been coughing blood.'

''Tis true,' said Gerald, a big, plump man with a short grey beard, 'and I shudder to think what will happen should he die. There's only Mary and Elizabeth in the succession and I can't imagine a woman running England in the state we're in now. The nobles will start fighting for the crown, like in my grandfather's day. Did I tell you he was killed at Bosworth Field?'

'You did,' said John. 'Several times. But it's not the nobles who worry me. It's the peasants. Another harvest like the last and they'll attack London, like they did Norwich. You and I will have our throats cut and Kate here will be raped by a gang of Kentish yokels.'

Kate shuddered. John could be coarse-mouthed at times.

'The peasants aren't a problem,' insisted Gerald. 'After all, they didn't hold Norwich. They camped outside the place until they were scattered and the ringleaders were hanged. They always go home after a bit of rioting. It's our high-born betters who'll be the ruin of us.'

'Fie on you all!' exclaimed Mary. 'If you had such little faith in England you'd be burying your silver, not coming all the way through the Kentish mud to invest it. I'm sure Sir Henry has a plan to save us. And here he is! Doesn't he have fine legs?'

Indeed he had. Sir Henry Sydney strode down the hall, flaunting his long, strong limbs, dressed in the latest Italian fashion: a scarlet and gold doublet, short breeches and red stockings. He mounted the dais at the end of the hall, followed by six other men, to open the meeting.

The dais was crowded.

'Do you know these people?' whispered Kate.

'That one,' replied John, 'the older man with the oaken face, is Richard Chancellor, Sir Henry's brother by adoption.'

'He doesn't look like an aristocrat.'

'He's the seaman who led the Turkey voyage. A real seaman, who gets further than the taverns of Antwerp. I imagine he'll lead our venture.'

'If he's to be captain, can I be cabin boy?'

She knew John liked her to be skittish, but she really would have preferred him to be a little more like Richard Chancellor. He was a man to make any woman's heart jump.

'I can't imagine you at sea, Kate!'

'Indeed, I have been to Antwerp with the Cloth Fleet, which, as you say, is as far as most English mariners ever go. I had a cabin boy too, a sturdy lad. Had it been a longer voyage I might have been tempted.'

John moved closer. 'Enough wantonness, Kate. You're a respectable widow.'

'Very well, I'll behave. Who's the military-looking man?'

'Sharp wench. That's Sir Hugh Willoughby, the one who burned Edinburgh two years back and the nearest England has to a war hero. God knows why we need a soldier on a merchant venture.'

'And the others? The old man with the big, white beard and the sinister, young one all in black? What an odd company! And what's under those velvet covers?'

Sir Henry lifted his hand and the assembly fell silent.

Sir Henry looked hot. His face was as red as his stockings, either from the heat, the wine or the excitement.

'Ladies, gentlemen, dear friends, I am honoured that so many of you have ridden down from London to be my guests and I am sure you will find the journey more than worthwhile. I am confident that you will join with me in a venture to save this realm of England from its manifold ills, to restore its riches and to bring it back to its true greatness among the nations of Christendom. A venture bolder than any out of England these past fifty years, which will make the vaunted ventures of the Spaniards and the Portuguese to the Indies seem but preludes to our grand design.'

'Sounds risky,' whispered Kate.

'If England could export empty talk, we'd be ne'er so rich,' grunted Sir John.

If Sir Henry heard the mutters of disrespect he ignored them. 'Tomorrow I will show you the plans for my house and garden, to turn this old-fashioned pile my father left me into a splendid mansion, which will be paid for from the return on my share of the venture which I now set before you. But first, to the content. Have any of you seen the like of these?' He turned and, with a flourish, tumbled the velvet covers from two large spheres suspended in wooden cradles.

Nobody ventured a word.

'Do I hear someone say two celestial globes to chart the movement of the stars? You are mistaken. Globes such as these have never yet been made in England. They come from the university at Louvain, home to the greatest cosmographers and cartographers of our age. It is England's shame that I have had to seek them on the Continent, but I accept the hardships on your behalf.' He smiled archly, hinting that he had other tastes to satisfy beyond the Channel.

There was no response. The audience began to fidget.

'To our great shame,' he hurried on, 'we left these arts to the Flemings and Spaniards, just as we no longer build great ships to sail the oceans. But see, I have brought these arts back to England! Their greatest practitioners sit before you. And, with your help, we will again build great ships to sail distant oceans and give work to the workless of London who feed upon the poor rate. Only thus…'

Kate sensed an indiscretion hover on Sir Henry's tongue. Would he dare speak out against the Emperor Charles, whose ever-growing sprawl of kingdoms and principalities reached across Europe from Hungary to Spain? But no, Sir Henry was giving no hostages to fortune. If Princess Mary succeeded her dying brother, as Kate fervently hoped she would, and if she were to marry the emperor's son, Philip of Spain, as was rumoured, it could be mere months before England was part of that empire.

'Only thus will England prosper,' he concluded, lamely.

'Why should we need great ships when the oceans of the world are closed against us?' called one of the older merchants.

'Aye,' called another. 'Enough of toys and fine words! Whither are we bound?'

'Whither? Whither but Cathay?'

Even the clock seemed to halt in astonishment and the crackling fire held its breath. The audience would have been less astounded had Sir Henry proposed a voyage to the stars.

Mary Knollys broke the stillness.

'You mean Marco Polo's Cathay, like in the *Marvels*? But wasn't that written three hundred years ago? Is it all true? There really is a marvellous land on the other side of the world that makes us all look like savages?'

'More or less,' Sir Henry replied with a smile. 'No European

16

has followed the silk road across the deserts to Cathay since Marco, for the Turks bar the route, and we cannot be sure if the Spaniards and Portuguese have found a way by sea, as they claim. But, wait, I have yet to show you the globes from Louvain, the heart and secret of our venture. Let the master at whose feet I sat in Paris explain them to you. I give you the most learned man in Christendom, despite his youth: Dr John Dee.'

The young man in black stepped forward, the learned scholar to the point of parody. His black gown trailed the floor and his sleek black hair trailed his shoulders. A close-trimmed black beard supported a pallid face topped by a high white brow lit by glittering dark eyes. Had he been old and female, thought Kate, he would have been hanged as a witch. He advanced on the two globes with a pair of large wooden dividers, like God at Creation.

Dr Dee opened his mouth and instead of the French or Flemish accent that Kate expected, out came a lilting, Welsh voice. 'Sir Henry flatters me, but I will do my poor best, ladies and gentlemen. These globes are indeed a pair, yet they differ. This is a celestial globe to chart the stars, with which you are doubtless familiar, but this other is of a type never yet seen in the British Empire.'

'What's the British Empire?' asked Kate.

'Shh!' whispered Sir John. 'He means England and Wales. The Welsh pretend the royal house is Welsh because of Owen Tudor, so as to make out that they rule us and we're all so-called British.'

'It is a terrestrial globe,' continued the doctor, with an icy stare. 'You are used to charts on scrolls or pages which can be spread flat, but this is a spherical chart which presents the world as it truly is.' He spun the globe and Europe, the Americas and Cathay flowed past. 'We British have long been deceived by pictures of the world on flat paper. They have us believe that Portugal and Spain are closer to Cathay than England, and that to reach there an English ship needs pass over the seas controlled by these peoples. But, see, Portugal and Spain are more distant from Cathay, since their merchants must pass by the southern reaches of Africa or the Americas, or transit across New Spain.' Dr Dee walked his dividers around the globe. 'England stands astride the shortest route to Cathay.'

In an instant the benches were vacant and the merchants crowded around the globe to see how the young wizard had reshaped the world in their favour.

The doctor's dividers bestrode the North Pole.

'But that's across the Frozen Ocean!'

'I cannot believe it! Not even Sir Henry could dream this!'

'Legend calls it the Frozen Ocean,' protested the doctor, indignation sharpening his lilt, 'but have you seen the ice? Do you know it is frozen all year from shore to shore? That icebergs float from the polar regions is no proof that the sea is impassable.'

'I'll ne'er launch my money among a fleet of icebergs,' declared one man.

'Nor I,' chorused several others.

'Histories tell us otherwise,' shrilled the doctor. 'The brothers Zeno travelled from Venice to Iceland, Greenland and beyond nearly two hundred years ago, although their chronicle was unpublished until this century, and they found Christian kings and open seas. And small, dark men with narrow eyes, who can only be from Cathay, have been found drowned on the coast of Norway. Where a drowned man can float a living sailor can navigate. The Portuguese and the Spaniards dared the equatorial zone, where men had said it was too hot to live and that that they would blacken and shrivel in the heat. But the legend proved to be a myth, like so many other legends disproved by discoveries. We British have never discovered to the north since the times of King Arthur, and so we live trapped in our legends, believing that we are at the end of the world.'

The assembly was fascinated but unconvinced.

'If the Portuguese or the Spaniards are already in Cathay,

they can hold the land against us with their forts, as in Guinea,' called another sceptic.

'They have not reached Cathay. They have reached tropic regions to the south. Cathay is to the north, on the latitude of London. But should they reach Cathay, the great khan is a powerful prince, not to be governed by handfuls of alien soldiers and a few cannon. He is to be won by diplomacy, not force. Cathay is not Guinea nor Mexico nor Peru.'

'Do we know that they will buy English cloth in Cathay?'

'Marco Polo tells us that the winters are cold and they heat their houses with sea coals. Such people need good woollen cloth and can trade silk for it, and spices and rhubarb.'

'What's that last one?' asked Kate.

'Rhubarb, Kate,' answered Sir John. 'An aphrodisiac that comes dried in sticks.'

'Where can we find ships for such a voyage?' called another merchant. 'You have studied maps but do you know navigation at sea, Doctor?'

Sir Henry came to the rescue. 'Dr Dee has shown you the message of the globe. He is the most learned cosmologist in Christendom. Now I present you Christendom's foremost pilot, Master Sebastian Cabot of Bristol. Thank you, Doctor. We shall need you again.'

Sebastian was a patriarch with the great white beard and rheumy eyes. His accent was as unexpected as Dr Dee's. It was unmistakably Italian. 'Ladies and gentlemen, honourable venturers of London, I am not worthy of Sir Henry's compliments…'

But the merchants were too excited for courtesies.

'Then sit down. Give us a mariner!'

'Yes,' called Gerald, 'and if you're from Bristol, then Widow Thomas here is a Carib.'

'I was born in Bristol,' called back Sebastian, 'and sailed thence with my late father, Zuan Caboto, in the *Matthew* when we discovered the New-found land.'

'God's teeth, that was in the last century!' exclaimed Mary. 'How ever old were you then?'

'Twelve. I could not sail with my father the next year, for he sent me to Venice to study cosmology. After my father failed to return there were no more English voyages, so I entered the service of Spain and led the expedition to the Argentinas.'

'And it was such a disaster that you never went to sea again,' observed one of the audience.

'In reward I was given an office in the *Casa* in Sevilla,' continued Sebastian, 'where I rose to become the pilot general of Spain, responsible for the award of master pilot certificates in all Spain and the Americas. From there I was promoted to Brussels, to fill the same office for all of the emperor's dominions: Spain, Italy, the Netherlands, everywhere! So I have a modest claim to maritime expertise. And now I return to my native land, too old, alas, to sail to Cathay, but ready with the wisdom of my years to be the chairman of your company.'

'Why do we need a chairman? We need no guild to share the profits when, and if, our ships come home.'

'To sail to Cathay is not like catching the ebb tide to Antwerp,' replied Sebastian. 'To reach Cathay one needs great ships, such as only Spaniards and Portuguese now build, ships for long voyages in tropic seas, sheathed in copper against worms, which eat away the timbers. There are no such ships for hire in England, so we – I – must teach our shipwrights to build them. This will cost more than can be recovered in a single voyage, so Sir Henry and his advisers have devised a new form of association: a marriage in commerce, as Sir Henry terms it. The capital will not be distributed on the return of the ships but will be the permanent capital of our association, The Company for the Discovery of New Lands, which will send ships for many years to come over the route which our first voyages will pioneer. The profit will also flow for many years to come, for you, your children and your grandchildren.'

'And suppose we need our money before we die?'

'The details are for tomorrow, but you will each have a bond or share with title to a commensurate part of the profit which the Company will share out from time to time, and these shares can be sold like expectations in an inheritance. You are merchants of the city of London and such an exchange cannot be beyond your wit.'

'You think it will work?'

'It will make London the envy of the Christian world.'

'We trust your skill and experience, Mr Cabot, but who will lead the voyage?'

Sir Henry hastened forward. 'Thank you, thank you, Master Cabot. You will advise us how to build our vessels and guide our deliberations. Now, friends, we have two gallant gentlemen to lead our ships to Cathay – England's greatest soldier and her greatest mariner. I present to you first, Sir Hugh Willoughby.'

2

Admiral and Pilot

There was a hush as falls on rival armies lined for battle, when the morning light first glints on the steel of levelled pikes. It was the audience that opened the engagement with a cannonade of questions.

'You're a soldier, why should we need you? Are we to trade with Cathay or conquer it?'

'You heard Dr Dee. We've no need of *conquistadores*.'

'It is a gentleman's highest honour to serve his country with his sword,' Sir Hugh replied, haughtily.

'And we pay for your glory. What good came of the Scottish war?'

How I despise you all, thought Sir Hugh, but Sir Henry needs you and I need Sir Henry. The Scottish war should have been my chance of glory, my first independent command. They were a feeble enemy, but the only enemy England was strong enough to attack and there had not been a war since old King Harry had been a young man. If only the Scots had stood and fought! If only I had seen the sunlight on their pikes – I would have made them stubble for our English swords! But they didn't offer battle; they had taken to the hills. True, we sacked and burnt Edinburgh, yet the booty was modest, the Scots still intrigue with the French and you money-grubbers treat me as if it had been a defeat.

If I were an eldest son from a family with influence I could hope for wealth and glory without grovelling to the likes of you, but, as it is, I need to carry off some great enterprise, if not on land, then at sea. I don't understand the learned babble of Dr Dee and Master Pilot Cabot, but to have Sir Henry as my patron could make me a person of note. He has married the daughter of the Duke of Northumberland, our boy king's regent, and if – when – Edward dies before coming of age, Northumberland will probably make himself king or put one of his Dudley clan on the throne. Sir Henry forbade me to wear a sword ('Just a black velvet doublet with modest facings and not too much lace'), so you see how I abase myself before you, you rabble of rag merchants!

These were the words that ran through Sir Hugh's mind, but were not those that he spoke.

'War is but armed diplomacy,' he said ingratiatingly. 'A means among many to persuade another prince to our view. Our relations with our Scots cousins have had rough episodes, but I have served my king, in both peace and war, as his ambassador in the north. I go to Cathay as one used to treating with princes, who is knowledgeable in French, Italian and Greek, and with letters of credence from King Edward to become England's ambassador to the great khan. The Spaniards and the Portuguese know only force, for they are used to treating with Moors and savages. We seek peace and trade with peoples of whatever faith.'

'Very wise,' he heard one of the audience whisper. 'Who knows what religion England may have by the time he reaches Cathay?'

'We will seek the protection of the khan,' continued Sir Hugh, 'and bear gifts to display the whole range of England's manufactures, to find them markets. Our strength lies not in pikes and powder but in the cunning of our craftsmen, so many of whom are now idle.'

The audience was beginning to soften. 'Do we know anything of the language of Cathay, to treat with them?'

'Letters of credence have been prepared in Hebrew and Arabic as well as European languages. Marco Polo himself became an emissary of the khan, so their tongue is not impossible for Christians.'

'You will be commanding seamen, not soldiers or diplomats. What do you know of the sea?'

'I know command and statecraft, and Sir Henry has chosen a pilot general as my advisor. I think you know Mr Richard Chancellor.'

It was better to say no more. Sir Hugh bowed to Sir Henry, who nodded to him to be seated.

Richard Chancellor had an advantage in that he already knew many of the audience. Several had invested in ventures he had led, although not always profitably. Against this lay one great disadvantage. He did not want to go to sea – or, to be more honest, he had begun to dread the sea.

I never chose the sea, he told himself as he awaited his turn to speak. I simply followed the trade of my birth father, as most men do, except that my birth father died when I was an infant and I was adopted by Sir William, to be brought up alongside Henry as his brother. They say my birth father died in Sir William's service, which is why he adopted me, though some whisper that I'm Sir William's bastard. Not that I look like a Sydney. Sir William didn't have to send me to sea, but he said it was my birth father's wish.

I love mathematics and learned enough to use an astrolabe and backstaff. I like to trade and learn languages, but I have never loved the sea. When I was young I never feared it; I believed I was immortal. Now, as I grow older, I fear each voyage will be my last. Last year I was lucky to get back from the Levant and not to have become a slave shackled to a Turkish oar, or drowned in the Bay of Biscay. There are so many reasons not to go to sea. I ought to be with Jane, now she is expecting our first child, and I need to finish the handbook on seamanship I'm writing with Dr Dee. Sir William is dead now but I still can't decide my own life. Now it is brother Henry who plans it for me, begs me to save England, make us a proud nation, feed the poor and rebuild Penshurst, tells me I will be England's Columbus.

What a strange boyhood we had, me the older brother but not our father's heir! Our tutors and servants always deferred to Henry; he chose the games and set the rules and now he is head of the family. I tried to hide behind Jane. Henry answered with his usual high-flown nonsense: 'Tell her, Rich, you would not love her half so much, loved you not honour more.' So, rather than confront my brother, I've agreed to cross the Frozen Ocean, although he promised this would be my last voyage and I would not stay as ambassador in Cathay, which why we brought in Sir Hugh.

Jane doesn't understand. She's sulked for over a week, says I love Cathay more than her or our child. She's so unfair, like most women. She says I lack affection only because I give her so much. Henry doesn't have these problems. Of course, all women are unreasonable when they're with child, which gives wives almost permanent licence until they're too old to conceive. She can't really believe I don't want to see our child until I get back from Cathay, which I fear means never.

So it was that Richard stepped forward to sell his audience what he himself most lacked: hope. 'Dear friends, you know me well. Some among you have risked your fortunes with me. Our recent venture to Turkey was not as profitable as we had hoped, but I brought you home a cargo of figs and currants that covered our costs. More importantly, I brought our ship and crew safely home, which has not been true of some other ventures, and we cheated the Turkish and Venetian galleys in the Greek Isles. But such small ventures can never mend our present ills. The fault, alas, lies in ourselves, for we are grown used to easy profit and little risk. Our good woollen cloth had such a market in the German Empire, which took all we cared to sell, that we made nothing else and took it nowhere but Antwerp, and we prospered and our pound sterling was the gauge of value throughout the Empire.'

Murmurs of agreement told Richard that he had the attention of his audience, if not yet their money.

'Our commerce, which once ranged from Iceland to Barbary, now gathered only for the Cloth Fleet to the Scheldt. And, now that the emperor has closed Antwerp against us to force down our prices, the Cloth Fleet cannot sail, our spinsters and weavers are idle, our townsfolk live on the poor rate, and when the harvest fails our peasants starve because there is no cloth to weave to buy corn. The country simmers with rebellion. The emperor controls England, because he controls Antwerp.'

The murmurs became cries of assent.

'Who are the heroes of this age, in the romances we read to our children? Cortes and Pizzaro, Magellan and Albuquerque, the conquerors and navigators of Spain and Portugal. Where are England's heroes? What is Spain, a kingdom born less than a century ago? There was a time when the king of Castile begged English archers to control his own people and save them from the Mohometans. And Portugal? It was the men of Bristol who won them Lisbon from the Moors. These were once poor lands on the bounds of Christendom, and now they dazzle Europe. What have they that England lacks?'

Richard waved aside the shower of answers. 'We know what they did. They went beyond the bounds of Christendom. They dared the ocean to claim new lands. England, too, is washed by the ocean and it beckons us to follow their example.'

'That's history, Richard,' lamented Sir John. 'The Spaniards and Portuguese have reached the Indies, West and East, and possess them for themselves.'

'The greatest prize is yet to be won,' replied Richard. 'Columbus was seeking Cathay when he found the Indies. For sure there is wealth there, but they are wild lands whose riches must be mined at great cost. The Portuguese have reached the Spice Islands, and yes, there is money in cloves and pepper, but what are these compared with the silks of Cathay? Cathay has yet to be reached by Christian ships. The prize sought by Columbus and da Gama over fifty years ago has still to be taken. Think,' he pleaded, dangling the word in the smoky air, 'think, could we but sell silks from London as well as woollens, who would close their ports against us? If we could reach Cathay and exchange woollens for silk and carry it to London in quantity by routes unguarded by the Spaniards or the Portuguese, then would we have wealth to make the Spaniards look as poor as the Scots.'

Richard caught the gaze of a comely young woman near the front of the audience with red hair and a pale face. She was looking at him with rapt attention. It looked as though he had won her silver; would that he could win more than that! Was it her father sitting so close against her? Probably not. Lucky man.

'But there is a prize in Cathay more wondrous than silk, which has never reached Europe in the centuries that the caravans have laboured over Asia, for it is too fragile. Yet it has been taken by sea to the Spice Islands whence the Portuguese have brought samples to Europe, one of which was purchased by Sir Henry. Look upon this!'

Richard stood aside to give a clear view of an object on a pedestal, still under its velvet cover. Two servants gently lifted the veil.

'Stand clear, lest it be damaged. You must worship at a distance.'

On the pedestal stood a vase. It was beautifully formed, but most of the merchants owned finely crafted ceramics. The wonder lay in the colour and texture. It was white and blue, with touches of colours for which Christians had no names. The colours were gorgeous, but the whiteness was impossible, whiter than dawn frost.

Dragons and strange plants writhed around the vase. They seemed not to be painted on the glaze, but rather woven into it as though it were frozen silk. A servant reached a taper into the vessel and lit the candle. The flame glowed soft through the fabric.

'*This* will be among our cargoes.'

The redhead clutched the greybeard's hand and Richard

caught her words: 'Have you ever seen such beauty?'

'Save only thyself, Kate,' whispered her companion.

Richard let the merchants savour their admiration for several seconds.

'Friends, Sir Henry's colleagues – men of science and learning – have pointed you the way to Cathay. I can take our ships there and bring them home. I do not ask you to put your money into a voyage of conquest or a crusade to convert the heathen. I am asking you to join me in what every good English husband has done for centuries. We are taking our cloth to market! Are we together?'

3

Letters and Laws

Edward VI, by the grace of God, king of England, France and Ireland, to all kings, princes, rulers, judges and governors of the earth, and all other having any excellent dignity on the same, in all places under the universal heaven: peace, tranquillity and honour unto you, and your lands and regions, which are under you, as is convenient.

Forasmuch as the great and almighty God has given unto mankind, above all other living creatures, such an heart and desire, that every man desires to join friendship with other, to love and be loved, also to give and receive mutual benefits: for the establishing and furtherance of which universal amity, certain men of our Realm have taken upon them a voyage by sea into far countries. We assenting to their petition, have licenced the right valiant and worthy Sir Hugh Willoughby, knight, and other our trusty and faithful servants, to go to countries to them heretofore unknown, so that hereby not only commodity may ensue, but also an indissoluble and perpetual league of friendship be established between us.

We therefore desire you, kings, princes, and all other to whom there is any power on Earth, to permit unto these our servants free passage, and to aid and help them in such things as they lack. Show yourselves so towards them, as you would that we and our subjects should show ourselves towards your servants.

Written in London, which is the chief city of our kingdom,

in the year from the creation of the world, 5515, in the month
of Jiar, in the fourteenth day of the month, and seventh year of
our reign.

Sebastian Cabot stroked the soft white beard which flowed across his chest (a mariner's beard, as he liked to think of it) and read the manuscript admiringly. If there was a thing the English were good at, it was calligraphy. Indeed, they were good at anything to do with words, and precious little else. They had such a lovely young language, newly blended from a dozen others, classic and modern, like a fine sherry. No wonder they were drunk with it, and sang, recited, wrote and gloried in it so immoderately.

Sebastian had dictated the ambassadorial letter in Italian, and had left it to John Dee to translate. He seemed to love the language of his nation's conquerors even more than they loved it themselves. Yes, the proclamation looked good and sounded good. He hoped that the Greek version, which Richard Chancellor was drafting, and all the other versions that were in hand were as elegant. Perhaps he should order printed copies.

Ordinances, instructions and advertisements of and for the
direction of the intended voyage for Cathay, compiled, made
and delivered by the right worshipful M. Sebastian Cabot
Esquire, governor of the mystery and company of the Merchants
adventurers for the discovery of Regions, Dominions, Islands and
places unknown, the ninth day of May, in the year of our Lord
God 1553, and in the seventh year of the reign of our most dread
sovereign Edward VI. By the grace of God, king of England,
France and Ireland, defender of the faith, and of the Church of
England and Ireland, in earth supreme head.

That was a good preamble, especially the title of the new company. Such a pity that it hid Sebastian's great innovation. This was not a company of merchant adventurers in the old sense, a group of traders who hired a ship to conduct their individual enterprises. This new creation was like Holy Mother Church, an entity which owned property and made legal acts like a living being but which was incorporeal and immortal – at least, so long as the business was fortunate and they were favoured by government.

But then words often obscured reality. The studious adolescent dying at Greenwich was hardly a 'most dread sovereign', and whether his successor, whoever that might be, would be in sympathy with the Church of England was unguessable. And it was nearly a century since the king of England had been king of France.

Sebastian had drafted thirty-three rules for the conduct of the voyage, drawn from his unhappy experiences on the River Plate. This was further than any English captain had sailed. How strange that an adventure which had nearly ruined him as a young man in Spain should be the foundation of his fame as an old man in England.

> *First, the captain general, with the pilot major, the masters, merchants and other officers, to be so knit and accorded in unity, love, conformity and obedience in every degree on all sides, that no dissension, variance or contention may rise or spring betwixt them and the mariners of this company, to the damage or hindrance of the voyage, for that dissension (by many experiences) has overthrown many notable intended and likely enterprises and exploits.*

How well he had learnt that lesson! Not that rules could bind men to love one another, whether Spaniards or English. Rule one went further than a marriage vow, and the English were notorious for their fickle marriages. Witness old King Harry! Sir Hugh Willoughby and Richard Chancellor were not a likely match. Sebastian could not freight their ships with love, but if he wrote love into the rules he would not be to blame for its absence.

He ran his eye down the list, reading everything he had learned in life: shipboard discipline, accounting, provisioning, hygiene, navigation.

> *Item twelve: that no blaspheming of God, or detestable swearing be used in any ship, nor communication of ribaldry, filthy tales or ungodly talk to be suffered in the company of any ship. Neither dicing, carding, tabling nor other devilish games to be frequented.*

No, that was not one of Sebastian's ideas; that was to please the Puritan merchants. Richard might be happy with it but Sebastian doubted that the rule would be long observed in Sir Hugh's ship once it had quit the Thames.

> *Item twenty-two: not to disclose to any nation the state of our religion, but to pass it over in silence, without any declaration of it, seeming to bear with such laws and rites as the place has, where you shall arrive.*

That was Sebastian's policy. It was not just that he disliked the Reformed religion which England had adopted since he had last lived in the country; he detested Catholic zealots equally. They had caused endless trouble with the savages in the Indies, smashing temples and idols and preferring tumult to trade.

Sebastian had included a great deal about savages in his rules. None of the English had had dealings with them, so Sebastian had given them his best advice, though some scoffed at it.

> *Item thirty: if you shall see them wear lions' or bears' skins, having longbows and arrows, be not afraid of that sight, for such are worn oftentimes more to frighten strangers than for other cause.*
>
> *Item thirty-one: there are people that can swim in the sea, havens and rivers, naked, having bows and shafts and coveting*

to draw nigh your ships, which, if they shall find them not well
watched, or warded, they will assault, desirous of the bodies of
men, which they covet for meat. If you resist them, they dive, and
so will flee, and therefore diligent watch is to be kept both day
and night in some islands.

That was what the English paid him so highly for: the experience of the half-century during which they had been left out of the wider world, a New World beyond their imagination.

It could so nearly have been so different! He closed his eyes and relived the scene he had relived so many times in the last fifty-six years. He had lied when he told the merchants he had been born in Bristol. He had been born in Venice; his father had been born in Amalfi and had grown up in Genoa. But it was on the quayside in Bristol that Sebastian had last seen his father.

His closed eyes saw Bristol suffocating under drapes and banners – purple and silver, crimson and gold. Papa's three ships were almost invisible beneath their flags. The mayor was at the quay with his dignitaries and the people were there with their music. Papa had drawn up his officers and men on the wharf. The English were even more conservative in their dress in those days, and Papa stood out like a peacock among geese in his short, tight, bright, Italian clothes.

Zuan Caboto had promised to succeed where Columbus had failed. He had known Columbus when he was just a gatekeeper's son in Genoa, and knew that he was a charlatan who had lied about reaching Asia. Now Zuan was taking the true route to Cathay, through the northern latitudes.

Papa also knew that Columbus had miscalculated the distance to Cathay, and since the ships of Papa's day were smaller than modern ones Papa knew that they needed staging posts to take on wood, water and victuals. He had made a reconnaissance the year before in the little *Matthew*, crossing the ocean to discover Terranova, which the English called Newfoundland.

This had all the wood and water, as well as other provisions, that voyagers might need to continue on to Cathay, and they could be taken freely.

Sebastian had sailed in the *Matthew* and boasted of it for the rest of his life. It had been three months of storms, seasickness and mortal terror. Papa had refused to let him sleep on the floor of his cabin and insisted that he slept with the crew in the forecastle. They had been worse than savages. One had tried to sodomise him and he had dared not tell his father for fear of being lost overboard in the next storm.

Papa had wanted to take him to Cathay the following year, but Sebastian had been so terrified that he had developed a fever. So now he sat at the quayside watching the ships depart. Some weeks later one of them returned, dismasted in a storm off Ireland. The others were never seen again. So the hard, brave father died while his soft, coward son lived.

Sebastian had lived and travelled in many countries since that day, but he had left his heart on the quayside in Bristol, and his soul was ever in Cathay.

4

Departures

Richard sat in the puddle of light spilling from the two lanthorns on his desk. Behind him the gathering night slowly possessed the stateroom of the *Edward Bonaventura*. The scratch of quill on paper was lost in the sound of music and laughter filtering from the maindeck.

'Did they never tire?' sighed Richard. It had been ceaseless revelry since they had left Ratcliffe Stairs four days ago, a victory parade down the Thames as if they had already brought home the silks and ceramics of Cathay. The fireworks at the stairs had set the sky crimson and silver – the Sydney colours – and all London had wrapped itself in banners. As they slipped by the great, red-brick front of Greenwich Palace, built straight against the foreshore, young King Edward had been carried to a window to see them pass. Or so they had been told, and some swore they had glimpsed the pale, consumptive face from the decks. To honour the king, the crew had paraded in the blue coats which they next expected to wear when they appeared before the great khan.

They had spent a day at Deptford loading new-cast cannon from the arsenal. Now, at last, the *Edward Bonaventura*, the *Bona Esperanza* and the *Bona Confidentzia* lay at anchor at Gravesend, between the woody hills of Kent and the Essex marshes, the sounds of the festival still vibrating in their timbers. This was the last revel. Tomorrow they dared the ocean.

If any ships could cross the Pole it must be these, thought

Richard. Two of them were indeed great ships, of 120 and 160 tonnes burthen, new-built following the Spanish design approved by Sebastian Cabot and still fragrant with sawn timber, new rope and fresh tar. Each had three masts and could carry eight linen sails, including the bowsprit staysail. The fore and stern castles stood high above the waist of each vessel, which was broad-beamed to take an ample cargo.

Sir Hugh, captain general of the fleet, sailed in the *Bona Esperanza*, and Richard, as pilot general, sailed in the *Edward Bonaventura*. The *Bona Confidentzia* was a lesser vessel of ninety tonnes, captained by Richard's sailing companion, Cornelius Danforth. As the papers in front of Richard recorded, there were 117 men in the fleet, all volunteers. Such was the hardship among the mariners in London that the licence which the king had given Sir Henry to take men from the prisons had been unused. Even so, eleven men had thought better of going to Cathay and had jumped ship on the cruise downriver. Richard's busy quill noted the replacements taken on at Gravesend.

Richard reached for another set of papers. Papers, papers, papers! The Company must import paper from Germany by the hundredweight. At least this was the last set before he sailed – maybe the last set he would ever complete. What could they know of the Frozen Ocean? And yet they set out detailed orders based on legends sometimes centuries old. Which coasts to follow, where to meet if the ships were separated, how to greet the natives of lands none had ever seen. John Dee and Sebastian Cabot had already mapped the world in their imagination.

He checked off the list of ordnance, mentally reviewing the lines of eight cannon that scowled from either side of the two great ships. Five more lined each side of the *Bona Confidenzia*. They were classed as minions, and each threw a four-pound shot. There were smaller cannon in the fore and stern castles. Richard had greeted the sleek, black cylinders as if they had been great iron slugs crawling aboard his ship. Cannon were ugly nuisances – awkward, heavy and dangerous, and they either cluttered the deck or took up valuable cargo space in the hull. Yet no ship dared sail the lawless oceans without armament, any more than a man would carry a bag of gold over Shooters Hill without an armed servant.

All the heavy guns were mounted on the main deck on timber sleds; the Company had not wanted to lose cargo space below deck, or pierce the hull for gun ports. Richard resolved to dismount the cannon on his ship at the first sign of bad weather and stow them down on the ballast. He had seen a sailor smashed to pulp by a cannon that had broken loose in the Bay of Biscay. Also, it would trim the vessel better to carry the weight lower down.

Richard had never liked cannon, but he hated these in particular because Sir Hugh doted on them. They were the only items in the fleet's equipment which seem to interest him.

'Your fine ships may be copied from Spain, but no nation can equal England's cast-iron ordnance! The only guns a man can trust to murder the enemy and not the gunners.' No good could come of giving Sir Hugh such killing power.

Now the cargo. Surely even Noah had had a simpler manifest? No vessels had ever sailed with such a motley loading. Most was woollen cloth of different weaves, but there were gloves and ribbons, steel needles, pewter mugs, knives, toys and samples of every object made by English hands, as well as several tuns of French wine. No wonder the tradespeople of London were delighted to see them sail with so much stock they had never expected to sell.

The door creaked open and Sir Hugh peered into the gloom. 'Still so melancholic, Richard? You should see old Mr Caboto at the dance. He can outstep the youngsters! He may think he's too old to sail to Cathay, but he's not too old to catch a wench. We're already heroes! Had Cortes been as sad as our Mr Chancellor here, the silver of Mexico would still be with the Indians.'

Richard looked up. 'Must you always behave like a play-actor? They're not rejoicing, they're trying to forget – smothering fear in music, wine and warm flesh. Having voyaged as far as Scotland, you are surely familiar with the perils of the sea.'

'A turd in your teeth, Mr Chancellor! I'm the admiral of this fleet, and your brother is no longer here to comfort your snivelling. You dishearten the men and are surly to our guests. They look to us to win an empire.'

'England gave up dreaming of empires two generations ago. All they expect of us is to rid them of a heap of unsalable English rubbish. This is a clear-out sale, not a military expedition, and I would remind you that, admiral or no, the Company has ordered that this expedition be governed by a council of twelve. You have indeed two votes to our one apiece, but that does not give you a majority.'

'Christ's arse, I've hanged better cowards than you and disembowelled them in front of the men. I came to say that it is noticed that you are not at the dance.'

'I have work to do, as ever, but if they want me I will join them. My wife would have joined us tonight, but her ladies are with her and the birth pains have started.'

Sixteen-year-old Arthur Petty was joining the *Bona Esperanza*. In particular, he was joining Jeremy Ketch, Martin Cook and Stephen Andrews as the fourth member of their mess. From now on they would be the most important people in his world. They would sleep together on the same few feet of the forecastle deck, usually slumped on top of each other in their sodden clothes. They would share the food and drink which one of them fetched from the galley. They would use the same seat of ease in the forepeak. They would joke, sing, dance, grumble and despair together, and, most likely, die together.

Jeremy was the oldest of the mess, and its self-appointed leader. 'This,' he explained to Arthur, 'is a two-watch ship. Me and Martin are on midnight to noon watch and you and Stephen are noon to midnight. You, lad, will collect our rations from the galley at noon. It's mostly salt fish on this ship. We do get meat, though seldom beef. The 'ens on the maindeck are for eggs for the officers, though doubtless they'll be eaten before the voyage is done – the 'ens I mean.' He sniggered at his joke. 'Do what we tells you, and you'll soon get used to the ways of the sea.'

'I've been to sea before, Granddad,' protested Arthur. 'I was born on a boat – not a floating one of course, one of them 'ulks on the foreshore.' He waved to the mudflats on either side of Gravesend, thick with the hulks of barges whose sailing days were done and now sheltered hundreds of families who earned their living from the river. They were almost a village in themselves, with walkways from one to another and slippery green timber causeways to the shore.

'God's bones, we've got a cocky one 'ere, shipmates. We needs to learn 'im respect. Where've you sailed to then, lad – Cathay?'

'Newcastle, for sea coals, and Antwerp with the Cloth Fleet. I was cabin boy to Lady Thomas.'

'And who might she be then? You remember your place and you won't come to no 'arm. Things sometimes do 'appen to boys who're cheeky.'

Arthur had indeed been to sea before, but never in ships like these, with such crowds of seamen. Apart from the brief voyage to Antwerp, the biggest craft he had sailed in had had a crew of ten.

'Did y' bring a wench?' queried Martin Cook.

'They said there was to be no womenfolk on this voyage, not even wives, or m' sister Meg would have joined,' replied Arthur. 'I could have vouched for her and at least she'd be fed aboard ship.'

At least I'll be fed, thought Arthur. Had the fleet not arrived he would have become another vagrant on the Kentish roads, peddling trifles at fairs and pilfering linen from hedges. Maybe he would have joined the gypsies. Maybe he should have done.

'I meant for tonight, not to sail with us. This is a bold and dangerous adventure and only men are allowed, like in a battle, but 'tis a pity. The wenches of Cathay may be willing, but we'll be a while getting there, so this is our last chance to fondle a lass for many a day.'

'I see'd you bought your fiddle aboard,' leered Stephen. 'It'll not be the only fiddlestick busy tonight.'

Kate had taken the ferry downstream to Gravesend on an impulse; it was her last chance to be impulsive before she married Sir John. As their wedding date drew closer she was growing nostalgic for widowhood.

All London wanted to see the ships, but Kate had a special reason to visit the fleet. Ever since Penshurst she had been haunted by Richard Chancellor's weather-tanned face: the clear blue eyes and the fair beard. Tonight she would steal some time to live out her fantasy, to dance with him and feel his strong mariner's arms on her waist. His wife would probably be there, of course, but surely he would have time to partner other women. After all, Kate was a stakeholder in the Company.

She left Will to mind the business and travelled to Gravesend alone, without a servant, taking a room at the inn close by St George's church. It was growing dusk when she crossed to the fleet. The tavern windows on the shore glowed bright in the gloom, and points of light bobbed across the black water as a flotilla of small craft shuttled the last arrivals to the dance. The ships' lanterns were lit, fiddles played and she could see the dancers on the open deck.

It was the merriest dance Kate had known, and the strangest. Beneath the merriment lurked an edge of defiance, like the gladiators of Rome dancing before going into the arena.

There was hardly space to dance, though much of the deck cargo still lay in the lighters tethered alongside. Men and women squeezed into an intimacy which would have been considered improper ashore. Kate did not lack strong sailors' arms to lift and twirl her to the sound of the viols and lutes. The evening was warm and the lanterns added to the heat. Wine passed around freely from open casks, but where was Richard?

Then there he was, alone – or, at least, without a woman. She pushed through the crowd. She had not thought what to say, but he must not escape.

'Mr Chancellor, I doubt you remember me but I am Kate Thomas. We met at Penshurst. I have become a stakeholder in your company.' She paused to catch her breath, and to think of a way to excuse her boldness. 'I come to wish you Godspeed and to give you a memento of England. Of course you already have some of my kerseys, but I would be favoured if you would accept this.' She pressed a small object into his hand.

'I had forgotten your name but could never forget such a face,' replied Richard. 'I am honoured that you should have joined us for our farewell.' He looked down at the tiny gift. It was a silver pendant on a thin chain, with the letters K and R joined in a love knot.

'It was given to me by my late father,' explained Kate, struggling to cover her confusion. She had not thought to give him anything, but he had looked so alone and melancholy that she had to make the encounter more meaningful. 'R is for Rawles, the name of my mother's family, which I bear as a second baptismal name.'

'I am overwhelmed that you should give me something so precious to you.'

Kate blushed. She blushed too easily; her skin was so pale. She could feel the heat sweep across her cheeks, and the more confused she became, the more she glowed. She hoped he could not notice in the candlelight.

'A bauble, a meagre trifle,' she protested. 'You are hazarding your life for our profit. Here, take these and give them to Sir Hugh and Mr Danforth. They are to remind you of the hopes you carry with you from England, and the thoughts we have of you while you are away.' She pulled off two rings which she had put on for the dance.

'And I will bring you back a worthy memento of Cathay. But while we yet have a few hours left, may I ask the honour of the next dance?'

The Thames was grey with dawn as the boat pulled away from the *Edward Bonaventura*, carrying the last of the womenfolk to the shore.

Kate had not needed the room at the inn. She looked anxiously at the other women in the boat. She had already studied them minutely while on deck. They were of all stations in society, and surely none would recognise her? Half were crying and all seemed caught in a private turmoil of emotion. Thank God the ships were sailing on the morning tide, and were not due back in England for three years. Thank God she had not brought a servant.

It had been a mad adventure which could prejudice her intended marriage. Any marriage. Not that she was eager to marry, but a woman in her position had no other option. Life was so much simpler for men.

She looked back at the ships. They were breaking the sails from the yards and she could imagine the sailors clustered around the capstan heads, slotting in the bars ready to wind the anchors from the stubborn Thames mud. She had been to sea only once, but she remembered every moment; the glitter of sweat on the straining muscles of the bare-backed seamen, the gasp of relief as the anchor came away, the sense of animal delight as the ship became a free creature, outward bound. If only she were leaving for Cathay.

5

Storm

The *Edward Bonaventura* shocked into the oncoming wave like a ram against a castle gate. Her timbers screamed, and every man aboard might have expected her to fly to pieces, except that they had heard her scream six times an hour for the past one hundred hours, and yet she had lived.

The blunt forepeak bit into the wave, sea cascaded across the forecastle and at the instant before annihilation the ship reared like a hound, flinging the water from her back and pointing her head towards the narrow window of grey sky between the towering rollers. Then began the long, slow crawl up the flank of the wave, until for a moment she hung triumphant at the crest in a mist of gale-whipped spume, the wind sobbing in the rigging and the ocean spread about her like a field ploughed by giants. Occasionally the crew would glimpse the other two ships in the fleet, before the *Edward* lowered her head and slithered into the next trough, gathering speed to smash against the base of the oncoming wave.

This time she did not rise so briskly from the sea, and the bow began to drag to one side. Richard Chancellor was at the rail in front of his cabin high on the aft deck, where he had been for the last four days, apart from snatches of rest in the cabin at his back. From here he could normally look down at the rest of the hull, but at the moment he had to look up to see the forecastle. Some trick of fatigue gave him the dreamlike sensation that he was looking at the ship from a point above the masts, watching his puny self through the clutter of spars and lines.

The bowsprit and yard had been carried away and were hanging over the larboard bow, held to the ship by the web of ropes which had hitherto kept them in place and operated the spritsail. The wreckage had become an auxiliary rudder, dragging the ship sideways. Once broadside to the waves she would roll over.

Richard was reluctant even to feel alarm. The end had been inevitable for so long. It had been a sorry adventure, for all the pomp and festivity of their departure from the Thames; twelve weeks of cramped monotony tacking for a wind in the German Ocean, and then four days of terror while the Norwegian Sea pounded them to splinters. And he could have stopped it just by telling his brother to be sane.

Seizing what remained of his willpower he screamed into the wind to the man a few feet away on the quarterdeck. 'Stephen, hold the rudder hard a-port, and send six men for'ard to clear the wreck afore we reach the crest!'

It was needless to spell out his orders; a nod would have sufficed. As the ship's master, Stephen Burroughs knew well what to do. How he did it was his affair. But Richard needed to shake off this numb fatalism.

Stephen was already on the stairs to the well of the ship. A huge man with a mat of beard that curled to his waist, he swung across the slanting deck like an ape. Unusually for an English sailor, he had sailed in distant waters and had learned to love the sea.

Two men were struggling to hold the whipstaff to port. For the moment they would have to manage. Stephen scampered onwards to discover a gaggle of seamen sheltering in the lee of the forecastle, water streaming onto them from the deck above. They could not see what had happened at the bow, but they could see the broken ropes flailing above their heads, and feel the ship beginning to wallow beneath their feet.

They were not deep-sea mariners. Before this voyage none of them had been out of sight of land, except when there was fog in the Channel, and never had they known or heard tell of such a tempest. For four sleepless days of toil, wet and cold they had been braver than they had known men could be brave. Now they had reached the end of their courage.

The thirteen-year-old from the London Bridewell was crying for a mother he had never known, and to the Virgin Mary, whom his country no longer officially worshipped. The others hung to ropes and stanchions and waited to drown. Stephen steadied himself and bellowed into the blank-faced huddle.

'Lively there! An axe each. Onto the forepeak and cut away the wreck.'

The axes were in front of them, lashed to the foremast. Not a man stirred.

Richard appeared at Stephen's side and stepped to the foremast, drew his knife and slashed free two axes.

'Yours, Jack,' he said, thrusting it at the nearest seaman, 'and a silver penny if you race me to the peak. And the same for each of you. Let's tell our grandchildren how we saved the *Bonny Edward*!'

Jack followed the captain to the stairway like a bewildered sheep. Richard thrust him forward to win the wager. Stephen started to follow, but Richard held him back.

'Stay down. If I'm lost they'll need you to bring 'em home.'

The ship was still at the quiet stage of the cycle, sheltered from the wind by the wave she was climbing, and it was easy, if frightening, to climb out onto the forepeak. The dark sea surged beneath them as they stepped across the square holes in the woodwork that in quieter weather served as latrines for the common sailors. It seemed impossible to hack away the tangled wreckage before the ship mounted the crest and began to slide sideways into the trough.

'As well to die busy as idle!' shouted Richard as they set to, hewing at the hemp and cursing their blunt axes and the good rope. In truth, the axes were sharp and the hemp was rotten after months at sea, which was in part the cause of the disaster. Then the miracle! The ropework began to unravel like wool and the shattered bowsprit, spritsail and yard swung free on their own voyage to Cathay.

Robert Bardwell of Greenhithe jumped aside an instant too late, and a snaking rope caught his ankles and flicked him into the ocean. The last they saw of him was the gape of surprise on his big, round face. His shipmates had time only for a pang of gratitude that it was not they who had been taken before scrambling to the slender safety of the foredeck.

The wind struck, but the ship was facing it and swooped purposefully into the next descent. The men on the foredeck put their axes under their belts and linked hands to climb down onto the maindeck.

It would have been better for them all, thought Richard, if it had pleased God to take me rather then Robert of Greenhithe. It would have freed them to go home.

6

Encounter

Like a capricious lover, the sea suddenly forgot its anger and fell as calm as Greenwich Reach. A shy, apologetic sun smiled onto the pale water. The exhausted sailors gazed out at an empty ocean.

'They are lost, Stephen.' Richard involuntarily crossed himself.

Stephen was used to soaking up Richard's pessimism, sand to his wet ink. 'Why lost? Their ships float as well as ours and their men are no less ill-found. Our gallant admiral must have turned back.'

'Not Sir Hugh. He loves glory more than life – his own or those of his men.'

'A landsman's courage is like his cock. It shrinks mightily in cold water.'

'But Stephen, *could* any ship turn about in such a storm?'

'Maybe not. If not, we must await them at Wardhouse, as Dr Dee advised if we separate. Those are the Company's orders.'

'*If* there's a Wardhouse. The doctor says the king of Denmark keeps a castle there at the end of Norway, but the doctor hoards legends. And to find Wardhouse we must first find Norway, and should we find both Norway and Wardhouse, we dare not wait there long. Fortune stole the summer from us in the German Ocean and may yet freeze us into the Norwegian Sea for the winter.'

'But if we don't give Gloryguts the chance of finding us we

may have to explain it in London before a court.'

'Which spares us the torment of choice. We'll put it to the council – those who are still with us.'

The sweet-smelling ship which had left Gravesend in May had become a picturesque wreck, stinking of human waste that washed down into the bilge during the days when it had been impossible for the men to relieve themselves over the side. The bowsprit had gone, and frayed, broken rigging dangled from every yard. The deck had been swept bare, the pinnace, the hen coops and the gun carriages all smashed and scattered to the waves. The cannon had been dismounted at the onset of the storm and lowered down the stairways at the cost of two broken limbs, but, lacking gun carriages, the ship was now effectively disarmed.

Sleep was the urgent need. Stephen reorganised the crew into three watches so that most of the men were free to collapse on the deck. The remainder struggled to bring order to the limping vessel and prayed for land.

A great rock loomed from the sea, wreathed in gulls, the first land since Harwich. The sight was doubly welcome. So distinctive a mark must surely be on the chart which John Dee had brought from Louvain. Richard and Stephen decided that it was probably Rost, the westernmost of the Lofoten islands. This was quickly confirmed as a line of sharp peaks lifted above the eastern horizon, like the teeth of a shipyard saw.

They steered into the channel between the islands and the mainland, hurried on by the strongest tide-race they had ever known. They kept close beside the islands, beneath tall cliffs rising to fields as steep as the roof of a house. Peasant families crowded the fields, all ages working busily together. They too were pleased to see the sun and waved cheerfully to the alien ships passing below. It felt strange to see such normal, happy activity so close at hand after the long abnormality of life at sea.

At the same time, it was disturbing. The peasants were making hay for the winter.

They groped northwards from the Lofotens along the Norwegian coast, through a maze of islands and stark mountains. Wardhouse was beyond the limit of Dr Dee's chart, but was reputedly a mighty stone fort, erected by the king of Denmark, who was also lord of Norway, so with care, they should be able to find it. There were no signs of habitation, and no indication as to what the legendary fort was intended to protect. At length, they came upon a granite cape, peering north into the ocean like a crouching bear. Beyond the cape the coast turned south-eastwards.

'Stephen, our first discovery! This is, surely, the northernmost point of Europe.'

'If the castle of Wardhouse is still ahead of us,' replied Stephen, 'then this cape must already have been discovered by the king of Denmark's men.'

'Why cavil? We are the first English ship to round this Cape, so why not give it an English name? The Spaniards and Portuguese give their names to the extremities of Africa and the Americas. We'll call it Cape Edward, after our king and our ship.'

'The Company mislikes imperial names. Why not North Cape?'

'Ever the diplomat, Stephen. And, I grant, it's a grander name. Mark it on the chart.'

They came upon Wardhouse soon after the Cape. It had stone walls and even cannon, but they could easily have passed it by, for the walls were low-built in the modern style, with broad platforms for the artillery. It stood on a flat, treeless island facing directly onto the ocean, guns gaping towards the Pole.

For all its martial appearance, the reception was friendly. The tiny garrison – about fifty tall, fair-haired Vikings with a score of squat, dark-haired women and a gaggle of mixed-blood children – was eager for civilised company and turned out on the quay to greet them. The quay was surprisingly large, although bare of commerce.

The commander was a giant of a man who spoke some Dutch. He took the newcomers to his granite lodgings and talked with them far into the night, plying them with beer before a high-banked fire and telling them about life in his remote outpost and his trade with the Lapps, the people from among whom the garrison recruited their womenfolk.

''Tis late in the season for visitors. The merchants from Bergen have all gone now,' explained the commander. 'We even had a Scots boat this summer. They stay for the summer months when it is ever daylight. Now the days are shortening and soon we'll say farewell to the sun for a full three months.'

'Three months of darkness?' exclaimed Richard.

'Quite, but night has its delights,' replied the Dane, giving his diminutive consort a hug. 'Don't misunderstand me. We're happy here. The Lapps are friendly – they do not even have a word for war. Our cannon supposedly protect the king's trade, but we have never needed to fire them. We have our several comforts and few dangers. Some of the Lapps are still on the seashore, hunting seals, but soon they'll take their reindeer inland and we'll have the coast to ourselves.'

'Reindeer?'

'You don't know reindeer? They teem on this coast in the summer. Big, three-horned deer which the Lapps hunt and also herd. They live from the deer in the winter and from the sea in summer.'

'Do you have much trade with the Lapps?'

'Knives, metalware and coloured cloth for train oil and furs, mainly train oil. They make it by boiling seal flesh all summer long in pits on the beach. That's the stink you can smell everywhere.'

'Train oil?'

'You English! Do you know nothing? In lamps.' He laughed. 'How else? Unless you can find some better use for it. Our merchants take all they can to sell in Bergen and Copenhagen. I've a few barrels left over from the last lading, if you'd like to buy some.'

'Perhaps on our return from Cathay. Do you ever travel eastwards?'

'My duty is here. Traders sometimes go east to meet the Lapps, but usually the Lapps seek them here.'

'Is there open water?'

'The sea never freezes here, but to the east it freezes in winter, although the Lapps say that there are seas where the ice never melts.'

The governor had no news of the *Bona Esperanza* or the *Bona Confidentzia*. Richard explained that he needed to wait for his companions, offering to pay for their victuals.

'We need no woollens, but you could trade us some of that French wine you brought with you,' said the commander. 'As for food, there's plenty for you and your company, if you're happy with reindeer, seal meat and fish. Stay all night if you wish – until March.'

'Three weeks and a day, Stephen,' counted Richard. 'Either Sir Hugh is lost or he's away to Cathay without us. So where's it to be for us – Gravesend, Cathay or Wardhouse?'

'Not Wardhouse. The *Bonny Edward* is ready for sea again and so are the men. Leave them longer and they'll both start to rot. All this work – setting the new bowsprit, mounting the guns, fitting out the pinnace – has kept them from thinking about tempests and the sea, but give them a little leisure and it will start them thinking, and then they'll start to desert. Before we know it we'll be recruiting Lapps to take us back to Gravesend.'

'So we go back?'

'How would we explain it to the Company?'

Richard knew he had no choice, but he wanted Stephen to argue the decision.

'We are not without gains. We've discovered the North Cape and a possible trade with the Lapps. We can take back some train oil and see how it sells in London.'

'Was that what they had in mind when they carried the young king to the palace window to see us pass?'

And could they rebuild Penshurst with train oil? Could Richard tell Henry that all he had done had been to visit a Danish fort? And what if Sir Hugh had reached Cathay?

'So the men are ready to go on? What about the winter ice?'

'There's none here at Wardhouse. The Danes say it never freezes, and so as long as the coast ahead trends south as well as east, the way should be clear.'

'Nature follows strange laws here, Stephen. Could we winter on the coast?'

'The Lapps might help us. We've more than enough trade goods.'

'But you heard that they winter inland with their deer?'

'We've victuals for eighteen months, though men seldom stay healthy without fresh stores. And we could lay on extra stores here, even if it means trading the wine.'

'You think there would there be fuel?'

'Not to be cut, if the land is as bare as here, but we have sea coals and there's driftwood from the beach. We would need to gather it before the snow.'

'So we propose to the council that we go on?'

'What else? Tell them we're taking our cloth to market.'

The wind plucked a song of triumph from the rigging, strumming like a hundred harps as the *Edward Bonaventura* surged through the straits towards Cathay.

For over a week they had groped along the gaunt, grey coast, noting every bay and inlet lest the freezing sea should force them to seek shelter. But the sea stayed open. It might yet be possible, thought Richard, to work their way to Cathay around the northern shore of Asia, rather than attempting the bold stroke across the Pole drawn by John Dee on his globe. According to the doctor, the Strait of Anian that separated Asia from America and gave passage to the Southern Ocean and Cathay lay directly facing England on the other side of the Frozen Ocean. No Christian had seen this strait; it might be much closer, or there might be no strait.

And then here it was, wider than the straits of Dover, opening southwards into a great, broad sea. South they swooped into the new ocean, joyfully casting away from the coast that had guided them for so long.

Yet, as the men and boys sang and danced and planned their nights in the taverns of Cathay, the captain fretted. The compass, the sun and the backstaff all told him they were travelling south, but still it grew colder. Each morning the sails became stiffer, frost lingered on the ropes all day and the sea was beginning to curdle. With the strait freezing behind them there would be no way back until the spring.

'Sail ho!'

The excited men crowded the gunwale. They had not seen another ship since they had lost the rest of the fleet. Were these the first natives of Cathay?

What they saw was both familiar and unexpected.

'Holy blood!' breathed Stephen. ''Tis a Christian ship.'

To call it a ship was flattery, thought Richard. It was more a small fishing boat with perhaps half a dozen men aboard, which meant that it could not be far from its home port. This was no exotic craft with the ribbed sails described by Marco Polo, but a small single-masted, single-sailed craft that would not have been out of place on the Thames. Had the Spaniards, the Portuguese, the Flemings or the Hansa reached this ocean ahead of them? But they would hardly have sent an inshore fishing craft, and this craft was clearly fishing.

The boat had already seen the *Edward Bonaventura* and was hauling in its net. The English ship changed tack to close with it, firing one of the remounted cannon to call it to halt. The strangers promptly cut their net, hoisted sail and made away.

The chase lasted four hours. What was the use in trying to escape, thought Richard? Did it mean their home port or some other refuge was within reach? Were they leading him under the guns of a Spanish fort? Or perhaps they were from some lost Viking colony, such as Dr Dee said existed in Greenland.

The strong breeze favoured the larger ship and, inexorably, she overhauled the fishing boat. At length the *Edward Bonaventura* was alongside and the Englishmen could stare down into the boat, a very ordinary fishing boat with a catch. The five men cowering among the fish could have been from Kent, except that they had rather fuller beards than was usual in England. They had fair skin, and fair to brown-grey hair. It seemed unlikely that they were Spanish or Portuguese. Their clothes were the usual shapeless grey slops expected of fishermen. They were of different ages, possibly different generations of the same family.

The Englishmen called down to them, but the strangers seemed disabled by fear or astonishment. Richard ordered five men into the boat, swords at their waists but not drawn. The strangers neither resisted nor co-operated, but let themselves be dragged onto the deck of the *Edward Bonaventura* where they lay face-down, refusing to stand or speak, as if awaiting execution.

The crew gathered to gape at them.

'Stand up, damn you! Stand up and face the captain! Speak!'

'Try 'em in Italian, Richard,' pleaded Stephen when Richard's English and Flemish gained no response. But no words in any language they could muster brought a response.

'Do we kill 'em, Richard?' asked Stephen. 'If we let them go they'll tell their fellows, and they'll send an armada to catch us.'

The Company had ordered them to be friendly to savages and the subjects of the great khan, but rival Europeans were problematic. The assumption was that they would be hostile. As both Richard and Stephen remembered, it was the Venetians who had harassed them through the Greek Isles on the Turkey voyage, and these had been England's allies.

'They know everything about us now,' Stephen argued. 'The cannon we mount, the number of our men, and that we're alone. And their boat's worth having, even for the cordage. 'Tis a pity they cut away the net.'

'Aye, kill 'em,' echoed the men. 'They won't speak – kill 'em!'

Richard never ceased to wonder that men who faced death so often themselves could be so careless with the lives of other poor mariners, as cheerful to see them die as if they were cockerels in a pit.

'The Company's orders are to befriend strangers and return them to their people,' replied Richard. 'These men are strangers, though they be not wild men in lions' skins. Ask them to lead us to their harbour. Better to winter in port than in the wilderness.'

'A port can be more dangerous, Richard. Our cargo is worth the taking. Suppose their port is held by an enemy of England? God knows we have few friends!'

'Then let's not multiply our enemies. Try to befriend them and discover the way to their port, but keep them prisoner and take their boat in tow. If their port is defended we will stand offshore and send an embassy to the governor, sending a single hostage to help treat with him. We have copies of the letters of credence from the king to all the princes of the earth, appointing Sir Hugh as the royal ambassador. For the moment, I will have to act Sir Hugh's part – we can explain later when we know they are friendly.'

The strangers still pressed their faces to the deck. Their hosts piled gifts around them: cloth of different sorts, caps and ribbons, pewter mugs and steel cutlery.

'Give 'em a drink,' advised one of the sailors. 'That'll loosen their tongues.'

They fetched a bottle of wine. Richard unsealed it and

poured a mugful for one of the strangers, who had timidly raised his head. The man shied away. Richard swallowed a mouthful. The stranger sat up, took a sip and spat it out.

The Englishmen laughed. 'He's no Frenchie or dago, for sure. Give him some honest ale.'

They brought beer and cider. The man tried both, preferred the cider and ventured a wary smile.

'*Harasho.*'

Now the others were sitting up, more mugs were filled and quickly emptied. '*Harasho! Harasho!*'

'*Harasho! Harasho!*' mimicked the English, beginning to learn the language before they knew what language it was.

At once the strangers were on their feet, embracing and kissing their captors. More cider was poured and what had risked being a massacre started to become a carousal.

'Show them the proclamations in all the languages,' ordered Richard.

'Were there ever fishermen who could read?'

'True, but there may be one who can recognise their alphabet.'

The fisherman frowned over the texts. Then one seized one of the papers and ran to the gunwale. The crew tried to restrain him, thinking he would destroy the document, but instead he gestured to the text and pointed to the horizon.

'I think he's trying to say,' said one of the men, 'that he can't read it, but he knows a man who can.'

'What language has he there?' asked Richard.

''Tis Greek.'

The little town sat in a bare landscape with neither fields nor farms, a small human footprint in a vast, untamed world. It was not on the seashore, which was mainly marsh, but several miles up a wide river, which curled lazily across the flat terrain. The settlement was on the outer bank of a big bend, where the deep water ran close inshore. Opposite was a broad beach, thronged with seabirds basking on the sand.

'They're moving south like us, before the sea freezes,' observed Stephen.

'Perhaps they know the way to Cathay.'

'More likely England, Richard. They look like the terns that winter in the Essex marshes.'

The houses were small and almost identical, like square timber boxes set along the riverside. They looked as if they had been shaped *en masse* at the same workshop. The wood was rough-hewn and used unsparingly, despite the lack of trees. Where do they get the wood, wondered Richard?

The only stone building was a fort on a low hill overlooking the town, but it was without visible cannon. If indeed they have no cannon, thought Richard, we control the town. It would burn well. From behind the walls of the fort loomed several buildings painted in blue and gold, topped by onion-shaped domes, like those seen on Greek churches.

The arrival of the ship and its prize brought the whole town to the quayside. They looked Christian enough, although in an old-fashioned style. Not that the poor had fashions in any country, but even the group standing at the end of the jetty, whom Richard took to be persons of quality, wore the long, loose robes and generous beards of the last century. He had the strange feeling that perhaps the ship had lost its way in time as well as space, and had chanced back on England a hundred years before its departure. The only exotic feature in the crowd was an abundance of fur hats, some particularly tall. If furs were plentiful, there was a chance for trade.

The *Edward Bonaventura* anchored in the river and Richard, with five men and one of their prisoner-guests, went ashore in the longboat. The Englishmen wore the blue coats last worn at Greenwich, and the ship's trumpeter sounded them onto the pier. Never could so mean a village have seen such a grand entry.

The captured fisherman led the way, calling out to the townsfolk and showing them the declaration in Greek. Whether any understood was not clear, but they seemed overawed. Even so, it was not Greek that they were speaking.

The crowd parted in hushed astonishment as the guide took them through the town and up the hill to the fort. Richard began to feel uneasy. The *Edward* might be able to destroy the town, but he would rather they did not have a murder to avenge.

The gates of the fort stood open, admitting them to a central courtyard surrounded by elaborately decorated wooden buildings. One looked like a bell tower, although it could also serve as a watchtower. Another was definitely a church, topped by a cross, although not a simple Latin cross but the triple-barred cross of the Greek church, which Richard recognised from Chios. He had already begun to suspect that this was perhaps not a military establishment when they were surrounded by a throng of brown-clad monks.

'Brother Antonis, your humble servant,' announced one of the younger brethren, speaking careful Greek. 'Welcome to the monastery of St Nicholas.'

'I am honoured to meet you,' answered Richard, in the same language. 'I am Richard Chancellor, sent as ambassador from His Dread Majesty King Edward the Sixth of England to your emperor.' He gestured to the letter, which the hostage had passed to Antonis. 'He is a great and mighty lord who desires traffic and friendship with all the peoples of the earth. We are come from his kingdom far beyond the sea.'

'Yes, indeed,' replied Antonis. 'We have heard of England. It lies beyond the German Ocean, does it not?'

Richard's carefully rehearsed speech vanished from his head. This undiscovered people knew about England? How could they, and could it be to England's advantage?

'Pray, forgive me,' continued Antonis, 'but the simple folk who brought you here would have had me believe you came from Heaven. For them Greek is the language of the church and, thus, the language of the angels. Now, I know where you are from, but I still do not understand how you reached us. The sea we fish in has no exit but to the Frozen Ocean. It is our lake. To meet a foreign ship has to be a miracle.'

In these few innocent words he murdered Richard's dream of Cathay. Richard had sailed into an enclosed sea, a bay with no exit save back into the Frozen Ocean, through a strait which was already freezing. Struggling to hide his dismay, he answered as evenly as he could.

'The ocean is passable in places and in certain months. His Majesty sent me to find a way to your ruler and he bids all I meet to help me find him.'

'We will spare no effort to help you, but it will not be possible for you meet the emperor before December.'

'December? Midwinter?'

'For us, winter is the season of travel. Our river will soon start to freeze, and when the ice is firm enough we will have a wide and easy highway to our emperor. Then we will send word of your arrival and we must await his permission to escort you to him.' He saw Richard's look of concern. 'Our sleighs fly across the ice like eagles – it will take less than six weeks to reach him.'

'Six weeks! Is your emperor so far?'

'It is a long way to Moscow.'

7

Ice

'Good riddance to him! Our great and skilful pilot general wasn't the sailor that he and his brother thought, and he's steered his fine ship to the bottom of the ocean. Either that or he's scurried back to his wife and brat. The fewer to share the glory and the profit when we come home from Cathay.'

Sir Hugh slammed his tankard onto the table. It was graceless to drink wine from a pewter tankard, but none of the admiral's glassware had survived the storm. At the rate that Sir Hugh and his officers were diminishing the stock of French wine, little would survive to reach Cathay.

The officers of the *Bona Esperanza* listened to Sir Hugh's outburst and remembered their friends.

'Issit cold out there?'

'Nay, 'ot as 'ell, Arfur! What d' y' think, you idle lad? While you've been a-snoring, we've been 'acking ice from the rigging to stop us turning over. There's more ice in the sea today and it ain't yet October.'

'D' y' think he'll turn back?'

'So our little seaman who'd sailed all the way to Newcastle is afrighted, issee? Nay, we'd need solid ice all over to change Sir Willie's mind, which won't be so very long perhaps. But for the nonce the wind's behind us and we're still northbound.'

'Did y' see the witch's lights again?'

'Y' don't wanna trouble your 'ead about them, lad.'

'Y' weren't so bold about the lights y'self yesternight,' sniggered Martin.

Jeremy had been the first man to see the lights. Like most of the crew, he had noticed small plays of lightning in a corner of the sky for several evenings past – not storm lightning, but little sparks which bothered nobody. And then, as he was watching them shortly after nightfall, they opened up right across the horizon in a sudden tapestry of multi-coloured fire. It hung for a moment in rippling folds, then vanished. Jeremy was looking about to see if anybody else had noticed when it happened again, and then again and again. The sea was calm, the air was clear and the night was silent. Nothing in nature explained it.

Jeremy had fallen to his knees and was still praying minutes later. Others hid and William Gefferson, the ship's master, ran to tell Sir Hugh.

'Magic lights! Witchcraft! Don't be a fool, man. Show them to me.'

Sir Hugh shuffled, cursing, onto the quarterdeck, muffled in a heavy cloak. The lights responded with an even more spectacular display.

Jeremy was directly below them on the maindeck and heard every word. 'They're dead ahead,' pleaded William. ''Tis an enchantment. They say ships can fall enchanted in the northern seas and sail for eternity without reaching port.'

'A turd in your teeth,' spat Sir Hugh. 'You're all ignorant fools with heads stuffed with stories of sea monsters and goblins. Give me a company of soldiers any day. Tell the men to get off their knees and get back to their duty.'

Sir Hugh returned to bed and Jeremy scurried back with the news to his messmates.

It lay before them, the reality behind the legend of the Frozen Ocean. When they had imagined the frozen sea they had envisaged it smooth and still, like the Thames in January above

London Bridge. What they saw today was a seething, writhing mass of ice, which cracked apart to open long leads of dark water and heaved together to throw up jumbled ridges as high as a ship, like a land gripped in a never-ending earthquake. Nor was it silent. It creaked and groaned, sighed and roared, and from time to time gave out sudden shrieks.

'We'll never pass through that, sir,' announced William Gefferson, with an air of satisfaction. 'We've found the Frozen Ocean and proved it impassable.'

'So then, God help us, we'll find a way around it,' replied Sir Hugh.

'We've done all that was asked of us,' protested William. 'When we took the sun at noon we were at seventy-five degrees north latitude – further north than any Christian ship, any ship in the history of the world, has ever sailed. We have discovered much and the season is late. 'Tis time to go home.'

'Did I hear that you'd seen land beyond the ice?'

'Aye, sir, but it is marvellous difficult to count distance at these latitudes. It may lie further than it shows. And it stretches north-south. I know Dr Dee maintains there is a passage from the Frozen Ocean to the Southern Ocean and Cathay, but I've heard that other doctors do say that the Frozen Ocean is a bay, with a shore that stretches from Asia to Greenland. The land we see may well be that shore, the head of the bay.'

'We will follow the edge of the ice east towards the land. There may yet be a way forward between the ice and the shore.'

'That, sir, is surely a matter for the council to decide.'

'Damn the council! Half of them have already gone to damnation and I'll decide for the rest. Besides, we don't need to consult the council because we're not changing course. I am keeping to course as best the ice allows.'

They followed the front of the pack ice towards the land, which emerged as a line of low, bare brown hills.

'My first discovery,' exclaimed Sir Hugh. 'This will be Willoughby Land. If need be, we shall winter here.'

They were halted not by the shore, but the shallows. Between them and the beach, more than a mile ahead, the sea lapped over flat black rocks. It was impossible to land, but for the moment, even Sir Hugh was not interested in visiting his discovery. It was a featureless land with no sign of life except thin, brown grass and thick, brown seaweed. Despite the ice on the sea, the shore was not under snow.

As Sir Hugh had hoped, the ice floe did not reach the shore and it was possible to coast northwards. They edged forward along the unwelcoming rocks and, as darkness fell, they anchored in a bay.

That night the wind changed and they awoke to see that the ice floe had closed on the shore and lay stretched across the mouth of the bay.

'We cannot land, sir, or at least, not without great difficulty, and to land stores would be nigh impossible,' insisted William Gefferson. 'And if we stay here we will be trapped in our ships, perhaps for the winter, and may be smashed by the ice. We must find a way back to the open sea.'

'So God gives you your own way at last, Mr Gefferson. I'm sure that pleases you. Get us out of here then and set course for Wardhouse.'

The ice across the mouth of the bay was broken ice from the edge of the floe, laced with passages of clear water. The ships had the chance of escape but the wind that was pushing the ice into the bay was pushing it closer together, so that the passages were narrowing even as they watched.

With the wind in their faces, the only way out of the bay was by towing or warping. To warp they loaded the for'ard anchors onto the ships' boats and rowed them ahead of the ships to drop them at a convenient point. The men on the ships then toiled at the windlasses to wind in the anchor chains. Once the anchors caught on the seabed, the ships winched forward with surprising speed until they were above the anchors, which were then hauled back onto the boats to repeat the cycle. It was hard work, but not so hard and slow as towing.

Warping brought the ships into the ice field, but once among the sinuous, shifting channels only towing was practicable. Sir Hugh paced the deck, cursing with impatience as they bumped and scraped through the bobbing ice at less than a walking pace.

The straining boat crews were cheered by the hope that, once out of the bay, the ice would be less crowded and they could turn southward with the wind behind them. But first they had to pass a zone where the jostling floes had collided and piled atop of each other. Gently the *Bona Esperanza* edged between two bergs, each scarcely smaller than the ship.

The closeness of the ice chilled the air. 'Where's my boy?' snapped Sir Hugh. 'Send for him to bring a flagon of malmsey, Mr Gefferson. Why isn't he on deck?'

William passed on the order and shortly a seaman appeared with the flagon.

'I asked for the boy. Where's that skulking lad? Why isn't he on deck?'

'He's afrighted, sir. Unfit to come on deck.'

'Frighted? Unfit? He's done nothing but pray half the night ever since we saw those damned lights. He seems to think he's the ship's priest. Get Samuel up here. I need him, *now!*'

The shivering thirteen-year-old was dragged on deck. At the same moment a shift of wind pushed the ship against the ice on the larboard side. The glittering white bulk loomed over the gunwale, close enough to taste. The boy screamed and ran to the opposite side of the deck. The vessel grated alongside the berg; the spar that carried the triangular sail on the mizzen mast struck the ice, swung about, broke free and clattered to the deck.

Those below easily dodged the falling timber, except for the crazed boy who ran clear into its path.

He died two days later. Sir Hugh spent most of the time at his bedside and left William Gefferson to bring the ships through the ice.

*

'What's your name, boy?'

'Arthur, sir.'

'A good name. A royal name. I've been watching you, Arthur. You've been a cabin boy before, so I'm told.'

'I attended Lady Thomas on a voyage with the Cloth Fleet.'

'Never heard of her. No matter. Now you're my attendant. Bring your things to the stateroom.'

Sir Hugh stood in the doorway, which opened into the stateroom from the cabin where he slept. It was a tiny cabin by landsmen's standards, luxury by the standards of the sea.

'Come on in, Arthur, I need you.'

Arthur was on the floor. A cabin boy always slept on the floor outside his master's door. He scrambled to his feet.

'Come inside.'

Sir Hugh drew the young man into the cabin. Most of it was occupied by the admiral's cot and a dressing table, both fixed against the bulkhead. Being a gentleman, Sir Hugh took off his clothes at night and now wore a linen nightshirt. Arthur usually slept in the clothes he had worn during the day, wet or dry.

'Let me take those filthy rags from you,' whispered Sir Hugh, unlacing the front of Arthur's shirt. 'If we work well together you shall be my page when I am the king's ambassador in Cathay, and I will dress you in naught but silks.'

Arthur stood, immobile, as Sir Hugh peeled away the shirt. He had the dead look of a Scots prisoner waiting to be hanged.

They set their course south-westwards, which they supposed to be the direction of Wardhouse, but the wind sent them where it willed. It blew both hard and soft and seldom for more than two hours from the same quarter. For two weeks they wandered like the enchanted ships of the legend, much of the time in heavy mist, keeping contact by firing cannon. At least they saw no more of the magic lights. The men began to show signs of scurvy, teeth loosening, gums bleeding and old scars opening like fresh wounds.

At last they saw land across the southern horizon. In an interval in the mist they saw mountains inland. This was a major landmass, presumably the northern shore of Europe and Asia. They turned west to find Wardhouse.

The further they sailed the less Sir Hugh welcomed the thought of meeting Richard Chancellor at the rendezvous. He had castigated Richard as a deserter, but he could yet be waiting at Wardhouse, in which case it was clearly Sir Hugh who had lost his way and disobeyed Company orders. Also, Sir Hugh's ships and men were sure to be in a much sorrier state than Richard's, a comparison he did not wish to make.

But, more than this, Wardhouse was halfway to abandoning the dream of Cathay. The council might well decide to sail back to London and Sir Hugh would never become ambassador to the khan, never escape the dreary pettiness of Protestant England.

'Mr Gefferson, we have passed several deep and sheltered bays and I think we could well winter in one of these.'

'Our orders were to meet at Wardhouse, sir.'

'Not my orders, Mr Gefferson. If Mr Chancellor ever reached Wardhouse, which is scarce probable, he will have left 'ere now. And if we go there the men will surely desert. Even soldiers would desert after a campaign such as ours. As I understand it, the Cloth Fleet routinely loses half its mariners in the taverns of Antwerp.'

'There'll be fewer taverns in Wardhouse, and little chance of another ship to England.'

'Aye, but if there is a castle there it must have something to protect. Look into the next bay.'

To Sir Hugh's surprise, William Gefferson put up no further argument. The next day they entered a broad, deep bay. At the entrance there was a narrow beach, and as they passed they noticed heaps of bones littering the shingle, as if a multitude of animals had been butchered there. There were also two deep pits and the remains of numerous shelters made from poles. Two ancient boats were drawn up above the waterline, although whether they had been drawn up for the winter or simply abandoned was not clear. How long this rubbish had lain on the beach was impossible to judge, nor whether its owners intended to return.

'Savages,' declared Sir Hugh. 'We must be on our guard. Nobody is to go ashore except in parties of ten or more. All men must carry arms and an armed man must always be on guard while the others work. And we must keep guards on deck, for savages are famous swimmers and can approach underwater and climb aboard.'

Sir Hugh was glad to see signs of the savages. Now they would need a soldier. He had not felt in command of this expedition since they had been becalmed in the German Ocean. During the long weeks when there had been almost nothing for the sailors to do, he had imposed a regime of gunnery practice, for he understood cannon better than ships. The men soon became better gunners than sailors. But Richard Chancellor and the rest of the council had put a stop even to this, complaining that he was depleting powder and shot.

Once on the move, especially once the bad weather set in, Sir Hugh had become almost totally redundant. His officers overruled or ignored his almost every order on grounds of maritime necessity. Now that the voyage was suspended he could reimpose his authority.

How he hated everybody in the fleet. Everybody except Samuel, of course. He had liked Samuel, perhaps loved him, but then Samuel had had an attack of religious fever after he had seen the lights in the sky and decided that it was a warning from God for sleeping in the admiral's bed. Sir Hugh had been angry, but he had not wanted Samuel to die. He had wanted him to be his page and companion in Cathay.

This new boy was a strange young man. He was good-looking

but said little, and had a sullen, independent manner. Still, they had all winter to learn to know each other.

The bay was deep, with deep water close inshore. They stopped beside a scree that offered a possible ascent of the steep banks. The four anchors splashed into the calm water and officers and men prepared to make this their home for the long winter.

William Gefferson rowed across to the *Bona Confidentzia*, supposedly to confer with Cornelius Durnforth about unloading stores.

'Why were you so consenting with the admiral to winter here, rather than sail for Wardhouse?' asked Cornelius. 'Wardhouse is our meeting point if the fleet is separated, and maybe the *Edward* awaits us there. Once the council is reunited we could scotch this mad fancy of the admiral's to try the ice again in the spring. 'Tis plain as God's truth that the Frozen Ocean is impassable and we'll all die trying to force it.'

'I doubt Richard Chancellor would still be at Wardhouse,' answered William, 'if indeed Wardhouse truly exists. And are you so sure that Mr Chancellor might not be minded to try the ice next year? A man who has ne'er seen it can ne'er imagine it. 'Tis better we decide our own fortune in the private of the wilderness. It's a goodly land and well watered.'

Cornelius shuffled uneasily. 'Do you speak of mutiny?'

'The council cannot mutiny against itself. There are seven of the council here, including the admiral and our two selves. If six are of one mind and the admiral refuses, he is the mutineer.'

'And if he goes against the council, as sure he will?'

'He can stay here and we can sail for Gravesend.'

Cornelius frowned. 'How do we explain that?'

'We tell the Company he met with an accident or was killed by his savages. If we officers all tell the same tale the men will ne'er deny us. They want to see England again as much as we. We must act when we know we are all of one mind.'

8

Death

Sir Hugh Willoughby sat in his stateroom at the head of the table. His silverware was set before him and a meagre meal of broth, biscuits and salt fish had been laid out. There was also a bowl of rather dry vegetables, mainly onions, for Sir Hugh had unusual opinions about food and made his officers eat unfashionable items to ward off scurvy. Two ranks of wineglasses stood along the table, some empty, some partly charged; more wine sat in two large decanters. Five other members of the council were seated around the table. William Gefferson sat next to Sir Hugh, and opposite him sat Cornelius Darnforth of the *Bona Confidenzia*, with the ship's master beside him. One chair lay upturned. Its former occupant was by the door, slumped against the bulkhead. The dead remains of a coal fire were banked in the hearth.

The man on the floor seemed fast asleep, as did everyone at the table.

A scraping sound beyond the door grew louder, followed by heavy blows and splintering wood. The door swung open and three men stood in the doorframe. Jeremy Ketch nursed an axe, Martin Cook held a crowbar and Stephen Andrews clutched a snow-caked shovel. A gust of cold air swept across the floor, forcing out the lingering warmth.

The three men turned and hauled Arthur Petty into the doorway. 'Go on then, boy, go on in. The gas'll thin out with the door open.'

'We shouldn't a' done this, Jeremy. No good'll come of it. We're accursed. None of us'll escape.'

'Avast snivelling, lad. 'Twas your doing, so go on in.'

'What if they still be alive?' whispered Arthur.

'Then we'll be 'eroes, come to save 'em, or we can help 'em on their way to 'eaven or wherever, if they're near enough dead.'

Arthur edged through the doorway and fearfully prodded the figure lying close by.

''Tis John Standish of the *Confidency*. He must have known something was awry and tried to force the door, God rest his soul.'

'See to the others,' hissed Jeremy.

'Nay. I'm not steppin' no further. I'd rather die. Let's leave 'em be and be gone.'

'The lad's right. Leave 'em be,' agreed Stephen, with a shudder. 'If the one be dead, so be they all.'

All four fell back and refastened the door.

'Unblock the chimney,' urged Jeremy. They climbed the icy steps to the poop deck and scraped the snow from the chimney vent. There was no smoke left to escape from the room below, and the invisible, slow gas from the smouldering coals, which had taken the occupants to their silent, sweet and unsuspecting death, had already been forced away.

'We shouldn't have done it! We're accursed,' whimpered Arthur.

''Twas your idea, boy,' hissed Jeremy, 'and you remember that. You don't want to go back to the ice agin, no more 'n we do. Do you want to die in the ice like the last cabin boy? Or did you want to be the admiral's fancy-boy in Cathay, like he wanted for you?'

Arthur shuddered and bit his lip.

'Aye,' continued Jeremy, ''twas you that told us those stories of yours, of 'ole families that'd been poisoned in their sleep on their 'ouseboats on the Thames by slow gas from their fires o' sea coals. You put us onto this plan, so that we could rid us of all the officers in one go and take the ships 'ome ourselves come the spring.'

'We didn't have to kill 'em all.'

'Yes we did, lad. That's just what we 'ad to do. They was havin' a meetin' on where to sail when the sea was clear. You told us so. We daren't wait 'til they decided. D' y' think Gloryguts would 'ave agreed to sail for 'ome? D' y' think the others would e're 'ave persuaded 'im? They used to stand up to 'im, but no longer. Didn't they let 'im make us build that stupid stone fort on the shore, and drag the guns up the cliff and wear oursel's out 'untin' savages through the 'ills, though we never so much as glimpsed the 'ide nor 'air of 'em?'

'The admiral was a vile man,' added Stephen. ''E was vile and unnatural to you. Y' told us so. We would all 'ave died. We's startin' dying already. We 'ad to get rid of all the officers for the sake of our mates who lie stiff on shore, waiting for the spring when we can bury 'em. 'Sides, they didn't know nothin' about it. Just thought they'd 'ad a bit too much of the wine they was supposed to be trading in Cathay. Dropped off after dinner and didn't wake up again.'

The other two men murmured agreement.

'Aye,' spat Jeremy, 'they died a sweeter death than they or any of us would have found in Willoughby Land or wherever we would 'ave fetched up – and a far sweeter death than the scurvy.'

'Anyway, 'tis done now and the rights and wrongs are for God,' said Martin impatiently. 'The arguing and the 'suading's over. You lit the fire that killed 'em, Arfur.'

'But I didn't never truly believe it'd work – none of us did!'

'But it did work, lad, better 'n we knew, and now we've got to stick together and see it through – see as we all gets 'ome. You'll see your mother agin on your little 'ouseboat you told us of, see if she's starved yet or no. You knowed our plan, though none of us knowed 'ow it would 'appen out. They're asleep now forever, dreamin' o' Cathay, and it's time for the rest of us to awake.'

*

As winter had closed in on the anchorage the men of the two ships had taken down the topmasts and upper yards, and used the spars and sails to build awnings over the maindecks. The two ships sat on the ice wrapped like chrysalids, waiting for the spring to shake off their wrappings and unfurl their wings.

The space under the awnings was heated by braziers, mainly burning sea coals now that the men found it too cold to go out and cut wood. It was never warm there, but they could survive and move around. Outside, the murderous cold was supreme. By December men seldom left the ships, even to cross the ice from one vessel to the other.

Today, however, all the men of both ships who were fit to stand were gathered on the main deck of the *Bona Esperanza* to hear the strange news. The sides of the awning had been reefed back, despite the cold, to let in the starlight reflected from the snow. It was night even at noon, but the Arctic starlight was bright enough to see by.

Jeremy, Martin and Stephen had climbed on the hen coops (the hens were long since eaten) to address the men. Like everybody present, they were muffled in the heavy over-garments made from the cloth that was intended for sale in Cathay, and they shuffled their feet constantly to keep the blood moving. The steam of the men's breath hung over the assembly and rimed their beards.

'Shipmates, you've all 'eard the news,' began Jeremy, 'of the strange and unnatural death of our admiral and 'is officers, and 'ow they was found dead at table with not a mark on their bodies, God rest their souls.'

Several men crossed themselves, although this was no longer part of the official religion.

''Twas doubtless the witchcraft of the savages,' continued Jeremy, 'that we've chased in the 'ills, and whose magic signs we've seen so oft in the skies. They sit there together still. Any man among you can go witness 'em.' He gestured to the steps behind him. The men shrank away. 'Arfur Petty 'ere found 'em when he came to clear the service. Arfur had been sent away while they had a privy meeting – 'tis said they was planning another voyage through the ice.'

A growl of hostility rippled through the assembly.

'Now they're gone, we needs elect new officers to order the ships and determine if to go on to Cathay or sail for England in the spring.'

To Jeremy, it seemed self-evident that they would chose new officers to bring them home. As a common seaman he could not expect – even if he might hope – to be elected as one of the officers, but he had his own candidates who were friendly to himself and ready to go back. But he had misread the wind.

'If the ship's bewitched we'll all be dead men too, if we tarry,' shouted Charles Tanner of the *Confidezia*.

'We'll escape when we can,' agreed Jeremy, 'but presently the ice 'olds us fast. We must await the thaw and, for the nonce, must elect a captain.'

'Christ's blood, why wait on death?' snarled Charles, and a shout of approval echoed across the deck. 'Leave the goddamned admiral in his enchantment. 'Is death is a stone lifted from our 'earts. If we stay 'ere longer we'll all be dead of the scurvy. The ships are cursed, the land is cursed – save ourselves now and away!'

'Away! Away!' The roar sent clouds of vapour steaming into the cold air.

Jeremy flinched. Most of the men had heard of the sudden death of their officers before the meeting, and many of them had clearly decided what to do and were determined to force it through. He had not expected the mass murder to succeed; the beauty of the plan had been that if it miscarried it would leave no trace. He had given little thought on how to handle success.

'Be sane, shipmates,' he pleaded above the tumult. ''Ow can you sail before the ice melts?'

'The ships are accursed,' shouted another sailor. 'To the boats!'

'How can we sail home once we're dead?' insisted Charles.

'We've still got the *Comfy*'s pinnace and we can take the small boat from the *Esperanza*. To the boats!'

The meeting began to break up.

''Ow will you navigate in the dark?' pleaded Jeremy.

'If you care not to come with us, Jeremy, stay here with the witches and the cadavers,' said Charles. 'We're taking the boats, and stores enough to reach Wardhouse.'

'And 'ow'll you find it?'

'The same way as we was lookin' for it, afore the admiral decided to winter 'ere. We'll follow the shore westwards.'

'You're fools, damned fools! 'Ow're you to launch the boats on the ice?'

'We'll drag 'em to the open water. There's open water beyond the landfast ice, as you well knows. We could see it from the fort. We'll take our chances. Jesus knows we know more about sailing through ice than any other Christian men alive.'

'And what'll you do about the sick?'

'They'll 'ave to stay here, those of 'em that'll meet their maker before we can reach Wardhouse. That cabin boy can minister to 'em till they pass on. 'Twill be a Christian duty which will atone for 'is sins.'

The cabin boy's sins needed no explanation.

'You seem to 'ave it all mightily well thought out, Charles. When did you become admiral?'

'When did you, Jeremy? Just because you and your messmates found the admiral's corpse doesn't give you the right to 'is shoes. The men of the *Confy* chose me as their leader afore we came over. Any of your ship can come with us or stay, except we're not having that cabin boy. 'E 'as the mark of Satan.'

Jeremy's brief reign was over. Without enough men to handle at least one ship, he had no choice but to join the exodus. The weeks of caged inactivity, darkness and cold, scurvy and magic lights, capped by the sudden, strange death of their admiral and all the senior officers, had left most of the men more ready to risk their lives on the darkened sea than stay an instant longer with the ships.

*

Before the men left they brought their sick comrades together on the *Bona Confidenzia*, leaving the *Bona Esperanza* to the frozen corpses in the stateroom. Seven men too sick to take to the boats were left in Arthur's care. They all died within the week. They expected to die and all that Arthur could do was to feed and clean them as best he could until they expired. Why men died of scurvy was a mystery. It was doubtless due to the air or the food on the ships, although many of the men had worked ashore before the cold set in. Even more mysterious was why some fell ill while others stayed sound, and why officers were slower to succumb than seamen. Unlike the plague, tending the sick seemed not to expose the carers to the disease. When the last patient died Arthur still had no signs of scurvy.

For the first time in his life he found himself alone. Until then he had seldom even shat in private. As a baby he had shared his parents' bed, and when he was old enough he had slept on the floor with his siblings. At sea he had always slept on the deck with the crew, except when he had become Sir Hugh's cabin boy. Now he had two great ships and an unknown waste of bay, mountain and forest to share only with the cadavers.

He decided to walk home. It would give him something to do, even if he died on the way. He knew he could not walk to Gravesend but he reasoned that he could walk to Antwerp and, once there, he could find Kate Thomas' agent to find him a ship to England. He would tell him that he knew Kate, which should get him a berth on the Cloth Fleet. He knew it was mad, but whatever he did, he would most likely die within the next several months. He deserved to die and his life was not so much to lose, but he was not yet ready to accept the end.

It never occurred to him as unfair that his shipmates should leave him behind, he who had been the instrument of their release. He had allowed himself to be cajoled and bullied into the plan to kill Sir Hugh, which none of them really expected to work, not to escape the ice but to escape becoming Sir Hugh's silken consort in Cathay. He had no nostalgia for England, although he did want to see his mother again, which was why he was setting out for Antwerp.

He became very busy, sewing a new set of clothes for the journey, including a hood and mittens. He found some new boots, which were too big so he packed them with oakum. After this he took one of the sleds they used as carriages for the cannon (a spare one, for he was not strong enough to dismount a cannon alone), and cut a square of sailcloth so that he could turn it into a tent when he slept, by tipping the sled on its side. He loaded it with dried fish and hard bread, enough for four or five days, several blankets from the officers' cabins, flint and steel, tinder, an iron kettle, an axe, a spare knife and a small crossbow and feathered bolts.

There was room for more food on the sled, but Arthur could not resist raiding the ship's cargo. He had never been to the cargo hold before. It was vaster than he had imagined, a great cavern whose depths stretched far beyond the light of his guttering candle. It was stacked with every artefact a household could need, in immense quantities. Besides all the woollen cloth, there were needles and pins, pewter mugs and plates, knives and spoons, mechanical toys, caps and ribbons, bonnets and laces, and so much else. He made up a sack with something of everything. Just owning them was a joy, but he reckoned that he might sell them from village to village once he reached a Christian country.

Last of all, he loaded a fiddle and bow. It was not the instrument he had brought aboard at Gravesend; that was in the stateroom among the incorrupt corpses. However, there were plenty of other instruments on the ship. The men who had taken to the boats had not been planning to make music.

His preparations complete, Arthur climbed down onto the ice and set out in the opposite direction to his former shipmates; southwards, up the bay away from the sea. Sir Hugh had sent out several exploring parties before the winter set in and, although

Arthur had not been on any of them, he had heard their reports. He knew the bay led a long way southwards into a land of forests. Once in the forest, he could gather wood and hunt game until he reached a Christian land to peddle his trade goods.

He made much better progress than he had seen his shipmates make across the snow, despite the laden sled and the bundle of firewood towed behind it – firewood chopped from the crew's mess-tables. Whereas the other men had trudged through the snow, he slid across it on long slats of wood lashed to the soles of his boots.

He had grown up on the Kentish mudflats, a mudlark since he could walk, slithering over the grey ooze on plank mudshoes, hunting driftwood and terns. The mudshoes worked even better on snow, with a staff to lever himself along. Skimming over the snow was like being a child again on the foreshore. The strange, twilit, black-and-white landscape began to look beautiful. It was so clean and silent after the stench and restlessness of the ship. This was a good place to die.

Since the night lasted all day and he had no hourglass, he had no way to measure the passage of time. He slept when drowsy, travelled when wakeful and ate sparingly when he could no longer contain his hunger. When he had used his bundle of firewood and had found nothing to hunt on the ice, he moved onto the land. The land was flatter now and the scattered trees had merged into a continuous forest.

The forest was not what he had hoped. The uneven ground made progress more difficult, and the small trees were set so far apart they offered little shelter from the wind, which plastered them with thick layers of ice so that they seemed to be carved from stone. Occasionally, a branch would snap and shed its burden of ice, but for the most part, this new world was motionless as well as timeless. From time to time he heard the cry of wolves and owls. They knew how to hunt in the dark, but Arthur could find little use for his crossbow.

He navigated by the slope of the ground, climbing a low ridge and descending into the valley beyond. Here he chanced upon a starlit path, carved through the forest by a frozen stream. Along its banks were the tracks of scores of deer, all pointing in the same direction. The trail was old, but he followed it. Perhaps a sick or injured animal might have fallen by the way and the wolves had left him something of its carcass.

Two days later he came upon an abandoned campsite. Whoever had pitched camp had been lucky hunters. The snow was scattered with animal bones and pieces of hide with fat still on them, which he chewed gratefully.

He supposed at first that the camp had belonged to the elusive savages, until he found a broken steel knife very like his own. He also found a small ice-free tree, sheltered by the banks of the stream, with dozens of scraps of cloth tied to the branches. This looked like some form of heathen worship, except that the rags were linen and wool and even a few shreds of silk, such as he had seen in Sir Hugh's wardrobe. Of course savages in the Arctic could not go naked as they did in Spanish romances, but did they really wear woollens and silks?

He tied a ribbon of his own to the tree and dumped most of his pewterware and other trade goods at its foot. They were too heavy. He kept the needles, for they were light and would sell well in any village he found.

He ate the last of his food the following day. After three days his hunger began to slacken and instead he began to have visions. At times, he sensed another self gliding along on mudshoes beside him, with the same juvenile stature and swaddled in the same way against the cold. Yet when he looked again there was only the twilight. And there were other shapes among the trees, shadow people moving faster than ever mortals could move, even on mudshoes.

His legs grew clumsy, and he began to lose the feeling in them. Particular rocks and trees began to repeat themselves, as though he were going in circles. The shadow people multiplied and drew closer. He abandoned his sled and shuffled on until he sank into the snow, the mudshoes still tied to his feet, pointing to the sky. The shadow people closed in and carried him away.

9

Overland

'Yelena,' asked Richard, hesitantly, 'why are you so unlike the other people I have met in Russia?'

Yelena was tending the stove, the glow of the burning logs reflecting on the silk of her long black hair. She was shorter than most English or Russian women, light-limbed, with a broad, smooth face and high cheekbones. Her eyes were the shape of almonds and very dark.

Richard was fascinated by her appearance. She was strikingly un-Russian, in a colony where everybody else was big-limbed, blue-eyed and brown-haired. One did not discuss personal matters with servants, but Richard finally persuaded himself that it was part of his mission to find out all he could about the inhabitants of the lands he discovered.

'You mean, why do I have slit eyes and a flat nose?'

She smiled, a strange, slow smile that started in her eyes and spread gently across her face like the dawn, until it flashed across her big, strong, white teeth.

'Forgive me, I did not mean to slight you. I mean – where are you from? Are you Greek? You speak Greek, you have a Greek name, but those were never Greek eyes.'

'I am a Russian slave. *Your* slave, given to you by the Russians. Did they not explain that I was a slave? They have slaves in Russia, although I think they no longer have them in other Christian countries. Do you have slaves in England?'

'No, although certain gentlemen have blackamoor servants

who were purchased in Lisbon. The Portuguese catch them in Africa. But in my country, Christians do not enslave each other. But it is I who am asking the questions, Yelena.'

'Christians enslave each other in Russia, often for debt, although the young tsar is trying to change this. But most slaves are captives taken from elsewhere, like myself. I call myself Yelena because I can speak Greek, but in my own land I was Gulmira.'

'And your land is?'

'I have no land. I am a Tartar. I was captured in a Russian raid on Kazan, on the great river Volga east of Moscow, but that is not my country. I was once a princess, in a land called Krim. It is rich and beautiful with a soft climate, and lies by the Euxine Sea. There are many Greeks there and we trade with Constantinople, so Greek is our second tongue.'

'Tell me about Krim.'

'Krim is ruled by a khan, the overlord of all the other Tartar khans of Astrakhan and Kazan, but they, like all subjects, quarrel with their overlords, which was fortunate for my mother and myself, or so we believed. My father was murdered in a dispute over the succession, so we fled to Kazan. Had we reached there, the khan of Kazan would probably have returned us to Krim, for Kazan was beset by the Russians and the khan wanted help from Krim, but it was God's will that the Russians found us first while we travelling on the Volga. In that way, we escaped the siege and plunder of Kazan by the tsar. My mother is now in Moscow and I was given to the abbot of St Nicholas, who wanted a Greek-speaking secretary. Which is how I came to be here, so far from Krim, and how I became your interpreter, your secretary and your slave.'

'Are Tartars Christians?'

'They follow Islam.'

'And you?'

'I call myself Yelena and am as Orthodox as the abbot expects me to be. And you, my lord?'

'In England religion is private. We do not seek windows into men's souls.'

'Only into the souls of female Tartar slaves?'

'Forgive me. Princess, remember that I am an ambassador and my trade is discretion. I am under orders not to discuss my country's religion. We call ourselves Christians, but what sort of Christians we are at the moment I honestly do not know. We were Catholic Christians once, following the Pope in Rome, until the late king changed our religion, which has set us apart from our neighbours. Not everybody in England is happy with the change, or the other changes since the old king died. King Edward, his son, is a boy and the country is ruled in his name by nobles who squabble for power. Nobody knows what will happen should Edward die, as he might well have done since I left, for of late he has been very sickly. This is more than I should say. It is not for an ambassador to advertise the weaknesses of his country.'

'Nor is it for a slave to repeat her master's secrets. As a female slave in a monastery, I, too, had to learn discretion.' She gave the broadest smile Richard had ever seen on a human face. 'I asked about your religion only to know if you had a preference about mine.'

'It's your soul, Yelena. But you say your people follow Islam, yet you are not Turks?'

'Our ancestors came from Kitai. We once ruled Russia. We trade with Kitai along the Volga, which is how the Russians get their silk.'

'Kitai?'

'To the east, beyond the desert.'

'You mean…Cathay?'

For the next six weeks the hiss of the sleigh runners over the river ice was background music to almost every waking hour. The convoy of nearly fifty sleighs had other sounds – the muffled hoof-beats of the horses in the snow, the coughs and snorts of the steaming animals, and murmurs of conversation among the hundred travellers – but apart from the occasional call of a horsemen to his horses or to another sleigh, these were all hushed noises, as if everyone was fearful of disturbing the silence of the forests, which grew thicker and darker along the riverbanks as they glided southwards.

The monastery and village of St Nicholas had not been totally alone in the Arctic wilderness. There was a slightly larger settlement about fifty English miles – or 100 versts, as the Russians measured it – further up the river Dvina, named Kholmogory. It was here that the *Edward Bonaventura* moved after several days at St Nicholas. Beyond Kholmogory, there were only two small settlements for the next 1,000 versts.

The little colonies beside the White Sea might as well have been islands, thought Richard. Even much of their food came from far away, and they often had to live for months on their stores. They found their own fish and salted and exported the surplus, they had some vegetable gardens and the huntsmen found game in the wilderness, but all the flour for their heavy black bread was brought from the south, beyond the great forest, as were all their woollen cloth and metal goods.

'This is a roadless land,' explained Yelena. 'Everything travels on the rivers. They spread a net across Russia from the Frozen Ocean to the Euxine Sea, the Black Sea as the Russians call it, but in summer they are often difficult to navigate and portages have to be made between headwaters. The winter turns them into highways of ice, broader and smoother than any road-maker could lay out. Then the settlements of the north can send their salt fish, sea salt and furs to Moscow and the tsar's other lands by sleigh. It was along these highways that my Tartar ancestors conquered Russia. We attacked in winter, when the ice opened the way for our horsemen. They call the winter Russia's friend, but on that occasion, she was a false friend.'

The people of St Nicholas and Kholmogory had been enraptured by the English ship and its cargo. Almost everybody who was able to climb or be carried aboard visited the ship, felt the thickness of her cables, caressed the metal of her guns, gaped at her towering masts and wondered at the spread of her canvas. The trade goods were equally fascinating, and the English were happy to exhibit them in the market square. However, there were no customers. The governor forbade all trade with the strangers until he had received a permit from the tsar, although this did not preclude exchanges of gifts, in kind or services. Yelena was a present from the abbot of St Nicholas.

'Your emperor must be powerful, Yelena,' wondered Richard, 'to be so feared so far away.'

'For the moment, they fear him. They call him Ivan the Terrible because of his stern face and black beard, but he has spent most of his life more terrified than terrible. Like your king, Edward, he was a boy king. His father died when he was three years old, his mother was poisoned by the boyars – the nobles – and he lived in fear of them throughout his childhood while they ruined the country with their quarrels. Things are better now that he is a man. The tsarina is greatly loved, and he has just won a war against the Tartars. But Russia is like cast iron. It is hard, but cracks easily.'

The stay at Kholmogory had lasted three months. It grew colder than the English imagined possible; the marshes became firm land and the sea and the great river turned to ice. People came and went from the ship by sleigh. It was warm enough below decks, but on deck it hurt to draw breath. The daylight dwindled to a brief twilight around noon.

At last the courier had returned from Moscow with the tsar's assent, plunging the listless town into a frenzy. The great convoy of sleighs was organised and loaded with people, supplies and trade goods. Amongst the samples of English wares was a great silver bowl intended as a present for the khan of Cathay. Its companion piece was with Sir Hugh on the *Bona Esperanza*. Richard and Stephen and eight other Englishmen were to travel to Moscow, the rest were left to guard the icebound ship.

*

They kept the campfire burning all night to keep away the cold and the wolves.

The evening meal was over and Richard slid gratefully beneath his bearskin at the privileged place closest to the fire. There was a bundle under the cover. He pushed it aside and it gave a playful laugh.

'Yelena, what are you doing here?'

'I am your slave, master. *You* must decide what I do.'

'Why are you here?'

'Don't you like me then? You prefer tall girls with yellow hair? You liked me in the bathhouse, although you pretended not to look at me.'

The Russian bathhouses confused and astonished the English. In England some richer folk took baths, Sir Henry for instance, but the old king had never bathed and it was unlikely that his children did. In general, wealthier men and women doused themselves in perfume and lesser mortals were happy as they were, sailors in particular. The men of the *Edward Bonaventura* were surprised that the Russians found them physically offensive, and shocked at the way in which they were expected to keep clean.

The Russians had no shyness about their bodies. They crowded naked, both sexes together, into the bathhouses, where they chatted, drank, cavorted, and did business or nothing at all in clouds of steam. Richard knew that the Turks had similar habits, but he had never been forced to share them.

He had been more intrigued than aroused by the sight of Yelena's body, seeing it as he did in such a public setting, but over the coming days the image of the stark contrast between her jet-black body hair and pale flesh kept sneaking into his mind, even in his sleep. It was difficult not to recall it whenever he saw her clothed. She was so lightly built that he had fantasies that if he became too excited making love to her there would be no room inside her and his semen would gush from her ears.

'I'm a husband with a young child.'

'Yes, I have seen the silver charm she gave you in your purse. But how do you know she still loves you, or even that she is still alive? Your England is further than the stars. You may never see it again. Do you really think Tsar Ivan is going to let you go, that he is bringing you to Moscow to exchange courtesies with a country that he never knew existed?'

'Then why are we going to Moscow?'

'Who knows? The tsar and his advisers have reasons beyond the understanding of we poor subjects. All you can know for sure is that your body knows that I am here beside you. *Inshallah.*'

'But everybody will see us…will hear us.'

'So they will.'

They left the Dvina at a little settlement named Ustyug and travelled up one of its tributaries, the Sucuma, to the town of Vologda, 1,000 versts from Kholmogory. For the first time in five weeks they slept under a roof.

Vologda, the largest Russian town Richard had yet seen, was built in the same way as all the others. All but the grandest houses were four-square little buildings of rounded fir logs, assembled from sections stored in timber yards, ready to add extra dwellings or replace ones destroyed by fire. Long avenues cut through the town, serving as firebreaks, and the roofs were sealed with earth to guard against sparks. Even such a large town as Vologda looked as if it had grown from the soil, rather than being the work of men.

The townsfolk feted the convoy. Every house was open to them and a bowl of salt stood at every doorway as a sign of welcome. It was the salt itself which made the visitors so welcome, for it was they who brought it from the White Sea.

The more important passengers stayed in the larger houses, yet even these were mostly single-roomed dwellings. Guests were given the 'fine corner' beneath the icons. A whole gallery of candlelit sacred pictures watched over Richard and Yelena, staring down on their noisy, adulterous unions.

'Do they never douse those lamps?' complained Richard.

'Never. It would be sacrilege. Every icon must have its *lampada* to light it day and night. They use our train oil. Even though the icons get filthy with soot, it is sacrilege to clean them or destroy them, so they just add new ones. That's what they do all the time in the monasteries. They paint icons and sell them to the faithful.'

At Vologda they ran out of river and the sleighs took to a bumpy track over the watershed to the Volga.

'Is this the river where they captured you, Yelena? It doesn't look very big.'

'I was captured a long way from here. There the river is big and by the time it reaches the sea, 3,000 versts from here, it is almost a sea in itself. This is the silk road to Kitai.'

Six days later they stood on a low hill looking over a city as vast as London. It was built in the standard Russian manner, with thousands of four-square timber boxes, except for the stone churches and a great fortress ringed by a huge crenelated red brick wall. At least two cathedrals lifted a cluster of golden domes above the battlements.

'There,' declared Yelena, 'is Moscow!'

10

Sami

The aspen twigs burnt with bright, fierce heat. They also gave off thick, white smoke, which was why the men squatting around the fire were coughing. The fire gave the Sami people warmth and life in their harsh land, and eventually killed most of them by clogging their lungs. This was not, however, why the present group were in such an ill humour.

They spoke of the hard winter, of the shortage of lichen for the reindeer, of the lack of trade for train oil during the summer and the price of imported cloth. Above all, they complained of the Muscovites, whom they had not yet learned to call Russians. The Muscovites were not content to trade with the Sami, as the merchants from Novgorod had been in the days before Novgorod had been subdued by Moscow. The Muscovites wanted to tax them in return for protecting them against enemies they had never had.

'They want to bleed us,' grumbled Pakku. 'They are richer than us, but they want to bleed us. They want to take by threats what they cannot get by trade.'

'If it were only so simple,' replied his friend, Atti. 'They want us to trade only with them, on their terms, and to make enemies of our friends because they are enemies of the Muscovites. Soon they will want to take away our men to fight their wars. If we do as they wish, the Swedes or the Danes will attack us, and if we refuse, the Muscovites will attack us themselves. They will burn our huts and leave us to die, as they did with the Suomi and the Eesti.'

'If they can catch us,' said another. 'Can you imagine them stumbling through the forest? We can make circles around them on our skis.'

'They can kill our herds and stop our trade,' said Atti. 'We need more than bows and spears if we are to defend ourselves and make it too costly for them to harass us.'

'Is the young stranger a Muscovite?'

'He looks like a Muscovite but he seems not to understand their language, nor Swedish nor Danish. Nobody understands where he is from. And he has brought gifts – valuable gifts – and he left gifts under the Wishing Tree. He was trying to find us by following the reindeer tracks.'

'Never trust a Muscovite bearing gifts!'

'The *no'adi* will enlighten us.'

'We have been here so long,' groaned Pakku. 'When will the *no'adi* come back from his flight? He stopped beating his drum so long ago, his spirit must have covered the world and flown behind the moon and the stars countless times. Why doesn't he speak to us?'

'Sometimes,' said Etta, from the other side of the fire, 'the *no'adi*'s spirit is trapped in the rocks or beneath a lake, and it may be several nights before it can return to his body. Sometimes it never returns and the *no'adi* dies. Perhaps his spirit is even now far away, struggling with a force greater than its own.'

'You are so helpful, Etta,' replied Atti. 'Our *no'adi* has always served our *seta* well. He healed you when you were sick. He laid his hands on you and sent his spirit to plead with our ancestors and bargain with the spirit of the mountain, and here you are with us, well again. Are you saying the *no'adi* is losing his power?'

Etta was silent. The *no'adi* was Atti's grandfather.

They were gathered in a pointed tent pitched within a wide, snow-covered circle of stones. At the centre of the circle, a short distance from the tent, was a small hut made of branches, with an entrance covered by a reindeer hide. Behind it, the shaman was communicating with the spirits of the ancestors. For some time he had been beating on the sacred drum, moving his pointer among the symbols dyed in red and black on the taut leather, and then he had fallen silent. The elders in the tent waited and waited. They could enter the sacred enclosure, but only the shaman could enter the sacred hut.

At last, the shaman emerged and moved across to the tent, wrapped in the long reindeer cloak with the hair on the outside that he wore when communicating with the spirit world.

'The boy is no Muscovite.'

'And we took so long to learn that,' muttered Etta, disrespectfully. The *no'adi* is getting too old, he thought. Any other man of his extreme age would have gone into the forest to die well before now. They should find a boy to become the *no'adi*'s apprentice before it was too late. Etta had a good candidate in his own family.

'I gave the boy a Muscovite icon,' added Etta, 'and when I spat on it he just smiled. No Muscovite would have done that. For a Muscovite, it would be like smashing a sacred stone or burning a drum.'

'You're a fool,' replied Atti. 'Suppose he had been a Muscovite, and suppose he had returned to his people and reported your profanity? It would have given them a further reason to attack us. We take their icons and worship them because they trade with us and it pleases them.'

The shaman ignored their chatter. He was still quivering from his voyage into the Other World. Besides, it was not for him to enter into arguments, merely to pronounce on behalf of the ancestors. 'He comes as an ambassador, not from Moscow, Denmark or Sweden, but from the far country he calls Graves-End. They have sent a youth so that he can live with us and learn our ways and our speech, and return as our ambassador. He has brought samples of their cloth and their metalware. Our ancestors command us to welcome him, foster him and return him to his people with a message of peace and trade.'

Questions showered like arrows.

'How did he get here?'

'Is he a shaman? Can he speak with the spirits?'

'How far is Graves-End?'

'The ancestors counsel that we choose him a consort,' continued the shaman, 'to teach him our language, to show him what we have to trade and what we need from his people.'

'A consort?'

'The spirits point to Leeuna.'

'Why Leeuna? Why not Seena?' objected Etta.

Leeuna was the shaman's niece and Atti's cousin, but Etta could not openly accuse the ancestors of nepotism.

'Leeuna is lame,' said another elder. 'It is a good choice. She cannot herd the reindeer, so let her teach the boy. Seena is no teacher. She is also too beautiful, and would lead him into quarrels with other men.'

So Leeuna it was.

Arthur was puzzled. These people were not like any savages he had imagined, though they clearly differed from civilised folk. They reminded him of the gypsies he knew in Kent: in society, but not of it.

He was still not sure if they were Christian or, if so, to which form of Christianity they belonged. They possessed Christian ornaments and one of them had shown him a Popish picture and then spat on it. He guessed this was a test of faith, but which way did they prefer him to lean? Most English people were Catholic by tradition, though ready to follow the law, and just now, the law was Protestant. His people, the creek-dwellers along the lower Thames, were different. They had been Protestant before it had been the safe choice. They had given refuge to Protestant fugitives from the Catholic risings in Devon and elsewhere, whose homes had been burnt by Catholic mobs. He had heard that in Spain and the Netherlands it was Protestant flesh, not just Protestant thatch, that was put to the fire.

A mariner in a foreign port should never speak of religion.

He had smiled awkwardly at the desecrated icon. In any case, if he pretended to be a Catholic they would soon find that he had not been instructed in the religion. Nobody had followed up this test, but it worried him.

At first sight they looked savage enough, covered in capes and hoods of deerskin, presumably from the large deer with three horns which grazed in infinite numbers around their settlement. For most of the time the deer were visible only by their haunches as they burrowed in the snow. They wore clappers and bells and their incessant clicking and tinkling was the background music to life in the settlement, like the hum of the rigging and the groan of the timbers aboard ship.

It was these deer whose tracks Arthur had been following, and the empty campsite he had found had belonged not to hunters but to herdsmen. He had not recognised the herdsmen's tracks, for they had been wearing long wooden gliders on their feet, not unlike his own mudshoes, although more delicately fashioned, with curved ends and a fur lining. This explained the supernatural speed of the men who had stalked him.

But strip off the deerskins and beneath were civilised clothes, woollens in all the colours in which European woollens were dyed. They had strange bows made from horn and familiar knives of German steel. Nor were their imports all tools and clothes. Men and women alike wore silver ornaments, sometimes in lavish quantities. They were fashioned to their own designs, but it seemed unlikely they had mined the metal.

How did they get these products? There was no obvious form of contact with the outside world. The settlement sat where the forest met the fells, with no tracks in any direction and no sign that it had ever been visited by strangers. Since he could not speak the language, there was no way he could solve this puzzle for the moment.

The encampment was quite unlike the neat rows of tents which Arthur had seen on woodcut prints of the Indians whom the Spaniards had found in America. Instead, there was a large, untidy mix of structures surrounded by a high bank of compacted snow topped by a hedge of smooth, white, sharp-pointed deer horns. The tallest structures were masts topped by wooden boxes. One of the savages fetched a ladder and showed him that these were meat stores. The meat was frozen by the chill wind and protected from animals, including their own dogs, by the tall, smooth pole. The other structures were mostly either leather tents or huts made from turf and stones. There were several shelters containing what appeared to be boats of different sizes, even though they were so far from the sea.

The savages seemed to grow no crops, living only on their deer, more on the milk than the meat. They stored the milk in large pots buried in the ground and preserved it by fermenting it and flavouring it with herbs. They called this brew *juobmo*, and pressed it onto Arthur with signs of great relish. It had a strange, fizzy taste and a strong smell, and was mildly intoxicating, so that the savages were often in a well-tempered haze, whiling away the darkness beating drums and singing long, tuneless ballads that they called *yoiks*. It seemed an idle and amiable life, much as Arthur imagined the monks had led before King Henry turned them out of their monasteries. Life at sea was much harder.

He was not sure if he was a prisoner. He was not physically restrained, nor confined. They had pointed him a place to sleep in a round tent made of two layers of furry skins stretched over a framework of poles, as cunningly carved and interlocked as the timbers of a ship. The frame supported an iron cooking pot on a long chain and many other things, including a baby hanging upright, strapped into a log cradle. A fire burned constantly at the centre of the tent, making it surprisingly warm, despite the sharp cold outside.

Five adults, three children and a dog occupied the tent, along with a big, elaborately carved wooden chest, which was the only piece of furniture. The remaining space was a dense litter of blankets, clothes and household items of all sorts, some homemade and others obviously made in Christendom. The occupants accepted him smilingly, fed him *juobmo* and refused to let him do any work. He slept with them under a pile of blankets, just as his family had slept in the houseboat at Greenhithe.

A party of older men visited the tent and questioned him repeatedly in several languages, none of which he understood, although one of them sounded rather like English. He had tried to tell them everything about himself. They seized upon the name Gravesend, and repeated it to each other as though it was magic. His stock of needles and trinkets had been taken and displayed under an awning, along with the pewterware, which had reappeared from the forest where he had left it under the tree with the strips of cloth. It was a focus of intense curiosity. The darkness was no problem, for, like the tents, the display was brightly lit by burning wicks floating in dishes of oil.

About a week after his arrival it seemed that a decision had been reached. The older men came to see him again, and one of them delivered a speech. The others murmured approval. It appeared that Arthur was expected to reply. For all he knew, they had just told him that he was to be killed and eaten; he could only stammer his thanks for the food and warmth he had received and that he hoped that they found his needles and mugs to their satisfaction.

The group leaped to their feet and delightedly stripped Arthur of his clothes. He knew by now that they had no shame in nakedness, but what was going to happen now?

What happened was that he was led, naked, into the snow, where a boisterous crowd led him to a small cabin, away from the living area but within the compound. He was pushed inside and found himself alone with a bench and a charcoal fire in a stone hearth.

He was frightened. He was shut in with a slow fire, just like

Sir Hugh in his stateroom. They were killing him in the same way he had killed Sir Hugh. He wanted to escape, but the door was heavy and probably barred. It would be useless. Better to die quietly. He deserved it. They said it was a sweet death. Was there some reason why they wanted him to die without a mark on his body?

He became very hot and began to sweat, with heat and fear. Then someone pulled open the door and threw a beaker of water onto the coals. Instead of lowering, the heat soared. They were torturing him. Were they expecting him to recant some unknown heresy?

The door was pulled open again and a dozen arms snatched him and rolled him in the snow. The crowd was on top of him, laughing and shouting as they whipped him with birch twigs and rubbed snow into his body and hair. Within minutes he was scoured and his skin glowed. When his attackers had decided he was clean enough he was set on his feet and daubed with a strange-smelling white grease. It had a sweet, animal scent, with hints of honey, warm milk and rancid butter.

Had they been skylarking on the maindeck or the beach, Arthur would have been happy to share in the fun, but he had heard stories about the Spanish conquerors in the Americas, and how the savages they vanquished had washed and anointed their captives before sacrificing them by ripping out their pulsing hearts on public altars. It made sense that sacrifices should be washed before being offered to the gods.

He was brought inside one of the round tents and they dressed him again, not in his own clothes but in their mix of savage and civilised finery; high sealskin boots, European breeches and tunic, a deerskin cloak fastened with an amber and silver brooch, a silk neckerchief and a white fur cap with ear-flaps. He was seated on a stool and people came to look at him and leave gifts around his feet – bundles of dried fish, pieces of meat and jugs of milk. Was this all part of the sacrifice? Were they bringing him things to feed on in the afterlife?

The noise outside rose like surf against a reef. Over the throb of several drums he heard the wailing *yoiks* and the chatter and laughter of families, like an English crowd awaiting a hanging. He had been to several hangings and seen an Anabaptist burn and the victims had never kept their dignity. He knew he would scream and soil himself, but until then he would try to keep calm. There was no escape. He had not got very far on his walk to Antwerp.

The thought of his unfinished journey carried his mind back to the *Bona Esperanza* and Sir Hugh's frozen corpse, which he supposed still sat at the fatal dinner table. God had strange ways of grinding out his justice; it had reached out to find him here in the heathen camp as it was, no doubt, finding his messmates on the Frozen Ocean. Nobody escaped divine judgement. He must not throw away these precious last moments seeking excuses for his sins. God had given him this chance to repent. It was his hands that had lit the fire, even if others had blocked the flue. He could have betrayed the plot.

Dear God, Holy Jesus, forgive me and let me ready myself for whatever the savages may do, so as not to be too fearful when the time comes.

They brought him out of the tent and he saw that the space where his wares had been displayed had been cleared. Around it were all the people of the settlement, nearly eighty in all. A bonfire at either side gave light and heat, and more light shone from a row of oil lamps on a low counter.

A man in a long, shaggy cloak was waving a pole, to which were tied a set of animal tails. He must be the heathen priest. A strong smell of *juobmo* mingled with the train oil of the lamps. At the sight of Arthur and his escort the drummers and the singer fell silent, and the crowd parted to let them enter the central space.

Not even a child stirred. The crowd parted again at the opposite end of the space and another party entered with a second prisoner, a young woman who dragged one foot. The second party advanced to meet Arthur's group and halted a yard in front of him. The prisoner raised her eyes and met his.

She was no older than himself, taller than most Sami and with round eyes, the first attractive girl he had seen in the camp. Her cap was white like his own and she wore a long gown and high boots, all elaborately decorated. At least a dozen strings of beads and silver ornaments hung around her shoulders or were woven into her hair.

The priest lifted a flint and steel. The audience held its breath. The priest struck steel on flint and at the first touch a spark flashed out, greeted by a general shout. The spark had lain within the stone and the touch of the steel had summoned it to life, as the touch of a husband summons new life from his bride. This would be a fertile marriage.

Suddenly everything made a very different sense. Understanding flooded Arthur's mind, like stumbling from darkness into light. Not an execution, but a wedding! Not death, but a bride! No groom ever gazed more joyfully on his beloved.

He took her hands in his own and, as she smiled back, he knew that he no longer wanted to walk to Antwerp.

11

Ivan

'So where is he now?'

'Beyond Red Square, Ivan Vasilevich, at the inn on the way to the Kitai Gorod. The inn you could see from the St Saviour Gate, before you began work on the Thanksgiving Cathedral.'

Sylvester was too close a friend of both Tsar Ivan and Tsarina Anastasia to use the grandiloquent titles normally demanded by emperors and their consorts, but he was also a monk trained to deference and formality, so he compromised by using the tsar's baptismal name followed by the patronymic. Besides, Ivan liked to be reminded that he was his father's son, for Vasily had been the great prince who had thrown off the Tartar yoke, even though Ivan had been orphaned too early to remember him.

'One can see most of Moscow from the St Saviour Gate, but I know the inn you mean. It is good to keep him close to the Kremlin.'

'He considers it an honour.'

'So he should, Sylvester. But tell me, what has that Greek girl of yours found out about him? Why are the English sending us an ambassador? And why did they discover a way through the Frozen Ocean rather than take the highway through Germany and Poland? I had thought that England was a tributary kingdom of the Hapsburg Empire, or am I mistaken?'

He scowled. Ivan's scowl was famous. This, more than any of his deeds, had earned him the name Ivan *grozny* – Ivan the Terrible. With his black hair and beard, gaunt face and deep-set, dark eyes, he had a truly awesome scowl. Sylvester was not awed, but it was wise to be careful, to watch out for one of Ivan's mad episodes.

So far as anybody governed the Russian empire, it was Sylvester. He had become the father that Ivan had never had, just as Anastasia Romanova had taken on the role of mother as well as empress. Without Anastasia even Sylvester's hold over the tsar would have been shaky. She alone could face him during his wilder moments without fear for her life.

Having taken the throne at the age of two, Ivan was used to being the supreme ruler who did as he was told. But the boyars who had chased Ivan under the bed when he was an infant had long since been fed to the Kremlin hounds. Now he had to be handled in other ways. He reminded Sylvester of one of the great cannon they had used to batter Kazan into submission. It was fiery and destructive – it gave the gunners tremendous power but could easily blow up in their faces.

Of course, all princes culled their enemies with the gibbet and the axe, reflected Sylvester, but they usually preferred to do so by putting pen to parchment. When Ivan scented treason he often usurped the executioner's role and exhausted himself in orgies of butchery on the public scaffold. These fits were usually followed by agonies of remorse in which Anastasia was hard-put to keep him from suicide. Controlling Ivan was not easy.

'Or am I mistaken?' repeated Ivan.

Sylvester started from his reverie and was saved by the entry of two servants. They fed the stove, lit the lamps and drew the heavy curtains to shut out the darkening view of the Kremlin battlements and the icicle-hung domes of the cathedral. The soft light glistened on the gilded ceiling.

'It seems,' replied Sylvester, gathering his thoughts, 'from the few indiscreet remarks that their ambassador has betrayed to his mistress, that England is at odds with her neighbours. The late king seized the lands of the church, like the king of Sweden, and the country has become the enemy of the Catholic powers.

Moreover, their king is still a boy, and the nobles who rule the country are uncertain of their future.'

'You mean we've found a foreign kingdom that is neither an enemy nor a friend of our enemies? This will be the first time in my life that we have received an embassy that has not threatened war or come to parley a truce.' Ivan laughed, but his interest in meeting a novel foreigner was unfeigned. As a virtual prisoner in the Kremlin, Ivan had spent much of his childhood in the library, making himself if not the best educated man in Russia, certainly the most widely read. Sylvester was more learned in the literature and traditions of the Orthodox church, and had studied at Mount Athos in Greece, but Ivan knew more of the Catholic and Islamic worlds, even though he had never been outside his own dominions.

'But we do not need an alliance with England to give ourselves fresh enemies,' Ivan continued. 'What do they want?'

'Their man speaks incessantly of trade. Yelena believes they have heard of our victory at Kazan, although he pretends otherwise. She thinks they want to open a route to import silk from Persia and Cathay along the Volga.'

'Do they, now? They know far more about us than we of them.'

'The whole world has heard of your victory at Kazan,' replied Sylvester. 'It is the first great triumph for Christendom since the fall of Constantinople – we are becoming the third Rome.'

'If you say so. Flattery becomes you. Do they have anything to trade that we might want?'

'Their cloth is good enough, but we have our own. Their manufactures are inferior to those from Germany, but they have good wine and excellent cannon. Not that they propose to sell us cannon, but the governor of Kholmogory reports very favourably on it. The English put on a display of gunnery, presumably to intimidate the town.'

'You mean that they have cannon that do not blow up in the gunners' faces, unlike ours at Kazan?'

'Indeed,' replied Sylvester, with a tremor of guilt, 'and they have silver. Their king sends you a great, finely wrought platter.'

Ivan loved to add to his hoard of silverware. That the English had silver was good news, for the silk from Cathay was paid for almost exclusively in silver.

'We will have a meeting of the chosen council,' declared Ivan. 'We must consider how to turn this man to our advantage.'

'Be cautious of Makary,' counselled Sylvester. 'He is even more suspicious of Lutherans than Catholics. At least Catholics respect church property.'

They both knew that they could not act in anything spiritual without the blessing of the patriarch of Moscow. Relations with states that were not true Christians, which meant all other states, were clearly a spiritual matter.

'But I think I have a plan,' continued Sylvester, 'which could make the Englishman extremely useful to us, and which should please the patriarch.'

'Tsar Ivan the Fourth, by the grace of God lord of all Russia, of Vladimir, Moscow, Novgorod, Pskov, Smolensk, Tver, Yugorsk, Perm, Vyatka, Bulgaria, Nizhny Novgorod, Chernigov, Ryazan, Volokolamsk, Rzhev, Belaia, Rostov, Yaroslavl, Beloozero, Udorsk, Obdorsk, Kandinsk, Kazan, Astrakhan and other places. Huhh! Did I get it right that time?'

'Bravo,' congratulated Yelena. 'But you need to say it more confidently. Again.'

'This is absurd,' Richard complained. 'Does the tsar really expect his visiting ambassadors to memorise such an absurd title?'

'Of course not, he wants them to get it wrong so that he can humiliate them, and if need be, have an excuse to dismiss them. Remember, you are the first ambassador Ivan has ever received from a friendly prince. The war with Kazan has opened up a war with my people, the Krim Tartars. The king of Sweden took advantage of the Kazan war to take Russian territory in Finland and Lapland, and the Kazan war was only possible because there was a truce with the Poles, which will soon run out. A foreign friend is new idea in Russia.'

'So perhaps Ivan may not be so strict with me. But show me, Yelena, where these places are! Then I can remember them like names on a chart, as a sailor does. And why does Ivan claim Bulgaria?'

'It is not the Bulgaria you know of, in Turkey,' she laughed, 'but Bulgaria on the Volga, where the Bulgars first lived. There is a reason for having so many titles. Most of these lands have their own princes who were once the equals of the tsar and now accept him as overlord. But as you say, if Ivan favours you, you have nothing to fear, and if he does not...'

'At least the waiting is over. We have been three weeks at this inn.'

'It is the best inn with the most beautiful view in Moscow.'

It was indeed a fine building by Moscow standards. The lower storey, built of stone, was set into the steep bank of the Moscow river, so that there was access at both the lower and upper levels. The upper storey was made of timber, covered with a steep roof of wooden tiles. A year earlier, a guest could have looked out of the inn directly at the wall of the Kremlin across the open space called Red Square ('red' and 'beautiful' shared the same word in Russian), but now the view was blocked by an outlandish, polychrome building, budding with twisted domes and still encased in scaffolding.

'That,' explained Yelena, 'is the new cathedral the tsar is building to celebrate the glorious victory at Kazan. They say it is so beautiful that Ivan ordered the architect to be executed, so that he can never design a better.'

'Is that so?'

'I doubt it, but the story pleases the tsar.'

'How many people will be at the feast?'

'Hundreds. The tsar wants to impress. He may also wish to bargain, so don't fall into the mead and remember to tell your friends to stay sober. They have already earned a reputation as drinkers.'

*

Richard's skin was hot, and the lighted candles had begun to wear haloes. There had been a great deal of wine and mead at the feast, and he was hoping to cool a little in the antechamber before going into the cold. He wondered if his condition was noticeable.

'I warned you about falling into the mead.' Yelena giggled.

'Am I so unsteady?'

'You stink of mead. It's in your beard. But I expect all of you smell the same.'

'They pushed Matthew's head into the bowl,' admitted Richard. 'They were trying to make him drink it up at one blow.'

'So you had an enjoyable feast?'

'I have been at royal feasts in England and France, but never such magnificence! I tell you, there must have been a score or more great bowls and platters as precious as the platter we brought from England, and every guest had a goblet set with amber or precious gems. And the servants were all in silks and there was such an abundance of strange dishes and wines, although most of us preferred the mead. And the emperor! He was on a stage, seated with his sceptre, and they changed his crown three times during the feast. And he called men one by one to his table – myself and each of my men – and fed us from his own knife from the meat set for him. And at the end of the feast he called out the name of every man present – as you said, there must have been two hundred people there!'

'Ivan has decided to dazzle his new ally,' murmured Yelena. 'He is good at it, but there is not always such state at the Kremlin. The servants are hired for the occasion and must return their silks after the feast, but the silverware is genuine. Sharing the emperor's food, which is now such an honour, began as a precaution against poisoning. I know you have more to tell me, but we will not be going back to the inn for a while. The emperor wishes to see you.'

'But we had the audience in the afternoon when I presented the platter.'

'No matter. Ivan wants to see you again, and now.'

'Your Imperial Majesty, lord of all Russia, of Vladmir, Moscow...'

'The tsar says you can dispense with the titles,' interrupted Sylvester, who was acting as translator from Greek into Russian. 'Out of his friendship for you and your king, you can call him Ivan Vassilevich and he will call you Richard Villemevich – I understand your father's name was William. The tsar has business to discuss.'

The three of them were alone in a small, sparsely furnished chamber, without even a servant. So private a meeting must be very important.

'My king seeks amity and trade, Ivan Vassilevich,' continued Richard, awkwardly. 'I have samples of the many goods our realm produces, above all thick, hard-wearing woollen cloth well suited to the Russian cold. In return, we seek seal oil and furs, fish and flax, honey, masts and ropes, and maybe other of your produce.'

The heat of the mead was giving way to cold panic. For the first time Richard was face-to-face with the enormity of his pretence. He had arrived in Russia by accident and still knew little more of the country than Yelena had told him. Nobody in England, except perhaps Dr Dee, had heard of this empire, yet here he was, feigning great interest in it on the part of the king of England. How Sir Hugh would have loved it!

He prayed that he would not have to stay long in Moscow, either on the orders of the emperor or the king. God willing, all he had to do was to sell his cargo at a good price and sail for home with goods vendible in London. Then another man could take over as ambassador.

'God has charged the rulers of all Christian kingdoms with a holy duty to advance the trade and prosperity of their subjects,' cooed Sylvester, 'but He has also chosen them for higher duties.

As your king so excellently phrases it in his message, trade is but the means by which God has chosen to further amity between nations. Ivan Vassilevich has it in mind to send an ambassador to England, and he wishes you to escort him to your king by the path you have discovered through the Frozen Ocean. In this way, he can avoid the lands of our enemies. The tsar has yet to choose the ambassador but he has chosen a worthy gift for your king, a gift the like of which has rarely been seen in a Christian land.'

'This is an honour for which I had never dared hope,' lied Richard.

Ivan and Sylvester had a brief animated exchange before Sylvester continued. 'Ivan Vasilevich has in mind to make an alliance with your king against their common enemies, to be confirmed by the marriage of your king to a Russian princess, if this should be to your king's pleasure. It may yet be your honour to escort a royal bride to your country.'

'I am overwhelmed,' said Richard, truthfully.

'You have a fine ship,' said Sylvester.

Richard was surprised at the sudden change of topic, particularly since Sylvester had never set eyes on the *Edward Bonaventura*.

'We believe it so,' he said, cautiously.

'It has many cannon?'

'It is no warship. The cannon are for our own defence against corsairs.'

'Indeed. Ivan Vasilevich is not without enemies who would be envious of our trade and friendship with your country. You were wise to come well armed. It is in the interest of both our peoples that the authority of the tsar should be secure in the northern lands.'

'We met with no enemies, nor anybody after leaving the king of Denmark's fortress at Wardhouse.'

'We have no quarrel with the king of Denmark. It is true that Ivan Vassilevich's father aided the Swedes in their revolt against their union with Denmark, for which the Swedes promised him Finland and Lapland. But the Swedes, having won their cause, have been false to their promise and took advantage of our sacred war against the Tartars to advance their frontiers in those regions, even to the shores of the White Sea. So now we must chastise Sweden and bring the heathen Lapps under the rule of Holy Russia.'

Richard began to sense the direction of the conversation. 'But my ship cannot sail across Lapland,' he pleaded. He remembered the stocky little Lapp women at Wardhouse. They seemed unlikely enemies.

'But your cannon may,' answered Sylvester.

Ivan, who seemed to be able to follow the conversation in Greek between Richard and Sylvester, laughed and added a comment in Russian.

'I am a man of religion with no knowledge of military matters,' the monk continued, 'but the tsar assures me that cannon can be mounted on sleighs and drawn over the ice. It has been done before, against the German knights in Livonia.'

This was everything the Company had forbidden: engagement in a war.

'My ship needs cannon to protect its cargo, and to protect your ambassador when the time comes. Much as my king would like to assist your empire in its holy cause, we have no ordnance that we can spare.'

'But you have already said that you met no enemies. Let me explain. The sea will become passable for your ship only after the land becomes impassable. You cannot sail before the ice melts in April, and Ivan Vassilevich must move against the Swedes and their allies before the thaw, or else he cannot move artillery across Lapland. At the moment, the tsar has no ordnance in the north, but neither have the Swedes. Your guns will give us the advantage that might well decide the issue. Our force will cross the White Sea on the ice, strike across Lapland and set up a fort on the Baltic shore. Once there, the tsar's men will build boats which can harass Swedish commerce when the sea is open, until such time as the Swedes withdraw their unjust claims.'

'You mean to use our English cannon for your fort? It would mean that we would sail to England without cannon.'

'We may not need all your cannon, and for those we take it would be simply an exchange. Ivan Vasilievich will order cannon to be sent along the Dvina from Moscow to Kholmogory. It will take time but they will be there when your ship is ready to sail, to replace the pieces you sent to Lapland.'

The scheme sounded plausible...or it could be a stratagem to disarm his ship.

'I have no authority to surrender my armament, even as a gesture of friendship. I am sent as an ambassador, not as a hostage.'

'Please, let us not play with words. You are a long way from your ship, your excellency. There are many official duties which could delay you a long time here in Moscow. However, if you could help us in our northern enterprise, the tsar will arrange for your immediate return to Kholmogory, and will give orders to the governor to purchase your entire cargo in exchange for goods of your choice. He will send presents for your king and his chosen ambassador will accompany you. Your cannon will be replaced by the time you sail, to safeguard yourself and your passengers.'

Richard grasped at a flaw in Ivan's plan. 'If you have no cannon in the north, how can you have gunners skilled enough to use the English cannon?'

'The tsar has considered that. That is why it is important, if you accept our proposal, that you to return to Kholmogory at once. Here in Russia, we are not so proud that we do not value the expertise of foreigners. This very fortress where we sit was designed by Italian engineers. The tsar will need English gunners with his force. He would be honoured if you yourself would lead them.'

12

Attack

Leeuna was new to happiness. She had grow up as the ugliest girl in the *seta*, the product of a union between her mother and one of the big yellow-haired men whom they met on the coast in the summer, who came across the sea to trade for seal skins and train oil. As if this was not misfortune enough she had been born crippled, the lame girl who could not wear her skis properly, unfit to herd deer.

All women married strangers; it was forbidden to marry within the *seta*. When the different *seta* met by the coast in the summer they exchanged womenfolk as well as reindeer. Leeuna had been like an untradeable deer; no other *seta* would take her. She had accepted that she would stay in her own *seta* for the rest of her life, making herself as useful as she could.

And then this wonderful stranger had been found in the forest. First she had been chosen to help thaw out his frozen limbs, gently with her own body heat, while he lay delirious, and then, astonishingly, the spirits had appointed her to be his bride. Now he was her husband and he was so obviously enraptured with her.

It was too good to last. They had explained to her that her duty was to prepare Arthur to go back to his own people. She doubted he would ever return. But with the *no'adi*'s blessing she would surely bear Arthur's baby; the flint had struck fire at first touch at the wedding. She would have something to keep when Arthur was gone, to make her special in the *seta*. With such a father, her child might grow up to become a *no'adi*, and she would be the *no'adi*'s mother.

In the meantime, there was so much to teach Arthur and so little time. The *seta* migrated eight times a year, following the eight seasons. The early summer migration would bring them to the sea coast where they would fish, hunt seals and trade with other *seta* and the men who came in ships from far away. There she would say goodbye to Arthur, and he would go away with the traders.

Before then Arthur had to learn the Sami language, what the Sami had to offer to Arthur's people and what the Sami needed from them. Leeuna was uncertain what Arthur's people were expected to provide, but the *no'adi* and the elders would teach him that.

Leeuna was a good teacher and Arthur an apt pupil. Soon he was beginning to speak and think in a mixture of Sami and English, becoming more Sami every day. Leeuna even learned some words of English to add to her small stock of Danish. She found that English and Danish were not dissimilar, which helped the tuition.

Even had Leeuna been fluent in English, there was much she could not have translated. The Sami language described the Sami world. There were at least a dozen names for different types of reindeer, according to age, sex, position in the herd and the work they performed. There were six varieties of snow, according to age and texture. And there were distinctions the Sami language did not have, which surprised Arthur, distinctions between singular and plural and between 'he', 'she' and 'it'.

Besides the language, Arthur learned to ski in the effortless Sami style, to bring down a reindeer with a noosed rope, to trap game in the forest and to help the reindeer find food. This was not difficult in this season, while the snow was still fine and loose and the deer could paw it away to reach the lichen. Later, the deer would need help to break the ice crust on the snow, and the deerherd might need to cut tree lichen for them in the forest. At present, his main duty was to ward off wolves and wolverines.

Leeuna managed to explain the eight migrations but whenever she tried to tell Arthur that he was going away in the early summer she cried too much to be understood. When she drew Arthur a ship, he drew her a sketch of the *Bona Esperanza* and the *Bona Confidenzia*, and tried to indicate where they lay and how much more cloth, needles and mugs there were for the taking. Neither could gauge how much the other understood.

The morning after they had consummated their marriage, Leeuna took Arthur to the *no'adi* to be given his *yoik*. Every adult in the *seta* had their own *yoik*, just as the *seta* itself had a *yoik*, the song-poem which expressed a person's identity and became part of it. Just as identities could shift and change, so too could *yoiks*. It was the *no'adi* who composed and gave people their *yoiks*.

Leeuna asked Arthur the meaning of his name, indicating that she was named after the moon. Arthur mimed one of the dancing bears he had seen in the streets of London. Leeuna and the shaman were awestruck. The bear was the most sacred animal of the forest, so sacred that its name was never spoken directly. It was referred to only in circumlocutions, such as 'he of the forest'.

The *no'adi* gave him his *yoik* and Leeuna taught it to him before he knew the meaning of the words.

I am he of the forest
The frozen dream
Become life
In the warmth of your tents
In the warmth of your love
In the warmth of your tents
In the warmth of your love

110

The *yoik* went on for many more verses, singing of love, friendship and world trade, but for the moment, Leeuna was content to teach Arthur the first verse.

'Christ's tears, Richard, you can't do this! It's against God, it's against nature and it's clean against Company orders!'

Stephen Burroughs glared across the half-mile of ice between the *Edward Bonaventura* and the quayside of Kholmogory, tightening his gloved hands around the rail of the quarter-deck The weak, Arctic sun hung like a blood orange, low on the horizon behind the ship, throwing long shadows across the ice and picking out the houses on the quay like a row of gold teeth. The three hours of thin light which the sun gave the town at this time of the year were almost over.

It was bitterly cold, despite the two braziers on the deck and the awning of sailcloth. The two men's breath frosted their beards and eyebrows. After three minutes on deck a man looked twenty years older. Both were both muffled, Russian-style, in long coats and fur hats. They had the deck to themselves, having sent the grateful deckwatch to the warmth below while they argued in private.

Richard's return from Moscow had seemed much shorter than the outward journey, although there was only a few days' difference. The men left behind on the *Edward Bonaventura* greeted their shipmates with stories of the incredible cold, which they insisted was much beyond anything possible in Moscow – how a man could fall stunned upon the deck by the sudden chill if he emerged incautiously from the fug below, kept going with their dwindling supply of sea coals. They marvelled at the troop of cavalry that escorted the party from Moscow, men on small ponies with long spears, short bows and shaggy cloaks. Most were Tartars in the Russian service, as squat and sturdy as their mounts. They brought with them a small contingent of men with long handguns, whom the English knew as arquebusiers and whom the Russians called *streltski*, after the long coils of match-cord on their shoulders.

The announcement that Richard intended to take some of the crew with ten of the cannon on a military expedition with the Russians on the far side of the Gulf, which they had learned to call the White Sea, set the men straightway at odds. Some had been caged too long and were eager to go, but others joined Stephen in cursing the plan.

'How can we defend ourselves while you're away?' stormed Stephen. 'The Russkis want you to take our cannon so as to take the ship when you're gone. Can't you see that, or has that girl bewitched you?'

'Stephen, even with ten fewer guns, yours will still be the only cannon in the north.'

'I don't trust 'em. It's the ship they want and stripping the cannon can only help with whatever devilish plan your emperor has in mind.'

'Let me explain, Stephen. The emperor in Moscow has far more important designs than seizing our ship. His father helped the Swedes in their struggle to free themselves from the king of Denmark and, in return, they promised him Lapland and Finland. Instead, they profited from the disorder in the Russian Empire while the present emperor was a boy, and reneged on their promise. Now that the emperor has come of age and has subdued the Tartars on the Volga, he has asked us to help him claim his lands in the north. His intent is to mount our ten cannon on heavy sleighs and to take them over the sea-ice and across the land on the far shore, which they call Lapland, to a reach of the Baltic which divides Lapland from Sweden. There the emperor's men plan to find a harbour, which they will shelter with a fort armed by our guns, and where they will build boats. When the ice melts they will sail forth and harry the Swedish trade throughout the Baltic until the Swedes accept the justice of the emperor's cause.'

'So we say farewell to our guns forever?'

'They will be replaced before we sail for England by Russian cannon brought downriver from Moscow.'

Stephen stamped his feet to keep the blood moving. 'They've taught you their story well, Richard. But we know nought of the rights and wrongs of such quarrels, and if we did, 'tis no business of Englishmen. And 'tis clean against the Company's rules to wage war. Mr Caboto told us so on the deck at Gravesend, and you yourself reminded Sir Hugh that the guns are to protect the ship.'

'But we are in the emperor's power, a handful of men in an empire.'

'Our cannon can drive 'em away if they come at us across the ice. We have stores enough to last till the ice melts, and then we can be away unhindered. We are in nobody's hands but God's.'

'Stephen, you have no idea of this empire! You didn't travel to Moscow, you haven't met the tsar or feasted at the Kremlin. You've hardly glimpsed this land.' He moved nearer the brazier and faced the heat. 'There are measureless riches here for English trade: spars, furs, honey, leather and silk!'

Richard saw that he had caught Stephen's attention. 'Yes, silk, Stephen – *silk* – which they get from Cathay. We too can reach the silk and even the porcelain of Cathay – I've seen it in the emperor's palace – by trading down the great river Volga. We have only to help the emperor briefly in his war, for we have the only heavy cannon in the Northlands, and we open Cathay for English trade.'

Stephen stood silent at the gunwale, brushing the snow from the wooden parapet with his glove. The snow was sticky, like English snow – snow for making snowballs and snowmen. It was no longer the fine, hard dust which had blown in under the awning and eddied across the deck like sand over the past weeks. He looked up and noted the lengthening icicles in the rigging. Spring was coming.

Richard fidgeted uneasily. He could, of course, act without Stephen's consent, but then Stephen might have just cause for complaint when they reached England. The Company's rules laid down that any major change of course required the consent of the majority of the council, or such of it as could be assembled. Obviously the *Edward Bonaventura* would not be taking any course anywhere for weeks to come, but the company had never envisaged their men crossing the sea by sleigh, which was surely a major change of course. There were four members of the council present: Richard, Stephen, Tom Lovelace the master-gunner, and Will Pearson, the factor. Tom and Will would follow whatever course Richard and Stephen agreed – if they could agree.

'Did your so-called tsar give the governor licence to trade with us?' grunted Stephen. 'The Russkis have been kind in giving us food and beer while you were away but they still won't trade.'

'Yes, we brought all kinds of trade-goods from Moscow, and they are cutting masts and spars for us in the forest which they will float downstream in the thaw. Tsar Ivan intends them as a present for King Edward in gratitude for our alliance – if we become allies.'

'Damn you!' cursed Stephen. 'You're bent on your folly and 'tis too late to turn away. But don't forget we are a Commonwealth on this ship, and while you and Tom are away 'tis I and Will who command the ships. If you're not here by the thaw we sail home.'

Two weeks later the convoy of sleighs, horses and men set off over the frozen river down to the frozen sea. There were over a hundred sleighs strung out in a long cortege, laden with stores, fodder, powder and shot, both for the journey and for the garrison to be left on the Baltic. The English cannon were drawn on the largest sleighs with cut-down sides, hauled by teams of horses who would be aided when need be by columns of men. Ahead of them was not just river-ice, but the ridged and tumbled ice of the inland sea.

There were almost as many horses as men, for each of the thirty cavalry had three mounts. Among the unmounted men were experienced boat-builders and engineers from the Tartar wars who were to supervise the eighty foot-soldiers who would build the fort and the boats and then transform themselves into pirates.

The White Sea was still hard and white, but on the far shore icicles were beginning to drip from the trees. They found a reindeer trail used by the natives, whom the Russians called *Lappi*, and followed it upwards towards the fells and the watershed between the White Sea and the Baltic.

Alexi Drugov, who commanded the soldiers, was raucous with delight.

'God willing,' said Yelena, translating for him and discreetly leaving out the obscenities, 'the *Lappi* are still in their winter encampments, with their herds. He says we can spoil their camps as the soldiers need some sport and the gunners need practice.'

'Spoil the *Lappi*?' answered Richard. 'To survive here is a miracle – how can they have anything to spoil?'

Alexi replied in Russian without waiting for the translation. 'Everybody knows that Lapps hoard treasure – you should see the silver on their women. They hide it in their winter camps, and that's where we'll find it. Besides, soldiers grow lazy and insolent without battle. They need to smell powder and blood. And Lapp women may be ugly, but they're all we'll find. And tell your master this, Yelena,' he added, before she could translate, 'lest he have any false ideas about the *Lappi*. The *Lappi* are not Christian souls. They are creatures of the forest, like the wolves and the bears. We give them icons and they hang them in their huts, but secretly, they worship stones and trees and practise black magic with their drums. When they have too many children to carry with them when they follow the deer, they kill and eat them. Tell your master this, and don't leave anything out. He has a lot to learn about the Northlands.'

The hedge of antlers along the rim of the enclosure was just becoming visible in the morning gloom. It reminded Arthur of the lace ruff around a gentleman's throat. The Sami began to stir.

They knew of the great convoy of sleighs, for the wolves had sensed it and alerted the reindeer. By the time the convoy emerged from the forest the herdsmen were watching for it, marvelling at its size and puzzling at its purpose. No outsiders had penetrated the high fells either in winter or summer in living memory. And why was the convoy so big? It was not the Sami instinct to attack strangers, even Muscovites, for they depended on outsiders for so many things they could not make for themselves. So they watched.

The Sami scouts hovered on the edges of the convoy, watchful and invisible. They counted the sleighs and the animals and when the strangers broke camp and moved on, they moved in to sift the debris. They brought their intelligence back to the *seta*, who tried to make sense of it.

The strangers were neither traders nor hunters; they were a people on the move with sleighs laden with heavy possessions, and with their herds. But they were migrating in the wrong direction for the season, from the coast into the uplands.

They were clearly not Sami, for they did not move like Sami, shout to each other like Sami, smell like Sami. Their herds were not reindeer, but unfamiliar animals which could not find their own winter feed and needed to be fed from stores carried on the sleighs. There were few women and no children among the strangers. They were most probably Muscovites, for they came from the east, but in their winter furs they could be from anywhere. Some said they spoke Russian, others Danish, and yet others that they spoke an unknown language.

As the strangers grew nearer, the reindeer ceased their search for food and gathered into a tight, nervous herd with the stags posted on the outer edge.

Now the strangers deployed in the darkness on the open ground in front of the settlement, about 200 paces from the enclosure.

*

Unbeknownst to the Sami, the Russian and English gunners had begun to argue.

'Tell her,' said Tom Lovelace, 'to tell Alexi that our cannon is for the fortress, not for field work. Not Jesus Christ himself and all his saints in Heaven could handle the kickback from a culverin carriaged on a sleigh on frozen ground. ''Twould be safer to be in front of the guns. And we can't tether 'em to stakes either, with the earth like cast iron.'

Alexi was adamant. His orders were to test the English artillery in the field, so they dug pits in the snow, with big banks of broken ice and loose moss to cushion the sleighs as they sprang back under the recoil.

'There'll be broken legs and crushed feet,' grunted Tom. 'Not as I'd care, except they'll be English legs and feet.'

The Sami scouts glided back with the puzzling news. The strangers were digging through the snow to find moss, as if they were reindeer. Had they come to build their own winter camp right alongside the Sami settlement? Yet winter was already moving into spring.

'They can't be Muscovites,' said Etta, 'or they would have demanded tribute. And they would never be collecting tribute at the end of winter, when all peoples' stocks are low. They are the stranger-youth's people come to take him back.'

Although this explained nothing of the strangers' behaviour, the frightened Sami seized on the idea.

'We should never have brought him in. He's bewitched. He's a child of the forest and the spirits of the forest have come to reclaim him.'

'Give him back to his own. Get him out of the *seta*.'

'The *no'adi* has failed us. He has angered the spirits.'

Even those who had taken their turn to thaw Arthur's frozen limbs with their own warmth now shouted for him to go. The shaman was hustled into the sacred hut to drum himself into a trance and take fresh and urgent advice from the ancestors. This time they favoured Etta's opinions.

'The stranger must return to his own.'

'And what of Leeuna? She says she is with child.'

'Then Leeuna must go with him. The child must be born among his own.'

They thrust Arthur and Leeuna through the gateway into the snowfield. They pushed out the gun-sled that Arthur had been towing when they had found him in the forest. Some said that they should return the knives, needles, mugs and other good things which had been on the sled, but these had been spread too widely among the *seta*. So they loaded the sled with white fox furs, which strangers always prized.

Arthur hitched the sled harness over his back and took Leeuna's hand.

'Why are they doing this to us?' sobbed Leeuna. 'I thought they loved you.'

'Let them think as they will, Leeuna. All that matters is that you love me. We must trust the strangers.'

Arthur's time with the Sami had always been so much like a dream that there was no surprise that it was ending. He had no idea who the strangers were, but why should he fear them?

Hand-in-hand, they walked across the open ground towards the other camp. As he peered into the lightening gloom Arthur's eyes caught the shape and sheen of a line of objects which were shockingly familiar. They were the objects he had toiled and sweated over repeatedly for almost a year, the cannon which the fleet had loaded at Woolwich. He counted six of them. (Tom had persuaded Alexi that there was no need to employ all ten.) The ghost of Sir Hugh had come to take his vengeance on Arthur and the *seta*, and he had brought his beloved cannon with him!

'It's a battery of cannon. They'll blow us all to pieces. We must warn them, Leeuna! Warn them!' He tried to make her understand, but there was no Sami word for cannon. 'Boom! Boom! Fire, blood! Dear God, how can we warn them? Get everybody on their skis and scatter.'

Leeuna stood bewildered. Arthur turned and ran to the gate, which had been closed against them. Beating on the timber, he shouted all the words of Sami that might alert them to their danger – 'Skis, skis, everyone skis – run, run, fire! Boom! Boom!'

For the moment he had forgotten that he, too, was about to be killed. He had to warn the *seta*, but they just waved him back. He screamed at them in a mixture of English and Sami.

'Fools, idiots, take cover! *Take cover!*'

The explosion crashed through the still, cold air and seemed to bounce from fell to fell. Tom Lovelace had opened the cannonade.

13

Counterstroke

Patches of black and brown sullied the white fells, and in the forest tiny avalanches of wet snow spilled from the trees. Spring was coming early and Richard Chancellor was worried.

'You are *always* worried, Richard,' said Yelena, pressing her cheek against his beard. 'I never knew a man to worry so much. You say it's because you are a sea captain. When you are not worrying about what might be, you worry about what might have been. At least worrying about the thaw will stop you worrying about the Lapps we pacified on our march.'

She felt him flinch.

'You witch! Why do you always talk about that? You know how it troubles me.'

He was unjust. She had never spoken of it before. It was his own brain which continually relived the bombardment, picking images from the turmoil, poking them into his thoughts and his dreams.

Just by closing his eyes he could see that Lapp tent carried bodily into the air by the passage of a round shot. It seemed to hover in space, the two sheets of hide unwrapping from the tent poles until they hung bare, the iron cooking pot swinging on its chain and the tight little cradle hooked to the poles, probably still cradling a tiny, swaddled baby. Then the whole arrangement collapsed back onto the smouldering hearth to be ploughed into the earth by the next cannon ball.

Not that they had had it all their own way. The first shot

fired by the sleigh-mounted English cannon had been a disaster that had kept Alexi and his comrades laughing for days. Tom Lovelace's work in banking and channelling the gun emplacement had not tamed the recoil of the gun. The moment he touched off the charge both cannon and sleigh leapt into the air like a startled horse, flew backwards at unimaginable speed and crashed onto one side, demolishing the sleigh and leaving Tom with a crushed foot. It was a wonder the entire gun crew was not annihilated.

Prudently, the other guns held their fire and for the next twenty minutes the crews toiled like frightened ants to weigh down the carriages with nets of round shot and anything else to hand. In the end the massacre went smoothly enough, but they had blown away the advantage of surprise and an unknown number of Lapps escaped. Richard told Alexi that it was better that way, that the refugees would carry the lesson of the tsar's power to the other Lapp settlements, but Alexi was not comforted. Once the Lapps were on their skis it was almost impossible to ride them down. Indeed the cavalry rode down only one of them, and she proved to be lame.

'I'm sorry, I'm sorry. I know how you feel,' pleaded Yelena. 'And you know I know how the Lapps feel. My family suffered in the tsar's wars. I am a Russian slave. The ruin of the *Lappi* camp was Kazan on a lesser scale – a much, much lesser scale. But this is how princes build empires, how my people built their empire. By joining the tsar's enterprise here you've become an empire builder. You're a sea captain, but you spent last week helping to build the tsar's pirate port to prey upon Swedish ships and that didn't seem to worry you.'

Richard was silent. Yelena hugged him.

'Please, please, we are in the hand of fate. *Inshallah.* It may be that the ice will have begun to break before we reach the White Sea, and we may not be able to pass over to St Nicholas by sleigh. So then we will have to wait until the sea clears and then pass over by boat. Alexi knows the country – he knows how to find food, shelter, boats. God will provide – or not, as

He pleases.' She pressed closer. 'And the sooner the ice melts, the sooner we sail to England. You do want me to come to England, don't you?'

'It is difficult, Yelena. We must talk about it later.'

'The governor of Kholmogory wants me to go as interpreter to the ambassador the tsar is sending to your king.'

'Not many people in England speak Greek, Yelena.'

'Surely your king speaks Greek?'

'Indeed. My brother tutored him.'

'Well, then. And you must teach me English. You always speak English when we make love. It is a beautiful language. It is the only time you stop worrying.'

Everything fed Richard's worries. He and his men had stayed only a week at the site chosen for the fort on the Baltic. It was difficult to believe that the empty, frozen sea was an arm of that same sea which carried the commerce of Copenhagen, Danzig and Riga. They had time enough only to position the cannon and give basic instruction to the Russian gunners. The powder and shot brought at such effort through the wilderness were too precious to use on target practice.

That done, the Englishmen left in a convoy of fifteen sleighs with an escort of fifteen cavalry and ten *streltski* under Alexi's command. Now that they were more familiar with the land they made faster progress, making better use of the many frozen lakes which threaded the country like veins in a block of marble.

Alexi seemed untroubled by the early thaw. 'A man has not seen Russia until he has seen the thaw,' he boomed. 'They call it the Terrible Season. Our Dvina casts off her majesty and becomes a wild torrent, swollen by the melting snow of the inland forests. You should see it! Great blocks of ice hurtle down the river, smash against each other, shattering anything in their path.'

'What does he say?' asked Richard.

'Just the usual, about how wonderful his country is. He says the Dvina floods in the spring and is full of ice floes.'

'But my ship! What of my ship?'

Alexi understood and laughed. 'Your precious ship, *Angelski*? The tsar has thought of that – who would lose such a gift from God? It will be hauled close to shore and sheltered by a log boom to fend off the ice.'

Yelena translated.

'Stephen will not agree to this,' said Richard.

'He has not seen the Dvina in the thaw,' replied Alexi.

The conversation was cut short by a disturbance further up the column. One of the sleighs had slewed to one side and a horse was on its knees.

'Hit a rock, no doubt,' growled Alexi, 'and probably lost a horse. Those Tartar bastards should take more care when we pass these narrows between lakes.'

But it was not a rock. A short, flint-tipped arrow had lodged in the horse's leg.

'There was a flight of arrows,' gabbled the excited driver. 'From over there, among the birches.'

'Shoot the horse and take one of the cavalry mounts,' ordered Alexi. 'I'll get the *streltski* to put a volley into the birch trees. That'll scare off the savages.'

'They're trying to slow us down,' said Richard, 'so that we miss the crossing to St Nicholas.'

'These are savages, not generals,' scoffed Alexi. 'They're horseflies, stinging us as we pass by so that when we're gone they can tell their friends it was a victory. We don't usually find them here so late in the winter.'

The horseflies continued to sting. Over the next four days the convoy lost three more horses and two more were injured but still able to keep pace. The convoy took to driving well out in the lake or keeping to open country wherever it could. As they descended below the tree line the opportunities for ambush multiplied. At night they built barricades of ice, rocks and branches around the camp, and the invisible Lapps kept them awake with their drums.

The English and Russians were well-armed and almost certainly more numerous than their enemy, but it was the enemy who possessed the forest and the darkness, who possessed everything outside the moving convoy and outside the light of the campfire when they rested.

The convoy reached an inlet of the White Sea and found the ice still firm. Alexi decided to move on south along the seashore and then cross over via the Solovetski Islands. Not only would the islands provide a refuge should the ice begin to break, but if they were stranded there the great Solovetski monastery would give them hospitality and the safety of its stone walls.

Paradoxically the thaw made the going easier, at least in the morning, for the top level of the snow melted in the afternoon and froze overnight. Their spirits rose as they left the shadow of the trees and skimmed over the frozen beach. Their brush with the Lapps was over without too much damage.

And then, as they rounded a small peninsula, they saw them for the first time. It was a convoy of six small, boat-shaped sleighs with single runners, each drawn by a single reindeer.

'After them! After them!' cheered Alexi, and the sleigh teams and the cavalry broke into a gallop.

The Lapps were quick to see danger and made for the shore, shrieking to their reindeer and lashing at the long reins, but the horses had the edge over them and closed in rapidly. The cavalry loosed several arrows from the saddle for the sheer joy of having a visible target, even though they were quite beyond range. The Lapps were headed for a passage between the shore and a small island.

'Stop them, Alexi!' screamed Richard. 'Stop! Stop! It's an ambush.'

There was no way to call back the cavalry. The only course was to follow behind and lend them the firepower of the *streltski* if they were attacked.

The Lapps disappeared around the point of the island. The cavalry swung around it in hot pursuit with the sleighs hard behind. The Lapps had vanished. There they were! They had changed direction to make for the island. The cavalry wheeled to head them off, racing towards a bare bluff rising above the beach. Not a single rider raised his eyes to see the cannon mounted in full view until a blast of grapeshot left seven horses and riders on the ice. The other eight horsemen scattered in panic.

'Keep on! Keep on!' screamed Richard across the ice. 'To the beach before they can reload. They can't depress the cannon.'

It was quite useless; the horsemen were too far away. They swerved aside as a second blast brought down two more of them. It was left to the sleighs to ground upon the beach, and for Richard to lead the English and the *streltski* up onto the bluff. There was no fight. When they reached the cannon it lay askew on a broken sleigh that had not been strong enough to withstand the shock of two detonations. The only trace of the gunners was their ski tracks.

Richard tapped the broad arrow cast on the breech of the cannon: the emblem of the Sydney family, who were masters of the royal ordnance. 'Tell Alexi that this cannon was cast last year at Woolwich. The savages are using our own ordnance against us. They must have captured the fort, which means they have other cannon.'

Yelena translated.

'Impossible,' exclaimed Alexi. 'You are mad. Even if they had captured the fort, how could they have brought the gun here ahead of us?'

'Does he have a better explanation?' replied Richard to Yelena. 'Does he think they've captured St Nicholas? Ask him that.'

Alexi shivered. 'Witchcraft – *Lappi* magic! We should never have meddled with them. We are dead men.'

From then on the convoy behaved like a routed army. That evening they burnt most of the animal fodder. They no longer had any thought of reaching St Nicholas, but only of seeking the

Solovetski monastery to shelter behind its stone walls and the prayers of the monks. The horses would then feed the men until rescue came. They gathered around the blaze, throwing on unwanted stores and equipment like some barbaric funeral. The slain horsemen were left where they had fallen.

The captured cannon was an embarrassment. Alexi refused to delay while they broke a hole in the ice to sink it, so they tumbled it onto the beach and hammered a stone into the muzzle. It would not have defeated Tom Lovelace's ingenuity to get it working again, but it would surely foil the Lapps.

They set out as soon as the slush had frozen. The Lapps appeared with the dawn. Their skis easily kept pace with the laden sleighs. Disdaining concealment, they kept up a loud, keening shout and made constant feint attacks. It was difficult to judge how many there were, but there were far more than expected.

'Throw them anything we can live without,' ordered Alexi. 'God willing, we'll glut the thieving swine with plunder.'

They whipped on the horses, leaving a trail of jettison: candles and cooking pots, spare clothing and boots, horse harness and horseshoes. The Lapps hovered just beyond bowshot, clustering inquisitively around each find as soon as was safe. However, rather than glutting them with spoil, each find merely seemed to whet their appetites.

The Russians and the English were forced to make more and more difficult choices. They dumped everything they had looted from the Lapps, the fox furs and the silver ornaments. Richard laid a hand on the heavy gold-framed icon that Alexi set up each night in the camp.

'Leave that, it belongs to God,' snapped Alexi.

'Tell him,' said Richard to Yelena, 'that if God saves us in his mercy, it will not be because of a brass idol.'

'Don't be mad! He'll kill you,' said Yelena.

'If we must spare weight,' continued Alexi, 'then we should rid ourselves of those who can no longer fight.' He glared meaningfully at Tom Lovelace, who was riding on the back of the sleigh.

Richard followed the glance and grasped his meaning. 'Tom is a skilled man. We need him. Throw them some of your own wounded. Tell him that, Yelena.'

'Do you really want me to ask him to throw them the two wounded Tartars and not the Englishman?' queried Yelena. 'I'll tell him that, if you wish.'

Her message was more diplomatic, but Alexi was afire. 'A skilled man? Who disabled his own gun at the first shot and couldn't knock over the two savages walking towards his cannon? Let the savages find a use for him. Have you not noticed that none of your men have weapons but their knives, unlike my *streltski*? I will tell them they can shoot any *Angelski* whenever it is necessary for the safety of the convoy.'

There was a sharp crack, as if Alexi had actually given the order to fire. The sleigh jumped, span round and turned over, spilling out people and goods. This time they had hit a rock. The attendant Lapps, watching for just this opportunity, came swooping in.

14

Rebirth

They brought him Leeuna's body on a scorched fold of reindeer hide. She was one of the few recognisable corpses. She had been lanced through the back by a Tartar horseman, she and their unborn baby. The lame foot which had kept her from herding reindeer, which had selected her to be Arthur's bride, had delivered her to the cavalry.

Arthur had been with her as they fled, had turned back when she screamed. There was nothing he could have done except to have died alongside her, yet he had fled on his skis and left her dying in the snow. He should have died at her side.

She looked so dead, like a new-caught codfish, as if she had never been alive. He remembered how they had lain together and he had held himself deep inside her after the climax of their love, feeling her heartbeat from within, as though they were no longer separate beings.

Arti, who was among the survivors, drew him away. 'Leeuna wanted you to live. You must live. The spirits chose her to teach you our ways so that you can go to your people and bring help to us. We need help more than ever. We can trade for the things we need, but you must bring them to us.'

Arthur understood the sense if not all the words, but for the present no words had any meaning.

Fifteen people had survived the massacre: seven men, five women, two children and a baby. Their first priority was to survive the night. The bombardment, the blaze and the pillage had left little for the Sami. Although the strangers had been mainly interested in silver and furs they had not despised axes, knives and pots. With difficulty, the survivors salvaged enough charred timbers to build a temporary shelter. They lit a fire and huddled around it in a warm, sweaty mass. There was no meat, for the strangers had cut down and robbed the meat masts, but the buried store of *juobmo* was untouched so there was some comfort for the evening. Tomorrow they would kill one of the bull reindeer, for they no longer needed so many animals to draw such sleighs as they still possessed, and they would roast the fat over the fire in the absence of a cooking pot.

Arthur's abiding memory of that night was the crying baby. The mother was dead; it was the baby's young sister who had snatched the log cradle from the blaze. Luckily, one of the surviving women was still in milk, for the Sami suckled their children until they were four or five. No Sami baby ever had such adult attention as that that tiny infant on that dreadful night. Everyone felt a sense of achievement when at last she was asleep, sucking on her bone marrow comforter. Outside lay the unhonoured dead and the wreckage of all they had built, but inside their rough shelter there was still a spark of life.

The next day they gathered the dead at the edge of the forest and made them a pyre from the charred remains of their huts and tents, and from fresh-cut birches. The recognisable bodies were dressed for the funeral. Leeuna wore a red conical hat trimmed with fur, like the one she had worn at her wedding. A strip of coloured cloth was tied to a holy tree in memory of each dead member of the *seta*. Then they fired the pyre and sang their *yoiks* while it was consumed.

Were heathen Sami allowed into heaven, wondered Arthur? Not that he had any hopes of getting there himself, but surely God would not deny an angel like Leeuna? Or did different faiths have different heavens, so that Leeuna had her own afterlife? Not that the Sami had a heaven in any Christian sense.

The ancestors seemed to be eternally present among the living, although they were not actual ghosts. Arthur decided to ask Arti more about this when he was more fluent in the language.

'Will you beat the drum,' asked Arti, 'now that we have no *no'adi?*'

He passed Arthur the sacred drum, which the raiders had declined – or feared – to steal.

Arthur would have preferred to play his fiddle, but it was now splinters. He took the drum and examined it closely. It was fashioned from a naturally curved strip of birchwood covered with tightly stretched reindeer hide, the tautness adjusted by cords, much in the manner of an English drum. The skin was marked by lines dividing it into three sections, each section speckled with painted symbols. Some he could understand, like the radiant sun, and others were unknowable. Arti gave him two sticks, one a drumstick and the other a pointer which he could press on the skin to vary the note.

Arthur beat the drum as he had heard the ship's drums beaten at funerals, which had become increasingly common while they were wintering at the bay. He beat softly and rhythmically in the shifting light of the pyre. Gradually he lost sense of time and place and the beat became steadier and stronger. It merged with the beating of his heart, as Leeuna's heartbeat had merged with his. He was no longer sitting at the pyre but was floating, flying above the *seta*, flying over the fell and the forest, over winding lakes and snowy hills until he could see the sea. He could see the two ships still on the ice, and as he swooped over the truncated masts he could see into the stateroom where Sir Hugh and the officers sat, frozen, at table, and he could count the cannon on the deck. He knew then what he had to do.

He had to destroy the ships, destroy Sir Hugh and his phantom men, else they would pursue him to the end of time and destroy all those who dared to love or befriend him. Even if he destroyed himself in so doing, it would break the curse.

Of a sudden he was conscious that he had ceased drumming

and the pyre had burned low. The others were looking at him and he was trembling.

'You are become our *no'adi*,' whispered Arti. 'You were sent to us by the spirits and we were punished for rejecting you. You will lead us, and I will help you explain the will of the spirits to those of us who have not yet joined them.'

'I know where to lead you,' replied Arthur. 'I shall take you to the sea, to find two enchanted ships. In the ships are blankets, needles, knives and guns. Many, many, many. You will have more things than any *seta* in all *Sameatnam*. Follow me?'

Before they sought the enchanted ships they had to find another *seta* to join, for they were now too few to survive as a group. *Seta* often combined or divided. They were all one blood through the exchanging of brides. In the winter *seta* seldom had contact, but the thaw was coming, the reindeer were getting ready to move, and soon they would be meeting other Sami. It was the reindeer who decided when to leave and where to go.

'Our grandfathers,' Arti explained, 'hunted the reindeer, following them from pasture to pasture. Now we protect the reindeer, but we still follow them along the same trails in the same seasons.' Whatever befell the *seta*, it had to move with the herd.

Arthur had hitherto known the Sami as indolent folk who spent their days dozing, drinking and singing. With the migration they were changed people. Everything was order and discipline. Five sleighs were made travel-worthy, the harness was prepared for the draught deer, new frames were carved for the tents, new tent covers were cut, and everything needed for the journey was stowed and packed in an order that would have been a credit to the Cloth Fleet.

The reindeer herd moved out two weeks after the massacre. The Sami followed, guided by the sound of the bells, travelling at night and in the early morning while the ground was still hard. The night they left the magic lights lit the sky with ribbons of green fire, which the new *no'adi* announced as a good omen.

After five days they made contact with another *seta* and were welcomed into their compound. Their hosts were astonished at their story. A supernatural youth found wandering in the forest they could accept, and a natural catastrophe that decimated a *seta* was understandable, but an unprovoked catastrophe at the hands of alien humans was unimaginable.

Arti and Arthur met with the elders and the *no'adi* of the host *seta* to explain their position, and to propose not merely a fusion of their two groups but a joint expedition to the coast to find the treasure ships. The *no'adi* of the host *seta* beat his drum and went into communion with the ancestors. Their message was not encouraging. Arthur's *seta* was pursued by evil spirits and it was dangerous to ally with them.

Arthur was desolated. Arti had done his best but if only Leeuna had been there; she could have explained it all so well. Leeuna, Leeuna, help me please! His hand burrowed into the pocket of his tunic, clutching at the packet of Redditch needles that he had given her, and which had been in her tunic when she was lanced. Her killer had been too interested in her silver to bother with steel points. Arthur clutched at the needles until they pierced his palm, as if trying to take in Leeuna's spirit through the pain in his hand.

Of course! The needles were the answer! All Sami were experts at needlecraft. He took out the slivers of steel and passed them around. The larger ones he gave to the men, because they were used to heavier sewing, and he asked them to call the women to show them the fine needles. The Redditch craftsmen could never have imagined the delight which greeted their handiwork.

'Feel them, how strong and sharp and bright they are. Follow me and I can give you more – more than there are trees in the forest – and knives, and bowls, and blankets, and cloth without end. Together, we will be the richest *seta* that has ever been. Yes, feel them, thread them! They are yours, but they are only the beginning.'

The speech was delivered in a mix of Sami and English.

Arti explained in greater detail. He was becoming almost as proficient in English as Arthur in Sami.

'If we combine, who will be our *no'adi*?' asked one of the elders.

'I will lead you to the enchanted treasure ships,' replied Arthur, 'and then I must leave you to return to my own people.'

The *no'adi* of the other *seta* nodded agreement.

The *Bona Esperanza* and the *Bona Confidenza* sat in the bay just as Arthur had left them, except that the ice around them was beginning to crack. Animals had broken into the ships' stores on the scree and split open some of the casks of salt fish, but otherwise all was undisturbed. As far as Arthur could see from the shore, each ship had a full complement of cannon. If one of them had been in action against the Sami it had since returned home.

They had left most of the newly-formed *seta* at the spring encampment, tending their combined herds. Arthur and Arti had gone on to the sea with a salvage party of twenty men and women with four sleighs. The bay was easy to find, for it was close by the shore they used for the summer fishing. They took their sleighs out onto the water, threading through the leads in the ice, for being built with keels in place of the runners the sleighs could do duty on land and water. Later they brought two lighter seal boats from the beach at the mouth of the bay, where they had left them after last year's hunt.

Arthur was the first aboard the *Bona Esperanza*, his stomach tight with fear. He half-expected to find Sir Hugh and his officers waiting for him, but the familiar deck was empty, the frost on the planks thick and undisturbed. Each ice-rimed cannon lay on its carriage at its proper place. Whatever magic might have transported them to the winter camp of the *seta* had returned them to their stations on the deck unmarked.

'Tell everybody,' said Arthur to Arti, 'that the big hut at the end of the ship is sacred. Whoever enters will disappear, and the ship will disappear.'

Arti did not dispute this so, for the while, Sir Hugh and his dinner party sat on undisturbed while the savages for whom Sir Hugh had hunted in vain ransacked his ship.

Cortes or Pizzaro were never as astounded by the gold of the Mexica or the Incas as the Sami at the sight of the English cargoes. For three days they stayed on the ships, breaking open the hatches and finding more and more treasures, so plentiful that they could only sample them. Arthur impressed upon them that they could come to the ships only once. After that the ships would be burnt.

The Sami cleared away the canopy which the English sailors had stretched over the decks, the better to get at the cargo holds. The masts and spars which had supported the canopy were pushed overboard and lashed together to form a raft. They loaded the raft as heavily as they dared and towed it out into the clearer water in the middle of the bay.

'Arti,' explained Arthur, 'the scree is too steep to unload our treasure here. We must go in two groups. You take some of our people in the sleighs along the shore to the end of the bay. I will take the others with me in the boats. We will tow the raft with our treasure to the end of the bay and meet you there. Then together we can load the sleighs and send the treasure to our camp.'

When they met at the head of the bay it was clear that there was far too much booty to take away on one journey. They hid some in the forest to fetch on later visits and loaded the rest onto the sleighs. Arthur, Arti and four others watched the sleigh party set off in high spirits along the same track that Arthur had followed when he had set out to walk to Antwerp, the walk that had taken him to Leeuna and his short-lived winter paradise. He waited until the tinkle of the sleigh bells had faded into the silence before he turned to the boats.

It was time to go back and burn the *Bona Esperanza* and the *Bona Confidetzia*.

*

'Perhaps you should talk with the ancestors once again,' suggested Arti. 'Much has changed since the night you became our *no'adi*. There are so many good things which we had to leave on the two big ships. The ancestors surely cannot wish to deny them to our people? Perhaps it would be better to leave the ships until we camp here in the summer, when we can unload what is left?'

'No. The spirits ordered me to burn them.'

Arthur was never sure how far Arti believed that he could commune with the Other World. He was not very sure himself. But he was well aware that he was Arti's instrument in governing the *seta*. The newly combined *seta* was still in the awkward position of having two *no'adi*, which made it important for Arti to show that his *no'adi* brought the greater gifts from the ancestors.

'There are things which even the ancestors cannot demand of our people,' said Arti. 'If you burn the ships our new *seta* may not be able to take you back.'

Arthur was troubled. Had it been Sir Hugh's cannon which had pounded the *seta*? Where else could they have come from? The horseman who killed Leeuna was certainly not one of Sir Hugh's company, but doubtless the phantom Sir Hugh had all sorts of devils at his command. Most of the survivors of the massacre spoke of their attackers as Muscovites, but then they did not know about Sir Hugh.

'If we do not burn the ships the strangers will come back and attack our new *seta* with their big guns, as they attacked us before.'

'Then let us take the guns for ourselves. You can teach us how to use them.'

'We could never unload the cannon into the seal boats.'

It was a mistake to argue practicalities with Arti, even about artillery.

'Maybe not. But there are two big guns already on the land, in a camp on the high ground. There are iron balls as well, for the guns to shoot. We can take gunpowder from the ships. You showed us where it was kept, so that we would not light a fire there.'

Of course two guns would not tip the balance of power; they could not be everywhere the strangers might strike. Nor could the Sami transport them overland on carriages designed for the deck of a ship. They would have to transport them without carriages and make or improvise them at the theatre of war. Nonetheless, Arti won the debate and Arthur allowed the ancestors to confirm it, although they had no advice to give on the problem of the carriages.

So they returned to the ships, not to burn them but to break open the powder magazines, unload the powder kegs and carry them up the scree to the earthwork on the headland. They also brought pikes and swords from the *Bona Confidenzia*'s armoury, so that the eventual gun crews could protect themselves against cavalry. As Arti had said, there was already sufficient shot at the fort – not only round shot but also grape and canister.

They returned to the head of the bay and when the next sleigh party arrived to ferry more cargo to the spring camp, they directed them to the fort. There they dismounted the two guns, wrapped them in deerskins and dragged them away, two bull reindeer to each cylinder of cast iron, in the manner that they towed the tent poles on the migration.

Before they dismounted the cannon Arti asked Arthur to perform a small ceremony to inspire their followers. Under Arthur's supervision, they loaded the guns with powder and wadding, tethered the carriages and lit two coils of slow match. The giggling gun crews were herded to a safe distance and Arthur and Arti touched off the cannon simultaneously. It was a perfect salute. The flash, bellow and billow of black smoke was a gunner's dream. The new gun crew, men and women indistinguishable under their layers of deerhide, fell upon each other in gleeful delirium. The Sami had firepower.

Wardhouse castle seldom had visitors in the winter, and never before visitors such as these. There were six of them, scarcely resembling humans. Blackened skin stretched over fleshless bones and wild eyes stared from greasy mats of hair.

They croaked a language that the governor recognised as English, although he could not understand it. They must be survivors from the English ship which had sailed east in August. The six wretches had sailed a small boat into the harbour by the castle during the noon twilight, guided by the smell of wood smoke and seal oil. The governor ordered them to be lodged at the castle until the trading season opened and then put them on the first ship going south to Bergen.

15

Ambush

Arthur lay face-down in the flinty silt of the cave and sobbed. The strangers or the Sami could take him and do as they liked with him.

It had all been so wonderful and so futile. Every time they had crested another rise on the long trail south they had looked back and wondered at the distance they had dragged the cannon, and all for nothing. Every time they had met another *seta*, the speeches they had made, the *yoiks* they had sung, the *juobmo* they had drunk, the joyous discharge of the cannon, and the dozens of eager men and women who had volunteered to drag the guns another stage or to join their growing little army – these had all been for nothing.

He remembered the challenges they had met, the storm that had pinned them down and the tall windbreaks they had fashioned from snow blocks to shelter the tents, the trees they had felled so that the hungry reindeer could eat the tree lichen. They had been so brave, so strong, so clever, and for what? For a half-hour skirmish in which they had lost their cannon and the Sami had run away without a fight.

They had had no clear idea of what to do with the cannon when they recovered them from the fort. They dragged them back to the spring pastures of their own *seta* and built them sled carriages, so as to fire another salute for their admiring families. They had a loose plan that they would then hide the cannon somewhere and pick them up again when they passed through the site in the autumn, so as to take them to the winter camp. The cannon were too cumbersome to follow the *seta* throughout the year of migration, so they would have to be used as fixed defences, although why the strangers had chosen to attack the winter camp and whether they would do so again was unknowable.

At this moment another *seta* arrived in the area with the story that they, too, had encountered a body of strangers crossing the high fells. This time the strangers were moving from west to east, while the Sami had broken camp and were moving northwards. The Sami herdsmen shadowed the strangers for a while but the strangers made no effort to raid the herd, and seemed unaware that they were being watched.

'Let us take the cannon south now,' said Arti, 'while the rest of the *seta* watches over the deer while they are in rut. We could catch the strangers. They would not expect to meet us on the fells in this season and they do not know that we have guns. We could trap them and avenge Leeuna.'

Arthur sorely wanted to avenge Leeuna but he was uncertain about another encounter with the strangers. But, as always, Arti won the argument and they moved south. They travelled in the opposite direction to the migration, parading their guns for each *seta* they met coming north. The news of the guns and their terrible power ran ahead of them like flame through dry grass. Within a week they had become a sizeable war band, with men and women from a dozen *seta*. With so many willing humans and ox-deer to pull the guns, progress was fast, despite the increasingly muddy terrain.

Without meaning to do so, they had created a new *seta* unlike any that had ever been in Sameatnum. They were much bigger than a normal *seta* – almost a hundred strong – and all of them young people with no children or elders. They had no reindeer other than those used to draw the sleighs, and they fed by hunting and from the hospitality of passing *seta*. Arthur and Arti wrote the band their own *yoik*.

We are the people of He of the forest
Masters of the iron trees
That carry the lightning
That carry the thunder
Across Sameatnum
We are become the hunters of the hunter
The hunter who devours the children of the Sami
The Sami are one seta
One pain is the pain of all
We are the daylight that ends the dream
We are the sunlight that ends the winter
The daylight that ends the dream
The sunlight that ends the winter

It was not a ballad that would have sold well in St Paul's Churchyard but the Sami liked it, and it was repeated in *seta* that the war-band never reached.

Arti instructed Arthur further on his role as the *no'adi*. He explained that the three divisions on the sacred drum represented this world, the World Above and the World Below. The symbols were spirits and deities found in each of these realms who could be contacted by the correct stick-work. He also taught Arthur to cure illnesses and injuries by the laying on of hands, which, for the Sami, meant a vigorous massage. Arti said that *no'adi* from different *seta* met in the summer by the sea to practise techniques on each other.

He also found Arthur an assistant. A good *no'adi* needed an assistant to help with the work, and to replace him if he died or was disabled. Arthur's predecessor had quarrelled with his assistant, who had died mysteriously, shortly before Arthur arrived. Arthur's assistant was a young woman named Seena who was so short and plump as to be almost a ball. She was, however, very energetic and an enthusiastic healer.

The plan had been to reach the site of the massacre before the ground thawed out and there to hide the guns, powder and shot under the protection of the spirits. When and if the Sami reoccupied the locality they could then build a fortified camp, although whether the powder would still be useable and whether the Sami would be able to serve their guns effectively were both uncertain. After hiding the guns the new war-band would, presumably, disband, although this would be a great disappointment to everybody but Arthur. The others were eager for battle with their new weapons.

It was the wolves who alerted the reindeer that the strangers were near, and the deer alerted their keepers. The Sami scouts quickly located the strangers' convoy. They were in much smaller numbers than expected, and without cannon. It might not have been the same group that had carried out the massacre, but they had no business being in this part of Sameatnum so the war-band at once began to harass them.

It was as if the ancestors were directing them straight into an ambush. The trap was set at Arrow Island, on the shore of the still-frozen sea – the White Sea thawed later than the northern ocean. Arthur had intended to site the cannon on opposing bluffs so that they could give each other covering fire, like the Thames batteries. Sadly, the cordage from the *Bona Esperanza* had hauled the cannon too far and gave way as they pulled the second gun up the slope. It slithered all the way down and buried itself in a snowdrift. So they had to fight with one cannon, which could not defend itself if the enemy came to close quarters.

The first shot had been very satisfying. It was a joy to see the horsemen go down. Perhaps one of them was the man who had killed Leeuna. The second shot went off prematurely, because they had failed to cool the barrel. It also wrecked the makeshift gun carriage. Arthur realised that they should have practised their gunnery before the ambush, but the sound would have carried too far in the wilderness. Even so, Tom Lovelace would have sent him to the masthead for the rest of the day for such incompetence; Tom had been a hard taskmaster and Arthur had been pleased when he was transferred to the *Edward Bonaventura*.

All this would not have mattered had not the strangers shown such resolution. The cavalry scattered but the infantry pressed on like the English at Agincourt, taking full advantage of the lie of the land. Arthur tried to rally the Sami, but they fled as soon as a few arquebus balls splattered against the rocks. So he, too, had fled once again. He had hidden in a cave at the far end of the island and now he was past fleeing. He would lie there and weep until they took him.

Somebody was embracing him, furry and Sami-smelling.

'Is that you, Leeuna?'

'No, I am not Leeuna,' answered Seena. 'I am come to fetch you. We need you.'

'Nobody needs me. Leave me be.'

Other arms were taking him, and they carried him out of the cave and across the beach and set him on the ice where they strapped on his skis. He co-operated numbly.

Yesterday's battlefield was around the headland. The eight dead horses and six dead horsemen lay where they had been shot down, still in their harness and furs. A group of Sami were stripping off the horsemen's boots.

Wisps of smoke still hung over the beach. This had been more than a campfire. The strangers had been burning stores and the Sami were raking the ashes. The cannon had been toppled from the bluff but lay on the beach, apparently intact. The scent of panic still lingered in the air. The strangers had fled and the Sami were spoiling the field.

It was like taking a gulp of Sir Hugh's brandy; it took some moments to take effect but when it did it was dramatic. This was not defeat, but victory! Arthur's limbs, which had been so heavy, now felt so light he wanted to fly. There were no words in English or Sami to say it all.

'Victory, Seena, victory!' he babbled, stupidly. 'We won, we won!' He seized her and lifted her clean off the ground, skis and all. But enough of triumph; he must take command. 'After them! Press them! Don't let them find their courage.' Arthur had become an avenging angel.

The Sami might well have given up the chase had not the strangers begun to jettison their loot.

'After them! After them!' shouted Arthur. 'Make them give us more!'

And they gave more. They threw away the loot they had taken from the winter camp, the silver and the furs, proving they were the strangers who had murdered their families. The stores and equipment thrown down by the leading sleighs began to create obstacles for the sleighs in the rear, forcing them to weave around the tangles of harness and empty kegs. The Sami kept up their high-pitched keening with which they used to panic wild deer, and which seemed just as effective against horses. An accident among the strangers' sleighs was inevitable.

One of the sleighs swerved to miss a tangle of abandoned ropes and poles, hit a ridge in the ice and spun over. The strangers' sleighs were much more stable than the Sami sleighs, but they were more difficult to right when overturned. The occupants did not wait to try, but picked themselves up from the snow and ran.

The shrieking Sami closed in, loosing arrows as they skied. But the strangers were not frightened deer.

Those ahead of the stricken sleigh dashed on towards the horizon, heedless of their comrades. Not so the three sleighs in the rear. They had no alternative but to swerve aside to pass the upturned sleigh and force a way through the milling Sami. The drivers stood on their benches and whipped their teams to a supreme effort. The passengers threw overboard everything except their weapons. Across the ice they hissed, the horsemen who formed the rearguard for the convoy galloping beside them. They galloped awkwardly, for they were mounted *streltski*, too large for their unfamiliar Tartar ponies, but they kept pace and kept their saddles.

Past the wreck they swept, past the fleeing passengers,

143

scattering aside the Sami, to pull up about 500 yards ahead. They halted in a loose horseshoe, its open arms reaching out to the six men and one woman struggling towards them.

The *streltski* leaped from their horses and sleighs. This was their form of war. They had been raised as the Kremlin guard and had put down many a Moscow riot. They worked in pairs, each arquebusier supported by a pikeman. The pikeman gave cover with his six-foot half-pike while the arquebusier loaded, levelled and fired his big, clumsy handgun, resting the barrel on a long, forked stand. This could take the better part of a minute, during which the gunman was effectively unarmed.

The sergeant passed along the line with a pot of fire, igniting the coil of slow match around each man's shoulder. They moved with the precision of dancers at the royal court, indifferent to the screams and chaos in front of them. The hedge of steel was set. The weak sun glinted on serried pikes and gun barrels, and the matches glowed and spat above the powder pans. The fugitives from the wrecked sleigh were now within earshot, with the Sami close behind. The sergeant shouted to them to throw themselves down.

The Sami instinct was to go for the sleigh and the horses. Arthur spurred them after the fleeing passengers. 'Kill them! Kill! Kill! Kill!'

He dug his ski pole, which also served as a spear, into the snow and shot into the lead. The strangers were running before him, looking more like animals than people in their heavy furs. One had fallen behind and was calling to the others. He was dragging his foot, the way Leeuna had dragged hers, the foot that had betrayed her to the horseman.

Arthur pushed himself faster and levelled his pole-spear. He was no longer a stealthy boy who murdered in secret but a warrior who killed face-to-face. He could already imagine his victim's scream, as he had heard Leeuna scream.

The man threw himself onto the snow. Arthur turned the points of his skis inward and skidded to a halt. He raised the pole to strike. The man rolled over. Arthur looked into his face and saw blue-grey eyes, heavy eyebrows and a bristly red beard.

Holy blood! Tom Lovelace.

Whether the shock of recognition would have been enough to check the death-thrust can never be known, for in the same instant Arthur felt a blow like the kick of a horse and then oblivion.

Part 2

16

Rebellion

The west wind was usually a cleansing wind, sweeping London's smoke eastwards to spread its soot over the warren of shacks huddled beyond the Tower, where the hopeful incomers from the shires eked out their precarious lives. Today it brought in smoke from further west, from the burning hamlets of Kensington and Knightsbridge, torched by the Kentish rebels who had forced a passage over the Thames at Kingston.

'Hurry, my lady, hurry! Before we're surrounded. We can still escape towards Essex. Will is burying the silver in the yard so we can discover it later.'

Kate Thomas looked at her two terrified apprentices and shook her head. 'You're good lads, but I'd never venture east of the Tower without an escort of pikes, even in days of peace. I'd rather trust myself to the mercies of Lord Wyatt and his Kentishmen than the vagabonds of Essex. And as for the silver, we've so little, we might as well leave it. If they find none they'll know it's hidden and they're sure to see the fresh-turned earth in the yard.'

'My lady, 'tis said Lord Wyatt has drawn up a list of the most desirable women in London, to be taken and shared amongst himself and his captains.'

'I'm flattered you think me listed.'

'They are sure to know of you, my lady, because of you were betrothed to Sir John.'

'Ah, a brief and accidental glory.'

'The boys are right,' said Richard Pierce, Kate's factor, who came, panting, into the hall. 'Remember what happened to Sir John. But weeks ago you were betrothed, and now he's dead in a Kentish ditch. These rebels are madmen, Protestants, who'll murder anybody not of their belief.'

'John was murdered by robbers, not rebels. He tried to escape back to London when his militia deserted at Strood. Nobody has seriously opposed these people until now, not until yesterday when the queen stood on the steps of St Paul's, pledged herself not to flee, and called upon us citizens to fight for our city and our sovereign. The queen is still in Whitehall so why should we desert her? Why aren't you on the city walls?'

'Are you in love with death, my lady? Nobody knows which way the Londoners will turn, and the rebels have cannon from the fleet.'

'Oh come, Richard, can you imagine dragging ships' cannon overland from Gravesend? If they had them they would have used them on the city when they took Southwark. As for our fellow Londoners, we should strengthen their temper by showing ourselves in the street in support our queen rather than set an example of panic.'

The two apprentices were crying. 'What have I ever done for you, that you should weep for me?' snapped Kate, pushing them away. 'Cease slobbering and do as you will. I'm staying. What matter if I die? Now that Sir John is dead, God rest him, I can no longer provide for you or myself, rebellion or no. I'll fend for my city and you can join me if you wish.'

'The rebels have been seen at Charing Cross,' said Richard.

'Then come with me to Ludgate and show defiance. We have had too much rebellion and strife since King Edward died, and if this rebellion triumphs it will not be the last.'

A mass of people and animals pressed eastwards through the streets around St Paul's. Kate and her little band pushed their way through in the opposite direction, ignoring the curses and warnings.

'Go back! They've forced Ludgate. They surprised the gate before it could be closed.'

'The queen is dead! Whitehall's burning!'

'Save yourselves while you can!'

The massive Gothic majesty of St Paul's looked down Ludgate Hill to the square towers of the gate in the city wall. Beyond the gate the road crossed the River Fleet and led on past the town houses of the nobility to the fields around Charing Cross. The popping of gunfire had been heard from that direction for some time. Somebody was engaging the rebels, possibly the forces of the loyalist nobility from the Midlands. The sprawling riverside palace of Whitehall was visible across the bend in the river, but whether it had been taken by the rebels, and whether Queen Mary, who had refused to quit her palace, was still alive, was unknowable. At least the palace was not ablaze, unlike the hamlets to the west.

The steep, cobbled street was all but deserted. A few bystanders had decided to watch events rather than flee, citizens who had nothing to save beyond their own wretched lives. The city gate stood open, as it had done throughout the long years of the Tudor peace. As Kate approached she realised that the rebels were already inside the wall. They had passed the gate and were standing in the street like lost pilgrims.

This was no terrible army, but a group of less than a hundred men with no cannon or cavalry. Most wore simple round iron helmets and carried pikes and a few had half-armour – backs and breasts. There were also some swords and handguns. As it was a raw morning with a hint of sleet, they were wet and muddy as well as breathless and confused. This could only be part of the rebel army, a contingent which had evaded the loyalists beyond Charing Cross and St James' and discovered the city gate still open. The man at their head was clearly a gentleman, although his finery was much bedraggled.

The leader decided to halt and make a speech to the scanty crowd. He could have pressed on to St Paul's and made an address from the cathedral steps, as the queen had done, but he seemed anxious not to go too far from the gate, more prepared to flee the city than sack it.

'Citizens of London, I am Lord Thomas Wyatt, loyal subject of Her Majesty, Queen Mary, come to London with other of her loyal subjects to save her and all her subjects from enslavement to a foreign prince. We have been forced to take arms to prevent the intended marriage of our queen with Prince Philip of Spain. Already the Spaniards are coming to rule us – we see them daily in great numbers on the road from Dover. Londoners, declare yourselves against the foreign despot before it is too late!'

It was a strangely apologetic speech. Most Londoners assumed that the revolt was a Protestant rebellion to overthrow Queen Mary and install her sister Elizabeth as queen. Nothing less justified treason. They had expected the Kentishmen to burst into the city with a shout – 'For God and Elizabeth!' Instead they had been treated to a timid lecture on foreign policy. The onlookers looked on in silence.

This should have been the moment of triumph for Sir Thomas, the culmination of the long march from Maidstone. He stood in the capital of the kingdom, which lay defenceless around him. He had reached his goal; could he grasp it?

Could he? His mind went back over the last few weeks. He had never intended to raise a rebellion in winter, but the conspiracy had been betrayed and he had been forced to raise his standard prematurely. Even in summer it would have been difficult to hold together a horde of unpaid volunteers for a prolonged campaign, but the cold and wet made matters far worse. The bad weather ate at the morale of his men and the mud clogged the wheels of his wagons and made it impossible to move heavy cannon.

At first all had gone well. Not only Kentishmen had joined them. The six hundred London militia, whom the queen had dressed in white coats and sent to hold Rochester Bridge, had deserted to the rebels as soon as they had lined up for battle. The five warships gathered at Gravesend to escort Prince Philip to England had also joined them. The rebels had no field carriages to convey the naval cannon overland, but the news that they had cannon threw London into panic.

If only they had taken London Bridge! Everything depended on the willingness of the Londoners to join the rebellion, but they had merely raised the drawbridge and watched passively as the rebels looted Southwark. After camping on the south bank for some time Sir Thomas realised he was getting nowhere. The queen refused to leave the capital and made her appeal to the citizens. News arrived of loyalist forces gathering in Buckinghamshire.

His only hope lay in crossing the river upstream and coming upon London from the landward side. Unlike foreign princes, the queen of England had no hired army at her command; she depended on a few hundred palace guards, the love of her people and the willingness of the nobility in the shires to bring their retainers to her aid. Sir Thomas had to get into the capital before the queen could gather loyal troops.

The rank and file of the rebels and even some of the gentlemen had already begun to drift home. The desertions grew when Sir Thomas struck camp and marched on Kingston. They were marching away from Kent. By the time he reached Middlesex his ranks had greatly thinned.

He had pressed on through the mud, desperate to reach the city. A confused running battle developed along his flanks as the advance guard of loyalists came up from the west. Groups of rebels turned aside to plunder Knightsbridge and Kensington. This was foreign territory to Kentish peasants and they claimed the spoils of war. Split into contingents, the dwindling hard core of rebels hurried across the fields of Charing Cross, up Fleet Street, and there was Ludgate, standing open. They walked through into a near-empty metropolis.

How should he appeal to the few remaining citizens?

Perhaps best not to attack the queen after the support she had roused by her recent speech. Nor had there been any sign of Protestant fervour. Better to play on their distrust of foreigners, Spaniards landing at Dover to take over the kingdom.

Sir Thomas had scarce finished his brief speech when a scuffle broke out to his rear, with the sound of clanging metal and timbers dragged over the cobbles. The rebels turned about. A small group of men and boys was shutting the gate.

Had the gate had been left open to lure them inside, and was it now being shut behind them? Who knew what ambushes lay ready in the lanes and alleyways of this vast, sullen, threatening city? The rebels gripped their pikes tighter, ready to fight their way out.

In front of the gate, full in line with every pike, sword and gun, stood a young woman. Her feet were planted astride, she had thrown back her hood and her red hair fell free, bejewelled with the drizzle.

Holding back her head, Kate shouted in as bold a voice as she could raise, 'God save the queen! God save Mary, our lawful queen!'

The rebels rushed the gate. John and Will snatched Kate from martyrdom by pulling her into the gutter and throwing themselves across her. Richard and the other prentices scattered as the rebels forced open the heavy timber doors.

Once one woman had shouted defiance, every Londoner became a patriot. 'God save the queen!' shouted the crowd, suddenly grown much bigger as the beggars, shopkeepers and honest citizens in the side streets came out of hiding. Faces appeared at windows, casements were opened, and chamber pots were flung down onto the rebel heads. 'God save the queen! God save the queen!'

The rebels spilled out into Fleet Street. Towards them along the street came a body of armed men, horsemen and foot soldiers. It was not a further contingent of rebels.

The fight was brief and confused. A few Kentishmen laid

about with their pikes and were difficult to subdue. Others surrendered without a struggle. Sir Thomas was found sitting on a bench outside a tavern, his head in his hands.

Seen close at hand, Queen Mary was much uglier than she had seemed from a distance on the steps of St Paul's. Kate Thomas knelt in front of her.

'So you are the young lady who saved London.' Mary smiled.

'Your Majesty, 'twas yourself who saved the city by refusing to leave us in our peril. You did not leave us and we stood loyal.'

'I am blessed in having such loyal subjects as yourself. Have you a husband?'

'Alas, I am a widow.'

'Then I must find you a worthy husband We may both be married before the year is out.'

Mary smiled again. She had survived thirty-seven years without a husband, led a successful rebellion against the puppet usurper Lady Jane Grey, become England's first queen regnant, and put down the Kentish rising, yet she smiled as sentimentally as a young milkmaid at the prospect of her forthcoming wedding.

The disloyal thought crossed Kate's mind that they might both do better without husbands.

'All I ask, Your Majesty, is to be able to support the enterprise and the household left to me by my late husband. My factors and prentices are my loyal subjects, for them I am the queen and I need to protect them as you protect your subjects.'

'I know little of enterprise or trade,' replied the queen, 'but I will ask my council to see you favoured.'

17

Ransom

'There is a man to see you, m' lady. At the gate.'

'What sort of man, Jane?' Jane was Kate Thomas' oldest servant, who had been with the household since Kate's late husband had been a child.

'A common man, m' lady. He says he is a gaoler from the Newgate prison, and that he brings you something from one of the prisoners, something which once was yours. He says 'tis urgent, for the man is due to hang at Tyburn next week.'

'A prisoner? Hang? You mean a rebel?'

'I take it to be so. What else?'

What else indeed? Boatloads of prisoners from Kent had been arriving in the city for weeks past, and it was a wonder there was room for them in the city's prisons. The mass hangings were due to start next week and most Londoners had a holiday to watch their former enemies choked, disembowelled and cut to pieces.

'Methinks,' continued Jane, 'he seeks to ransom some of his prisoners as servants and prentices to masters in the city.'

'And we may well need them,' replied Kate, 'if the queen favours us as she promised. We'll meet him in the courtyard – no need to have gaol fever in the house – and see that he is alone and that Will and Tom are close at hand.'

Kate had never met a gaoler, but this man looked more like a mariner, with a loose, open shirt and loose breeches hanging to his knees. Doubtless there was more employment in the prisons than on the river.

The man nodded a perfunctory deference. 'I am come from the Newgate, as I told your woman, m' lady. I have this to give you from one of my charges. He asked me to take you to him, and told me you would reward me, should you so wish.'

He held out his fist and opened a calloused palm. In it nestled the silver brooch she had given to Richard Chancellor, that night in Gravesend.

In deference to her rank, they allowed Kate a room at the Newgate to meet her prisoner. Most of the traffic between prisoners and gaolers and the crowd outside took place through the gratings which looked down from the street into the prison basements. Some came merely to gape at the prisoners but many brought bread, beer and other comforts, which they passed down to them. There was a brisk trade in ransoms, from friends and families and from masters seeking workers for the households, workshops and whorehouses of London.

How fickle they are, thought Kate. But three months ago these same people were fleeing for their lives, to escape the men they now came to feed. It had been a mistake for the queen to execute Lady Jane. She was so obviously innocent of any conspiracy with Lord Wyatt, yet her beautiful young head – she was only eighteen – had been one of the first to roll after the Kentish rising. Now it seemed that Mary was bent on sending another beautiful head rolling. It was rumoured that her half-sister, Princess Elizabeth, had been taken to the Tower only last night.

Lord Wyatt was dead but people were beginning to pay more heed to what he had told them about the Spaniards now that the queen's marriage to Philip of Spain had been fixed for July. Already Spanish nobles were arriving in London with their servants and guards, and two Spanish soldiers had been killed in a brawl at the Sun last Tuesday. England was inching back to blood and chaos.

The door opened to admit the prisoner. Kate hoped that Jane and Will could not see her agitation. Was this unknown man trying to save his life by blackmailing her about her escapade at Gravesend? How did he come by the brooch? The *Edward Bonaventura* had sailed for Cathay and there had been no news of a shipwreck on the English coast.

The prisoner was like any other: dirty, ragged and too young to have a beard, with a half-healed wound on the side of his head. She felt a surge of relief. She had half-expected it to be Richard Chancellor himself.

The youth fell at her feet. 'Mistress Thomas, heaven be praised! I've crossed the world to find you!'

'Do I know you, then?'

'You will not recall me, m' lady, but I was your attendant on the voyage to Antwerp, four years back. I recognised you on the deck of the *Edward* when you danced with Mr Chancellor the night we sailed for Cathay. I was playing the fiddle to your dance. I knew you are a great lady, and that you are close to the rulers of the Company which commanded our fleet, which is why I came from the Frozen Ocean to find you. I know that you can save Sameatnum.'

'I'm not sure I know you, though you may be the lad who was with me on the Cloth Fleet. If so, you are greatly changed. How do you come to be in the Newgate? Were you with Lord Wyatt?' But how could you have been, if you sailed with the fleet to Cathay, thought Kate? And if you did, how can you be here at all?

'In God's truth, m' lady, I am no rebel. I had the misfortune to leave ship at Gravesend, to seek out my mother and sister on the houseboat – I was born and raised on the foreshore.' The words tumbled out in ever-greater confusion. 'I was but new-landed and knew nothing of the rebellion, I swear it. Of course, I knew that the young king had died – the Danes told me that at Bergen and 'twas no surprise – and that England was Papist again – I mean Catholic, m' lady – but I swear I had never heard of the Lady Jane Grey, or of Lord Wyatt. Mother was telling me of it all, how we – I mean, the rebels – sacked Knightsbridge and Whitehall and nearly took the city, and would have done so but for the lack of cannon. When they came to search the boats for rebels, they took me because of the shot wound in my head. I told them 'twas done by the Muscovites on the ice, but nobody wanted to understand. They took about thirty of us and brought us by barge to London and put us here in Newgate.'

Kate lifted her hand to silence him. 'I cannot understand a word you say, but I am ready to accept that you were never a rebel. We will take you, feed and clean you and then you must rest, and after that you can tell us your story. But first,' she lowered her voice instinctively, although it served only to make Jane and Will listen more closely, 'who gave you the brooch? Did you steal it?'

'Seena gave it to me. She found it on the ice after the sleigh overturned. I knew it was yours from the time I was your attendant. I had fastened your cloak with it many a time. They found it, of course, when they searched me at the Newgate but I said it was my mother's and they let me take it with me to the gallows. But in truth, I had always planned to send it to you, to prove my story. It was God's will that I should find you.'

So he was not trying to blackmail her, though he may have known about her night with Richard. And he had news of Richard. Her heart was beating faster again. She must take this youth away, calm him and discover what he was trying to tell her.

'So you say your artilleryman, Tom Lovelace, is still with the savages?'

'The Sami, my lady.'

'So be it. We are all God's creatures.'

It was dark and the candles had been lit throughout the house. Kate had ordered that she and Arthur be left in private for Arthur to tell his story. There might be parts of the story which it was best for the servants not to know. Jane was anxious about leaving her mistress alone with a condemned rebel but

Kate reassured her that, in such a crowded dwelling with its warren of rooms, help was always close by and Arthur could hardly expect to escape, should he try to harm her.

'Tom told me that I fell upon him when I was shot and that he lay beneath me thinking I was dead, waiting for Mister Chancellor and the Muscovites – the Russians, as he calls them – to recover him. But after a time when nothing had happened and he was fearful of freezing to death he pushed me aside and found himself alone on the battlefield amid the wreckage of the fight. Then the Sami came back and discovered Tom and myself. The Muscovites had beaten us but left us with the battlefield, just as they had done before. Tom reckons that Mister Chancellor and the Muscovite captain left him behind to lighten their sleigh and make good their own escape. 'Twas our gain, for we needed a master gunner. I had never been more than a powder monkey and I was insensible for the next several days.'

'You were fortunate to live.'

'Seena is a great healer and a young man's wounds mend fast. But 'twas clear I'd never lead the Sami to battle again. 'Tis not so much the wound to my head as the ball in my shoulder which hampers me with the skis. What troubles me is that once the Muscovites get to their own land they will come back in terrible force and treat the Sami as Queen Mary's men presently treat Kent – if you forgive me, m' lady.'

'Stop excusing yourself, Arthur, and tell me what you expect me to do.'

'M' lady, I want you – the Sami people want you – to raise your voice in the councils of the Company to send out another ship. Then you can bring back Mister Chancellor, who wages war on the Sami, and make it clear to the Russians that you will trade with them only if there is peace in the Northlands. And, of course, you will be able to open trade with the Sami.'

'I have but a small share in the Company. However, the shares are not so valued at present and perhaps it will not be difficult to become a major stakeholder. But what of Mr Chancellor?'

'When I left Sameatnum Mister Chancellor and the Muscovites had taken refuge at a monastery, a great stone fortress on an island in the White Sea. That is the name of the gulf discovered by Mister Chancellor, and which he mistook for the Southern Ocean, or so Tom Lovelace told me. The Sami have invested the fort and Tom is sure that with our two cannon he can beat down the wall. They will kill them all if the monastery falls, but I fear this will bring an even more terrible vengeance.'

'But how can we in England prevent this? We are at the other side of the world.'

'The sea is now too difficult for the Muscovites to navigate through the floating ice, at least with their craft, for they have no great ships so they cannot send help to the monastery. ''Twill not be passable 'til the summer. M' lady, if the Company wishes to rescue Mister Chancellor, recover all the Company's fleet, bring the two sides to reason and make a great commerce with both Muscovy and Sameatnum, there is yet time. We can reach the monastery as soon as they. The Company must send another ship, with all God's speed.'

'Arthur, you are brave and venturesome, but you are also very lucky to be alive. Is it not time for you to forget the Sami and your beloved Leeuna?' She spoke softly and laid her hand on his arm. 'God has spared you to join us in our trading house. You will be safe here. If you serve us well I will set aside a sum of money for you each year and, in time, you can use it to buy a share in our cargoes and so share our profits. Many a London merchant has started as a prentice. For the moment leave matters of commerce and statecraft to older and wiser heads.'

'If a wise head needs grey thatch, why are you so beautiful?'

Kate's cheeks burnt crimson and she plucked away her hand as if she had touched a bread oven.

'*How dare you*? How dare you abuse our kindness? Remember that you are a servant lately snatched from the hangman!' She calmed a little. 'Do I need to spell it out for your lovesick ears? It took Mister Chancellor more than a summer to reach Muscovy.

How can we get a ship there before the Muscovites have crushed the Sami, and Richard has met whatever fate God holds for him? And do you know the Muscovites have no great ships? What of the *Edward*?'

'Forgive me, forgive me please, m' lady. In saying you are beautiful, I only dared to say that being young yourself, and wise and just withal, you might not despise a lad like me. I am an unlettered, crippled youth, but I have thought hard and talked to older and wiser men. Hear me, please.'

Taking her silence for assent, he plunged on.

''Tis true it took Mister Chancellor four months to reach Muscovy, but our fleet was cursed with ill winds – too light in the German Ocean and too brisk in the Norwegian Sea – but more to the matter, Mister Chancellor was looking for Cathay, not Muscovy, which he came upon by chance. Now that we know where to go and the way there, we should, with but reasonable good fortune, be able to send a ship there in four weeks. Everything is easier the second time. I was in Sameatnum four weeks ago, not counting the three days in Newgate. As for the *Bonny Edward*, I have thought of that too and Tom Lovelace is certain that the governor of Kholmogory would never seize the ship without the direct command of the emperor. He would not even buy a kersey without licence from Moscow.'

Kate looked unconvinced.

'M' lady, we in England cannot imagine Muscovy! Tom tells me it is vaster than the ocean. He has never been to Moscow, but Mister Chancellor took six weeks to reach it – a city he said was greater than London – and that was travelling fast over frozen rivers. He reckoned it would take longer in the summer, for the rivers are shallow in many places and difficult to navigate. In spring the way is impassable, for the rivers are swollen and full of floating ice, and the roads are lost in mud. 'Tis the same throughout the Northlands.'

'Are you saying that it is easier to reach the White Sea from London than Moscow?'

'Yes indeed, in the present season. Nor do we need build a special ship to reach Muscovy. Any of several vessels now lying in the Thames, English and strangers', would serve well enough and many are idle, for I saw they had stowed their top-yards as we passed upriver.'

'You noted which ships were idle on your way to the gallows? You were never born to hang, Arthur. You are a born merchant. But if Muscovy is as great as you say, then it must serve the Company and the queen better to make an alliance with the emperor than with his savage enemies. There may be honour in helping the Sami, but little profit.'

'M' lady, I beg you – the Sami understand trade and have wealth of their own. On my way through Norway I was given a barrel of train oil to take to London, and which I suppose is still aboard ship. The Sami get it from the seals that swarm around their coasts. Send me to the ship and I will bring you the train oil and light your house with it, with lamps as the Sami do. You will never wish to use candles again, and your maids can use it for the cooking. The Sami will trade it for your kerseys. You will be able light London and be the richest merchant in the city! You need never fear if the Cloth Fleet does not sail, or how English money exchanges at Antwerp or whether the emperor of Germany pays his debts. You will be beholden to no man.'

He looked into her eyes to watch her reaction. It was like looking at a woman in love: her pupils were so wide that her eyes were almost black.

She lowered her voice. 'I will send a servant to the ship on which you arrived in England, if you tell me her name and where you think she lies, and perhaps tomorrow you can teach me to light my lamps. Then we must set about building up my stake in the Company, and call on Mr Cabot and perhaps Dr Dee. And we will ask if Sir Henry is in London. But you have yet to tell me how you reached England. Was it Sami magic?'

'I came the same way as the others from the fleet. The Sami sent me by fast sleigh to the Northern Ocean. The sea was open but it was too early to meet the Danish traders, so Seena took me in a Sami boat to the Danish fort at Vardo – Wardhouse, to we English. She had been there before and knew it well. From there I took ship to Bergen, for there was train oil from the last season still waiting to go, and from Bergen to Antwerp and thence to Gravesend. We had fair winds and no mishaps.'

'The same way as which others from the fleet, Arthur?'

'The sailors from Sir Hugh's fleet who sailed away in the boats, or at least those six who lived to reach Wardhouse. The Danes told me they had left not long before myself, for they had to wait for a vessel. I had supposed them to be here in England.'

18

Philip and Mary

'At just this spot,' observed the boatman, gesturing to the southern bank, 'I passed the very barge carrying the Princess Elizabeth herself but two days ago. They was a-taking her to the Tower, God help her. They do say that the queen is in such haste to lop off her sister's pretty red head, not because she is a Protestant or because the Kentish rebels wanted to make her queen, but because she's afrighted that her husband-to-be will take a fancy to her when he sets foot in England.'

Plain sedition, thought Kate. Every London boatman seems to believe that his trade gives licence to babble treason the length of the Thames. But there again, he might be a government spy.

'It is reported that the princess has been accepted into the Holy Church and is taking religious instruction,' replied Kate noncommittally.

'The less reason for Prince Philip to refuse her, then. Not that any man would want to refuse her. A pretty little vixen she is. 'Tis hard for a queen to have a younger sister like that. For sure, our queen is brave and steadfast, more so than many a man, but none can say she's comely.'

'That's not a matter for her subjects to discuss.'

'No offence to you, m' lady. You're the comeliest cargo I've had on my bark for a twelvemonth. But I reckon 'twould be best for England if Prince Philip of Spain married Princess Elizabeth. Providing she escapes the axe, she should live a deal longer than her sister, whom they do say is a sickly woman, and the princess is more likely to give her husband a healthy brood of children, and a lot more pleasure for him in the making of 'em.'

'I hired you to take us to Mortlake, not for your opinions on how the royal house should arrange their marriages. Are we nearly there?'

'It's either a union with Spain or France. It has to be – England is too small now to stand on its own in the world.'

'Perchance. Can we see Dr Dee's house from here?'

''Tis yonder, among the meadows, with its own watergate.'

'A large house for so young a scholar.'

''Twas his father's house. He was one of King Harry's masters of the royal household at Hampton Court.' He saw Kate's look of surprise. 'I see you know the doctor, and that he fancies himself as a Welshman. 'Twas his father and mother who was Welsh. The doctor himself has lived at Mortlake all his life, save when he went overseas. Many's the story I could tell you about him.'

'I'm sure. Tie us up and go tell them to send a servant for us. Tell them Widow Thomas wants to see Dr Dee and Mr Cabot with important news about the Company for the Discovery of New Lands. And if they hesitate to receive us,' she added, nodding to Arthur who sat beside her in the boat, 'you may tell them that Widow Thomas is now the largest shareholder in the Company after Sir Henry.'

This was true, for she had spent the day before buying up shares in return for bills of credit on her own enterprise, which now had far better credit than the Company. It was during this tour that she had learned that Sebastian Cabot was with John Dee at his house at Mortlake.

The boatman steered for the shore and tied the boat. 'Do be wary, m' lady. They do say,' he whispered, 'that Dr Dee dabbles in the black arts.'

'All right then, if you must. Tell me about it.'

''Tis only to warn you what they do say, m' lady, seeing as you've never visited here afore. That building over there, the doctor had it built himself. That is where he conjures up the spirits of the dead and communes with them, so they say.'

'That sounds like an employment for you, Arthur,' remarked Kate.

'Aye, m' lady,' said the boatman. 'He pays young scryers to look into his crystal and tell him what they sees. Youths and maidens can see things denied to older folks, but first the doctor puts them in a swoon with strange spells, and then they look into the crystal and see and speak with the spirits. The doctor tells his scryers what to ask and they tell him what the spirits answer.'

'I am sure Arthur is happy in my household, but if he should need other employment I will bear the doctor in mind.'

'Mistress Thomas, how honoured I am by this unexpected pleasure! The very heroine of Ludgate herself.'

Was there a shadow of mockery in the doctor's welcome? He rose to greet her from the table at which he had been sitting beside Sebastian Cabot, a scatter of papers before them. John's father must indeed have been a person of substance, for he had bequeathed his son a handsome house. The bustle, noise and stenches of the city might have been on another star compared with the cathedral-like space and calm of the Mortlake residence. The great window behind the two men, emblazoned with heraldic devices, would not have been out of place in a small cathedral.

'I hear you wish to speak about the Company's business,' said Sebastian, rising with a formal Spanish bow. 'I am at your service. However, if you should wish to purchase any of my holdings in the Company, I have a factor in the city.'

'Pray be seated. Indeed, I have contacted your factor, and I have already taken the occasion to increase my stake in the Company. I understand that both yourself and Doctor Dee have been selling your shares of late. Hardly a propitious moment in these disordered times.'

The two men looked at each other uneasily.

'I am an old man,' said Sebastian, 'and soon to have no use for wealth.'

'I am sure Saint Peter would prefer you to depart this life with ready money rather than shares in the Cathay Company.' Kate smiled, then turned to John Dee.

'I,' said the young man, truculently, 'am a scholar. I have here a library finer than that of either of our ancient universities – to their shame, perhaps, but 'tis true. I need money to acquire books, charts, manuscripts, and materials for my experiments. I have sold my stake in the Company for the sake of learning.'

'I trust your learning rests at the disposal of the Company?'

'I was explaining to Mister Cabot that I was planning a visit to the court of King Sigismund at Prague. It has become the greatest centre of learning in Europe.'

'Well, I have news for you both. One of the rebels taken in Kent has confessed himself to have been one of the ship's company on the *Bona Esperanza*.'

'Scarce a surprise, Mistress Thomas,' replied Sebastian. 'There were numerous mariners among the rebels. The ships below Gravesend, which were readied to escort Prince Philip from Spain, all deserted to Lord Wyatt's cause. You will recall that they landed some of their great cannon but the winter mud forced them to leave them by the way on Shooters Hill. Otherwise your adventure at Ludgate might have ended very differently.' He spoke as though he regretted that she had not been pulped by a cannonball.

'Mister Cabot, the last news we had from the *Bona Esperanza*, at least to the knowledge of the shareholders, was a full six months before Lord Wyatt's rising. How, then, is it scarce a surprise that some of her company were in the fleet waiting to sail for Spain at the beginning of this year?'

'Mister Cabot meant to say,' intruded Doctor Dee, 'that there is no surprise that there were many mariners among the rebels. Some, indeed, might have served briefly in the Company's fleet, for there were men who deserted in the several days spent dropping down the river and loading the cannon, and I believe others were landed later at Yarmouth, miscreants and sick.'

'You are lying, and most clumsily for such a distinguished scholar. The mariner in question is standing beside me. I do not know what lies the other sailors who have reached England have told you or how you silenced them, but he tells me that the *Bona Esperanza* and the *Bona Confidenzia* were deserted by their crews in a bay in the Arctic, where they still ride at anchor. I am sure you both had some intelligence of this and suppressed it, so as not to damage the value of your stake in the Company while you sold it in preparation for your departure into the service of the king of Bohemia. Is this what you meant by your "marriage in commerce", your new fashion of ownership with the stakes in the Company freely traded on the Exchange?'

'Who is this lad, with such a strange tale?'

'Arthur Petty, Your Excellencies,' explained Arthur without being invited to speak. 'I was Sir Hugh's cabin boy, before he perished of the cold. After the admiral died the mariners left the ship and took to the boats. They left me to tend the sick who were unable to travel. After they had all died of the scurvy I walked into the forest in hope of reaching the Netherlands and was taken up by a group of the forest people and became their priest – not a Christian priest, of course, but one who spoke for them with their ancestors.'

Doctor Dee's eyes widened.

''Tis a tangled tale,' Arthur continued, 'but I swear that the *Esperanza* and the *Confidenzia* are still afloat, as is the *Bonny Edward*, although the *Bonny Edward* took a different course and is in port with its men. Mister Chancellor is alive, although in great danger for he has ventured into a war with the forest people.'

'I think,' added Kate, 'that we should save the full story for Sir Henry.'

*

169

'Kate, how honoured I am to see you.' Sir Henry had not met Kate above twice, and that only briefly, yet he took the aristocrat's privilege of using her Christian name. But this was not the flamboyant young aristocrat whose shapely legs had aroused Kate's admiration at the Company meeting eighteen months before. He seemed distracted and fidgety and was dressed in an altogether more sombre style, as though not to attract attention. 'Alas, if you have come on Company business, I regret that I probably cannot be of help to you. Mister Cabot and Doctor Dee handle all the Company's affairs.'

'Thank you, but they have already shared their wisdom with me, Sir Henry,' replied Kate, taking the seat which he offered her, 'which is why I have sought you here. I had feared you might be at Penshurst.'

Sir Henry seated himself wearily and Arthur, whom Sir Henry had ignored, remained standing behind Kate's chair.

'Kent is still too disordered, I am afraid, and besides, I need to wait on the queen here in London.'

'Sir Henry, I will be direct with you. Have you had any intelligence of the Company's fleet since it left the German Ocean?'

'As doubtless you know, Kate, the fleet was greatly delayed in the German Ocean and did not reach the Norwegian Sea until late in the season, meaning that they may need to overwinter in the Frozen Ocean before reaching Cathay. We have, of course, provided for that by provisioning the ships for eighteen months. So, giving a round voyage of three years, it could be another two years before we hear from them.'

Kate rose to her feet with a fierce rustle of skirts. Her cheeks were afire, her eyes gleamed and even her red hair seemed bright with anger.

'I am far from sure that you are being frank with me! What would you say, Sir Henry, if I told you that there stands beside me a seaman who less than two months ago stood on the decks of the *Bona Esperanza*? He is not one of the mutinous scum who deserted the fleet ere midwinter, and brought news to England that the ships were lost – news which your chairman Mister Cabot and your astrologer Doctor Dee suppressed while they sold their stakes in the Company and prepared their flight to Bohemia – but one with news that the ships are still whole and sound. Two lie abandoned in a desert bay in the Northlands and the third is in the power of the emperor of Muscovy. Sir Hugh is dead but your brother is alive, although in grave peril. What do you say to that?'

Sir Henry looked up at Kate and Arthur with a tired gaze, like an exhausted deer surrendering to the hounds. This was no longer a man who would open the world to English trade, or even try to save his brother.

'Mistress Thomas, I am not sure what you are asking...' He ducked as an inkstand flew past his head and crashed into the panelling. The servant nearest the door stepped forward and laid his hand on Kate's arm. In doing so, he stepped in front of Arthur, who seized the outstretched wrist and pinioned him in a single movement. There was a glint of metal on the far side of the room as the other servant uncovered a dagger from his doublet.

'Unhand him, Arthur. And you,' she added, turning to the man with the naked steel, 'put that away. So, Sir Henry, this is why you declined to dismiss your servants when I asked to speak in private: so that you could have armed men to protect you from an irate woman.'

'Kate, these are the queen's men, not mine. This is not the same England my brother left.' He did not need to explain that, while the fleet was tacking around the German Ocean, the boy king had coughed his last and the king's regent, Sir Henry's brother-in-law, had seized London and proclaimed his daughter-in-law, Sir Henry's niece, as queen. The girl and her equally young husband had now gone to the headsman's block, as had the father-in-law. But a busy axe grows thirsty, and its shadow now stretched over Sir Henry. Not that he had joined the Kentish rising, openly at least, but Penshurst had been occupied by the rebels and weapons from Sir Henry's armoury had been used at the battle on Wrotham Heath.

'A different England indeed, but one in which you claim to be a distinguished and loyal servant of the queen,' lied Kate. 'And forgive me, but in my excitement I forgot to congratulate you on the birth of your son. I believe you are calling him Philip, in honour of the queen's bridegroom, and that you have asked that when the prince comes to England he might become the child's godfather. Philip Sydney: a truly royal name.'

'Thank you, Kate,' answered Sir Henry, flinching at her contempt. 'And now I think we need close our meeting. May I wish you good day.'

Kate was still on her feet, but instead of taking her leave she sat down again.

'I think it may be to your profit if we continue our conversation awhile. You may know that I have the ear of the Bishop of London, who is close to the queen. You may also know that the queen is looking for an emissary to France, and I was speaking to the bishop of your skill in languages – that you know Paris well, that you are more than fluent in French, and that you have studied at the university there, where I believe you met Doctor Dee. Familiarity with France has now become quite rare among our English nobility. I do not know if you are minded to go to France, but I said that if the queen commands you would not decline the honour.'

Sir Henry continued to look sullen. Kate was lying when she claimed to have spoken about his suitability for the Paris mission, and Sir Henry probably knew this. Nonetheless, Kate was a Catholic who had the ear of the bishop and was favoured by the queen, so it was not impossible for her to promote this appointment. Sir Henry would be safer in Paris than in London.

Kate leaned forward and lowered her voice to a hiss. The two guards moved closer to monitor the conversation. 'Listen to me. There is a ship at anchor off the Tower. She is called *The Trades Increase*, and is open for charter. My people are talking to the captain on your behalf to hire her for the Company to carry a cargo of kerseys to the Northlands. She will be provisioned for two months. If need be, she can re-provision in Norway. We will rename the ship *Philip and Mary*, and her true mission will be to recover our lost fleet and our honour, bring home your brother before he seals an anti-Spanish alliance with Muscovy, and open trade with all the peoples of the Northlands. There is much to our profit. If you do not feel able to commit the Company to this venture I must try to find the money myself by uniting with other merchants, or seeking the help of some of the Spanish courtiers lately arrived in London. In which case, I may not have time to discuss the matter of the mission to France with the bishop. Are we together?'

Sir Henry remained silent.

'I take it that we *are* together,' said Kate, 'for both our sakes, and for the sake of your brother and your newborn son.'

''Tis Arthur, my lady. His screams shake the house. Please come! Only you can calm him.'

'Thank you, Jane. We must stop this. He has become quite deranged, and if this goes on we will soon all be as deranged as he.'

Mistress and servant hurried upstairs to the prentice quarters. Two of the boys were trying to restrain Arthur, who was sobbing and thrashing as though pursued by the Devil.

'Arthur! Arthur, my child, what troubles you so?'

Arthur became aware of her presence and struggled to form coherent English. ''Twas Leeuna, my lady, in the crystal. She was talking to me in Sami. I couldn't make out all she said. I wanted to go, but the doctor made me go on. I can't go back. I won't go to Mortlake again. I've been there twice. I'd rather face the *streltski*. They won't go away, even here, among the family.'

'Who are "they"?'

'Leeuna and others, so many others. There is a gentlewoman that Doctorr Dee says was Mister Chancellor's wife.'

'*Was* his wife. Is he become a widower then?'

'Doctor Dee said she died of fever after the childbirth. Mister Chancellor had a son born while he was away. The doctor was very excited when I described her.'

'How very interesting. But I expect he has a Muscovite wife by now. You're a strange child, Arthur. You can lead a charge into the cannon's mouth and yet sob like an infant after an afternoon at Mortlake. I thought you were used to magic?'

'Being a *no'adi* is not like being bewitched by the doctor, my lady. He looks into my eyes and says strange words, over and over, like the beating of the Sami drum. I go into a dream. Then he bids me scry into the crystal. I can't fully remember the scrying but I remember when the doctor brings me back and the faces and voices whirl in my head. I keep seeing Leeuna, the way she was when we laid her to burn. The doctor is in league with the Devil.'

'You have done well, Arthur. We have evidence enough to have the doctor hanged as a sorcerer, should I but tell the bishop.'

'Would you do such a thing, my lady?'

'If I threaten it I must be ready to carry it through, but I do not think that it need arise. If the bishop has his way there are many who will burn, but it is not to our purpose to hang Doctor Dee. I have called a meeting of the Company, those of us who are left, and I intend that the doctor will speak at it to support our cause, and in return we will promise not to talk to the bishop about black magic.'

'You think the Company will support our venture, m' lady?'

'The doctor will speak for us to save his neck, Sir Henry to save his head and Mister Cabot to save his fortune. Between them, we shall send the *Philip and Mary* on her way with everybody's blessing. I'm minded to sail in her myself, which should please them all.'

*

Sebastian Cabot bent over the vellum. This time he did not delight in the language he was transcribing. So much had happened since Sir Hugh's ships had left Gravesend, and the night he had danced with all the comeliest girls on the deck of the *Edward*, including Widow Thomas herself, he recalled with a shudder. Two of the ships had been lost and the third was, it seemed, in the hands of the duke of Muscovy, who apparently possessed a vast empire unnoticed by the rest of the world, and now the Company was in the power of that dreadful, scheming woman.

It had happened everywhere. A queen regnant would have been unthinkable when he was young, and now women ruled in England, Scotland and France. Thank God he had lived most of his life while men still mattered.

The revised Proclamation to the Princes of the Earth, which was to accompany the next expedition, had been drafted in anticipation of the queen's marriage to Prince Philip, which should have taken place by the time the ship reached Russia.

We, Philip and Mary, by the grace of God king and queen of England, France, Naples, Jerusalem, Ireland; defenders of the faith, princes of Spain and Sicily, archdukes of Austria, dukes of Milan, Burgundy and Brabant, counts of Habsburg, Flanders and Tyrol, to all kings, princes, rulers, judges and governors of the earth...

We have licenced our beloved and right worthy servant Mistress Katherine Thomas, gentlewoman, and other our trusty and faithful servants to go to countries heretofore unknown, so that hereby not only commodity may ensue, but also that an indissoluble and perpetual league of friendship be established between us...

'What a difference a year makes,' sighed Sebastian.

Part 3

19

Siege

Yelena paced the battlements. I really am a princess imprisoned in a tower, she thought, gazing dreamily across the ice-strewn water towards the mainland, although my only mortal danger is dying of boredom. Not that that seems to worry Richard. Her real problem, she decided, was that she was simply jealous. A woman jealous of a monk! Who could have imagined it?

Throughout their travels across Russia and Lapland, Yelena had been the only person with whom Richard could have a private conversation, albeit in Greek. It was through her that he learned everything about the country, and it was only to her that he could talk about his own country and himself. Even his conversations with others were through her lips and, like all good interpreters, she was a diplomat, leaving out the words better left unsaid and occasionally putting in words of her own.

At the Solovetsky monastery her usefulness abruptly declined. All the monks spoke some Greek and Abbot Philip was fluent, even though he had never studied in Greece. Philip and Richard had become close companions and spent hours in conversation. They were probably together now, while she faced the chill breeze from the White Sea.

Is this what it will be like in England, she wondered? Richard's ex-interpreter, the woman he no longer needs.

Philip was certainly an impressive man. Yelena would not have minded being his consort. She had learned through Richard that, although he was not the man who had founded the monastery, it was he who had made it the grand place it was now. Ten years ago there had been merely a crude granite altar on these remote islands, with a cross of walrus tusks. Now Philip ruled over a complex of churches and fortifications more imposing than any kremlin outside Moscow.

Like the Moscow Kremlin, it had two churches, one for the monks and the other open to the laity, each with its five onion domes, a tall, free-standing bell tower, the abbot's lodging, and the domestic buildings for the monks, their visitors and their horses. The whole was surrounded by a battlemented wall, a deliberate copy of the Moscow Kremlin, although, unlike Moscow, it was built not of brick but stone.

Philip had brought in peasants from the overcrowded farms beyond the forests and settled them on the mainland south of the Solovetsky Islands. They delivered their food rents and a proportion of the furs from their traps at the monastery. Not that the monks had forgotten how to labour for themselves, thought Yelena, for they had carved their own broad fields from the woods on the islands.

She watched the great blocks of ice swirling in the water. These should keep us safe from the Lapps for a while. The straits were easily crossed when they were frozen in winter, and by water in the summer, but it was very different in the spring thaw.

How glad they had been to reach Solovetsky! After that devastating volley from the *streltski* the Lapps had ceased to harass their convoy but they had dared not relax until they were behind stone walls and melting ice. Not that the Lapps had gone away. They attacked the peasants bringing their rents and carried off the farm equipment and boats, but that was beyond the water.

The monastery was now totally isolated, both from the mainland and the other islands, but that always happened in the thaw. Abbot Philip had turned down any idea of sending to Kholmogory for help. Anybody who reached the mainland would still have to cross the swollen Dvina to reach the town.

I wonder if the Lapps are watching me now, she thought? Even as she looked she saw a puff of smoke from among the trees on the other bank, followed by the boom of a cannon, and the wall jerked beneath her feet. There was a rattle of falling stones. Incautiously, she leaned over the parapet. She knew enough of artillery to know that it would take the gunners some time to reload and she knew they had only one cannon, presumably the one Richard had tried to disable after the last skirmish. The dust of a second impact blinded her for several moments, and stinging splinters of stone peppered her face. They had more than one gun.

Below her monks and soldiers swarmed into the courtyard like startled wasps. Dust-caked and dishevelled, her face beginning to bleed, she ran down the steps and pushed through the crowd.

'Let me see Captain Richard! Take me to Captain Richard!'

Richard and Abbot Philip were already emerging from the abbot's lodging.

She threw herself at their feet. 'The Lapps! The Lapps! They're bombarding the wall. They have at least two guns, maybe more.'

To prove the point, two more shots slammed into the masonry.

'Lenarushka, you're hurt! Philip, get someone to attend to Yelena.'

She felt warm inside. He had thought of her first, using the affectionate form of her name. It was worth being splattered with dirt by a cannon ball.

'Mere dust,' she said, 'but there's a battery of cannon on the point and they have our range.'

'I believe I told you, Philip,' said Richard, turning to the abbot, 'that we retook one of our own cannon from the Lapps, though how they possessed it or moved it over the country I never understood. Alexi is convinced they use magic. We tried to spike it, but perhaps not effectively. It now seems that it was not their only gun, so perhaps they really have overrun the fort on the Baltic. Our walls are thick,' he said, turning to Yelena. 'We have nothing to fear.'

'As long as we trust in God, we have nothing to fear,' agreed Philip. 'But we built the walls to the glory of God, and to be proof against arrows, not cannon. Between the two skins of masonry there is only a rubble filling. The Lapp gunners may have discovered this.'

'We could capture the battery?' pleaded Yelena. 'Lapps never stand and fight.'

'No,' said Philip. 'It's too dangerous to cross the strait before the ice has cleared.'

'Then that means they can't attack us, even if they breach the wall?'

'Yes. For the moment we are safe, and who knows what will arrive when the sea is clear? God will provide.'

'And, in the meantime, we must look after you, Lena,' said Richard. 'Philip, if you can send for water and cloths, I'll attend Yelena myself.'

The Lapps did not bombard the wall for long. They smashed a stretch of the external masonry and spilled the rubble filling onto the beach below in a noisy cascade. After that they turned their guns onto the boats drawn up on the beach and shot them into firewood. There were other boats on the far side of the island, but if the monastery had to be evacuated the remaining boats could take not take all the soldiers and sailors, let alone the monks. After this the cannon fell silent for some days, although the Lapp campfires still smoked and glowed along the shore.

When the cannon next opened fire the first shot flew over the wall and landed in the courtyard. It lay there, fizzing and smoking. The monks rushed to warn the abbot.

'Greek fire! The shot is painted with burning pitch. It burns even in water!'

'Probably seal fat,' said Philip. 'They're aiming for the thatch. Put men on the roofs with buckets of sand.'

It was too late to save the big stable block. The second shot allowed for the wind and landed square on the thatch. The wind, which had made the aim difficult, fanned the flames. At first the Lapp gunners did not try to spread the blaze but carried on shooting into the fire, building it up beyond the firefighters' control.

The smoke rose in a column, which towered over the island. The monks released the frightened horses but the crazed animals only added to the confusion. As the roof beams began to crash showers of sparks ignited the thatch on other buildings. The gunners shifted their aim to help the new fires.

Now the wood tiles of the two churches were beginning to burn, and then the gilded domes, for the gold paint overlay wood. Fighting the fire became useless. The men retreated from the heat and falling timbers and crowded onto the narrow beach on the seaward side of the island, taking with them such animals and possession as they could salvage. An explosion in one of the stone buildings told the *streltski* that they had lost their gunpowder.

The gilded domes flamed like enormous candles, creating a great beacon that must have been visible for leagues across the sea. Smoke poured from the windows in the towers which held the domes aloft, but these were stone and could never be burned. And then the impossible. One of the two larger domes collapsed and the blazing debris fell inwards, avalanching down the interior of the tower through floor after floor. As the cross-bracing collapsed the tower shimmered and sank with slow, upright dignity into a heap of dust. The rumble was still in the ears of the onlookers when the second tower collapsed.

All day long and most of the night the monastery burned. At least the fugitives on the beach were warm. By dawn the blacked walls stood broken and roofless and the monks and their guests returned to sift the hot ash.

The fire brought the Lapps no nearer to taking the monastery, but it made life uncomfortable for the besieged. The most immediate victims were the horses. All the fodder had been burned, so they became food themselves. The islanders now had cavalry without horses to complement their infantry without gunpowder. With the extra meat, the people were not short of food but they had only makeshift tents to keep themselves from the night air.

The next night a sentinel was found with an arrow through his throat. Somebody had crossed to the island in the darkness, carried out the silent murder and sailed back through the ice floes. The watch was doubled, adding loss of sleep to their other miseries.

The Lapps now began to show themselves and make themselves heard, beating their drums and singing their keening dirges into the night. They were thrifty with their powder and shot, but opened up occasionally to show the variety of missiles they possessed.

'We must get a messenger to St Nicholas or Kholmogory,' urged Richard. 'The Devil knows what other tricks they have in mind. I must send orders to Stephen to ready the ship so that as soon as the sea is clear he can sail to our aid. Then we'll teach them about gunnery.'

'I'll go,' said Yelena. 'You don't need me here. I'll go.'

'You're a woman,' objected Richard.

'I am glad you've not forgotten. But the Lapps have women too among their fighters. Where they can go, so can I. I even look like a Lapp.' She stretched the corners of her eyes to exaggerate the oriental slant. 'I've been a fugitive before,' she added.

'And you were caught and enslaved.'

'So I am just a slave who can easily be spared. But your man Stephen speaks some Greek, so I can explain to him directly what you want. Please, I want to go.'

They found a surviving pony for her and took them both

over to the mainland in a small boat, under cover of darkness. It was a perilous journey, constantly fending off the ice and twice unloading the boat and dragging it across larger floes thick with slush. It was impossible to bring Yelena to the shore, so they put her down on the landfast ice.

'God be with you, Lena, or Allah, or whomever you prefer to watch over you.'

'With so many religions, I'll be the best protected woman in the Northlands.'

'I would go with you, but I must bring the ship back to England.'

'I know. They can't risk losing you.'

'I don't know how I'll manage without you.'

'Quite well, I imagine.'

'I'll take you with me to England.'

'Just let me get to Kholmogory first.'

20

Alert

'Who is this madwoman? Can't she see that we don't understand her?' asked Kate. 'I suppose she's speaking Russian, but it could as well be Greek to me.' Both Kate's brothers had learned Greek, but her father had not thought it necessary for a girl.

Yelena cried. She was bewildered, frustrated and desperate. She had told her story in Greek, Russian and Tartar, but each met with the same blank incomprehension. She knew the woman was speaking English, but Richard had never tried to teach her the language.

Everything had gone so well. The journey to the Dvina had been long and she had been frightened all the way, but there had been no real difficulties and she had a purpose in life once again. She met nobody, friend or enemy. The few homesteads she discovered were deserted. The abbot's peasants had fled; where to, only God knew. The granaries and barns were bare, but there were enough sweepings on the floor for a few days' porridge for herself and some grain for the pony. She lived like a Tartar cavalryman, eating oatmeal and water and cutting a shelter for herself each night. Eventually she had reached the Dvina near its mouth and decided to cross there, if she could find a ferryman. The river was wider there than at Kholmogory, but for that reason the current was weaker and there was less danger from floating ice.

She found a fisherman who was ready to take the pony in exchange for a passage to St Nicholas. There was, he told

186

her, a strange, big ship moored off St Nicholas, with three tall masts. So Stephen must have moved the *Edward Bonaventura* downstream, thought Yelena, which would save her the journey to Kholmogory, and would save Stephen two days on the passage to Solovetsky.

Yelena asked the boatman to take her straight to the ship. Her pulse leaped as she saw the topmasts rise above the bank as they rounded the bend in the river. She had doubted she would survive crossing of the wilderness. Now she had done it, she had reached the ship and could yet save Richard and make him surely hers.

As they drew nearer her triumph began to wilt. The ship seemed smaller than she had remembered it and the sterncastle was not so high; yet there could be no other ocean-going ship in the White Sea, and her acquaintance with the ship had been quite brief. As she set foot on the deck suspicion became alarm. This was definitely not the *Edward Bonaventura*.

What ship was it? Whence had it come? Nobody understood her. They helped her on deck and looked puzzled as she ranted at them in every language she knew. They brought a succession of people to talk to her until she was faced with a woman. At first Yelena took her to be an interpreter, but the person she had taken to be the captain treated her too deferentially. Nor did she seem to be a passenger, for she gave orders with an air of command. Beside her was a young male attendant, a pleasant lad with clear, blue eyes. Instinctively, Yelana knew that he would help her.

It was certainly English they were speaking, but the whole purpose in choosing Yelena to carry the message from Solovetsky had been that she could speak Greek with Stephen. But where was Stephen?

'She's a madwoman,' said Kate. 'Arthur, do you understand anything of this?'

'No, m' lady. 'Tis not Sami, nor Danish, nor Dutch and I've never heard Russian.'

Yelena climbed to her feet, smiled at Arthur and began to hum loudly.

'I knew it. She is a madwoman,' said Kate. ''Tis dark now. Feed her and her boatman and land them tomorrow.'

'Listen – listen to her tune!' said Arthur. 'You know *Greensleeves*, m' lady? The tune we played at the dance in Gravesend the night before we sailed?'

Kate's pulse jumped at the memory. 'Yes, indeed. And she can only have learnt it from an Englishman, and there has only ever been one English ship in these waters before us.'

Arthur turned back to Yelena. 'English? The English sent you?' *'Da, Angelski, Angelski.'*

'Who is she, then?' asked Kate. 'Ask her if she knows Richard.' *'Richard Chancellor,'* said Arthur, slowly and carefully. 'Do you know him?'

'Da. Rishart Dzaencellya,' cried Yelena, jumping up and down joyfully, She pillowed her hand against her cheek and made a convincing imitation of a love cry.

'Please, not in front of the crew,' said Kate. 'Is she trying to say that she's Richard's concubine, or is she a dockside strumpet looking for custom?'

'I think you were right first time, m' lady. Tom Lovelace told me that that Mr Chancellor had an interpreter who was his secretary and mistress – an ugly little woman.'

Kate felt a stab of jealousy. 'The picture fits,' she said, studying Yelena. 'This one looks more as though she comes from Cathay than Russia. But if this is her, why doesn't she speak English?'

'M' lady, forgive my being so bold, but Mr Chancellor was surely the first person ever to speak English in Russia, so his interpreter must have spoken with him in some other language that he had, a trader's language.'

'Like Low German or Italian?'

'Perhaps. I've never heard Italian but 'tis not the Low German they speak in Antwerp.'

Yelena pointed emphatically at the furled sails, billowed out her arms and gestured to the open sea.

'Does she mean,' asked Kate, 'that Richard and the *Edward* have already sailed?'

'She is too distressed for such a simple message, m' lady. There is more to it. Her boat came not from upstream, but from the sea. And she is more than ordinarily travel-stained.'

This was a polite description, for Yelena was filthy and unkempt and had clearly lived and slept in the same clothes for some days, in close company with her pony.

'I would hazard that Mr Chancellor has not yet rejoined the *Edward*, and that this wench was with him and his men in Sameatnum. I reckon Mr Chancellor is still beleaguered at the fort in which he was seeking shelter on the islands in the White Sea, or else has met with some disaster and the wench here was sent to bring help. By God's providence she has found us.'

Yelena was weeping with relief. Allah be praised! The young man had understood and was pleading for her.

'That's an elaborate tale you've woven from very little thread, Arthur, but it bears belief. Captain Rodgers, how fast can you get this ship to sea?'

'The wind is offshore, my lady. We need only wait to fetch the shore party.'

'Leave them. They will come to no harm and we will be back soon.'

'But it is darkening and we have no pilot.'

'The boatman she came with must know the coast. She can explain to him what's afoot. Let us hope you have understood Mistress Slant-Eyes correctly, Arthur, or Captain Rodgers will most displeased.'

They put out to sea, leaving the bewildered shore party on the quay. Once out of the river Yelena pointed along the coast. Captain Rodgers was justifiably reluctant to follow a strange shore in the dark, and after further argument they hove to for the night and sent back for the men at St Nicholas.

With the dawn they began to grope along the unfamiliar, treacherous coast. Yelena and the boatman stood in the forepeak, debating the course and gesticulating to the helmsman. They halted at night. The nights were now shorter than the days as they moved towards the season of the midnight sun.

Yelena did not spend all her time on the forepeak. Whenever Captain Rodgers considered he could do without her she liked to talk with Arthur, as best she could. She knew that the people around her, the great lady included, looked on her as a freak and she sensed their sniggers and giggles. The Russians had been the same at Kholmogory. Arthur treated her as a normal being. He asked her to teach him her language, so she started to teach him Russian. Who needed Tartar?

Kate watched them from the rail in front of her cabin on the stern. The pair were in the waist of the ship and Yelena was trying to teach Arthur the stresses in Russian verbs. She held her face close to his and made him follow the movement of her lips. They were leaning together, fascinated by each other's eyes, his round and blue and hers almond and black.

Kate looked away in pain. She had tried so hard to be everything that a man should be, to run her enterprise and protect her servants, travelling overseas to open new trade, but still she behaved like a stupid woman. Worse than a woman – like a lovesick maid. She had told herself that she did not need a man, and that Sir John's sad death had been for the better. Arthur had won her for his enterprise by saying that if it succeeded she would be beholden to no man, and then here he was, enslaving her without trying.

He was so good and correct. He knew his station, always called her 'my lady', evidently worshipped her and would never dare an impropriety. In any case, he was in love with the ghost of his Sami bride. He slept on the floor outside the little cell she had as a cabin. He had always slept on the floor, for he had always been a servant, except for his time as a Sami priest and she did not suppose the Sami had beds.

She would have to find a husband to stop fantasising about cabin boys. It was all right for men. Plenty of successful merchants had their way with serving wenches and nobody cared. Well, they did of course, or she would not have known, but it was nothing to the humiliation which would be heaped upon a respectable widow who consorted with an apprentice.

She must let him be and hope he enjoyed the slant-eyed girl. Richard Chancellor would want her again once he had been rescued.

21

Sortie

The Lapps married diplomacy with gunpowder. The day after Yelena's departure a boat crossed the strait carrying an old man and a boy, peasants from one of the abbot's farmsteads. The old man asked to see Abbot Philip at once, pleading that he had a message from the Lapps who had been holding him captive for over a month.

As soon as the old man began his story Philip ordered everybody from his presence and summoned Richard and Alexei. The peasant was reluctant to go on with his story, but, under threat of torture, continued. The Lapps offered to allow the abbot and his monks safe conduct to St Nicholas, promising that they could reoccupy the monastery in the summer. Only the fighting men on the island were their enemies.

'Richard, have your men imprison this wretch at once and find his son quickly. Keep them in a separate cell with only English-speaking guards. They must not communicate with anybody. As a monk, I cannot ask you to kill them, though you may find it more convenient. If this gets out it will set every man against his brother.'

It was already out. That night the watchmen intercepted three men trying to launch a skiff from the beach. Two were monks, and the third a soldier with a borrowed habit. The soldier was hanged and the monks were confined for six days without food. Only the shortage of boats prevented more desertions.

*

'Your Holiness, myself and my men have become a danger to you and we must leave. You will be able to treat with the Lapps in our absence.'

'Thank you for your consideration, Alexi, but how do you propose to leave? The sea is clear but we have only two boats capable of the journey to St Nicholas. They can hold but twelve men at the most.'

'With a little crowding they can take my officers and myself, and the *streltski*. We could land from time to time along the coast for food and water. We would leave you with the Tartars and the English.'

'Which would not spare us from an attack, merely leave us less defended.'

'Your Holiness, the Tartars and the English are not true Christians. You could hand them to the Lapps and the Christian monks would be spared.'

'And suppose our heretics do not agree to be handed to the Lapps?'

'My men would be happy to assist you in overcoming them before we leave. We could carry it out in the night. When we have them bound we can ready the boats and depart, and you can then invite the Lapps to take away the heretics and raise the siege.'

'And if Tsar Ivan were to hear of this we would both be impaled slowly, painfully and publicly.'

'Who would tell the tsar, Your Holiness? The Lapps? We would say the English and Tartars deserted, hoping the savages would spare them because they were not Russians. They will not be able to deny that to the tsar because the Lapps will have killed them in revenge for bombarding their camp.'

'An interesting idea.' Philip ran his hand along the rough edge of the table. The lower floor of the abbot's lodging had been refurbished after the fire and crude furniture had been fashioned from salvaged parts. 'It reminds of us our humble beginnings,' the abbot had remarked. 'This would save the monastery, but what you propose is nonetheless treason. Richard Chancellor is an accredited ambassador to the tsar – an ambassador from a friendly power, something new in our country. I will have to discuss this with those of my brothers who might be loyal to the plan.'

Alexi kissed the abbot's feet and retired through the curtained doorway.

The problem was the guard rota. A way had to be found for all the *stretlski* to be on the same watch while the Tartars and the English slept. Philip proposed to Alexi that they suggest to Richard that, in view of the imminent Lapp assault, the watches should be reorganised, so that all the men with the same language were on the same watch. Richard would see the sense in this, and it would be popular with the men.

'Let us also ask Richard to prepare the two boats for sea, ready to evacuate the survivors, should the Lapp attack prevail. The English are sailors so the task is appropriate. For your men to do it would arouse suspicion.'

There was no doubt now that the Lapps were preparing an attack. They were no longer thrifty with powder and shot, and set about demolishing the wall with a will. The garrison, in turn, prepared a re-defence of barricades and ditches behind the breach, to create a killing ground in which to trap the Lapp assault force. Monks and soldiers toiled together in the dust of falling stones and the ricocheting shot, taking casualties as they went. There was no sign of Lapp boats, but they must be somewhere.

The coup was swift and bloodless. The duty watch seized and bound their sleeping colleagues at one hour past midnight, on the signal of a double stroke from the monastery bell. It had survived the collapse of the bell-tower and was now on a tripod in the main courtyard. As soon as the prisoners were in the cellars, under a guard of loyal monks, the two seaworthy boats were launched and Philip came to the beach for the blessing and farewell.

'God be with you all,' said Philip. 'We will pray for you.'

'I think it is Alexei and his Russians who need your prayers,' replied Richard. 'The Lapps will not be merciful if you have to deliver them into their hands. Thank you for warning me of their treachery and helping me forestall it. I will not forget it. If you can draw out your parleys with the savages my ship will arrive in time to relieve you, and we can bring Alexei to face the tsar's justice.'

The moonlit sea was as smooth and polished as the abbot's silver chalice. The two boats stood out sharp and clear as they rounded the end of the island, the oars beating a soft, even stroke. The masts and sails had not been raised, for the only breath of wind was set towards the shore.

If the Lapps were only moderately watchful they must see the escapers. That they had some boats was certain, but if they were ready for sea, and if they were the sort of craft which could pursue them into open water was unknowable. The sea was bright but the land lay black and secret.

The men in the boats felt like ants crawling on a mirror. The island on which the monastery was set lay in a wide bay, bounded on the north by a long promontory. Once round the headland they would put out into the open sea and try to hide among the banks of mist. This was not the shortest route to the Dvina and they would have to come back towards the mainland at some time to find fresh water, but for the moment they feared the Lapps more than thirst.

Slowly, so slowly, they crept across the mirror and passed the dark finger of the headland. Ahead lay open sea and sheltering mist. A sigh of wind stirred the water, this time blowing from the land. They raised the masts and unfurled the sails.

At the same moment splinters appeared to flake away from the dark edge of the land. They spread out across the water, and became a flotilla of small boats. The hateful drums started their clamour and the boats began to weave about, forming up for the pursuit.

'They was waiting for us all the time, Mister Chancellor,' whispered the man next to Richard. It was Robin Green, the man who had followed Richard onto the forepeak in the tempest on the Norwegian Sea. 'Waiting for us all the time. That holy bastard has betrayed us.'

'Aye, I think our cunning abbot may have outwitted us all, or maybe we have run against the fleet the savages have gathered to attack the monastery. Either way, we'll give them a good chase.'

It was the chase across the ice all over again, but this time over water with the English and Tartars in boats instead of sleighs, and the Lapps in boat-sleighs rather than on skis. The light Lapp craft could easily have overhauled the heavier English boats, despite their sails, but rather than racing each other, they held together in close formation. It would have been foolhardy for an unsupported boat to press home an attack. The English and Tartars had no firearms, for they had no powder, but they had short Tartar bows and no lack of arrows and spears, weapons enough to match the Lapps.

The Lapps hovered just beyond bow shot, gathering strength for a concerted attack. Occasionally a boat would venture into range and loose a volley of arrows, receiving a shower in return. Little damage was done on either side but it broke the fugitive's oar stroke and gave time for more sleigh-boats to come up from the shore. This time the fugitives had nothing to jettison, except the wounded. The Lapps were using the tactics of the seal hunt. A man stood with his harpoon in the bow of each Lapp boat.

'Wait until they close and aim for the men with the harpoons,' ordered Richard. 'If a harpoons strikes the boat, cut it loose.'

A keening noise rose from the crescent of boats, the drums beat faster and on they came. The two sailboats drew together for mutual protection.

The first attack was beaten off. Perhaps it was never meant to be driven home, but merely to tighten the pressure. Several

Lapps were killed or wounded and two of Richard's men, one English and one Tartar, were wounded and unlikely to recover. Almost everyone had minor injuries, although few noticed them in the heat of the fray. The lull lasted almost an hour, more frightening than the battle. The keening dropped to a low mumble as the Lapps sang the *yoik* for the spirits of their prey. The drumming became a gentle rattle.

A thin cloud had covered the moon, but the darkening night gave no comfort to the fugitives. They were almost surrounded and the wind had backed round to blow towards the land. They loosed the sails and let them flap.

'Come on then, come and take us, you 'eathen cowards!' shouted Robin, jumping onto a thwart and daring the Lapp arrows. 'Come on, come and take us!'

Richard pulled him down onto the seat. 'God'll take you in his own time. Don't be impatient.'

The Lapps had pointed their prows inwards, so close together that they stood up to use their oars as paddles. The signal was a wolf call and they thrust in for the kill.

'Your time is come, Mister Chancellor, damn your soul!' came a rasping voice over the water.

''S blood, it's Tom Lovelace!' gasped Richard, clutching Robin's shoulder. 'We left him for dead on the ice. No wonder their guns were so well served.' It was Richard's turn to leap onto the thwart. 'You'll swing for this, Tom!' he bellowed. 'So God help me, I'll see you swing for this!'

He never did. A round shot carried away the prow of the boat on which Tom stood, taking Tom with it.

It was a lucky shot in poor light at long range. Other cannonballs were skipping over the water, and the combatants on both sides heard the rumble of gunfire. Ahead of them a colourless shape glided from the darkness, a tall, three-masted ship with a high sterncastle and all sails set.

'Lena! Lenarushka, you did it, you got through! You brought the *Bonny Edward*!' Richard threw his arms around Robin and kissed him rapturously. All around them Englishmen and Tartars – men who had steeled themselves to be cut to pieces and knew now that they were saved – embraced, mixing tears, sweat, blood and kisses.

The Lapps were fleeing and the *Edward Bonaventura* was turning after them. Although the wind was light it was a lee shore and the ship dared not chase them far. For the moment, however, the Lapps were helpless. They were lucky that the *Edward* had only half its complement of guns, for once a Lapp boat was struck it soon broke apart.

For maybe fifteen minutes the Lapps struggled, pell-mell, to reach land, only to find their way blocked. As they neared the shore another shape detached itself from the dark mass of the land. A second three-masted seagoing ship lay in their path, smaller than the first, but darting as many tongues of flame. The *Philip and Mary* was firing bar shot, designed to cut down an opponent's rigging. Tangled loops of hemp cascaded onto the *Edward*'s deck, rents appeared in the sails and spars swung wild as the stays snapped. The Lapps were being avenged.

22

Combat

'Fire on her, for Christ Jesus' sake! Shoot!'

'My lady, suppose 'tis Mister Chancellor's ship? There can be no other in these waters.'

'I don't care if we are being attacked by Noah's ark. We are at anchor on a lee shore, as you pointed out, Captain, and there is a large ship coming towards us firing its cannon. Don't ask why. Sink it if you must! Disable it! Make it go away!'

God's bones, why are folk so slow to the obvious? They stand and watch as the world crashes about them. It's Ludgate all over again. The rebels enter the city and the citizens stand and gape, hoping that nothing unpleasant will happen, leaving a frightened woman and a clutch of apprentices to go out and shut the gate.

'Go on, do something! Shoot!'

Although the captain had given no orders, the men from both watches were already on deck, roused by the gunfire. All merchant ships sailed in fear of pirates, especially if sailing alone, and Captain Rodgers had drilled the crew to ready themselves for action on any sign of danger without waiting for a command. While the men readied the cannon and lit their fuses the women and girls below decks were already laying out cloths and hot water for the surgeons and helping the boys refill powder kegs from the magazine. As befitted her name, the *Philip and Mary* had no prohibition on females among the crew.

'Do you wish to give the order to shoot, Captain Rodgers, or would you rather I did?'

A sharp slap against the bow signalled that the ship had taken its first hit. Two further shots skittered across the deck, sending long black splinters from the gunwales. None of the shots had much force. They were probably ricochets, hopping across the water, but the enemy were drawing closer.

'Larboard guns, *fire!*' shouted a young voice from the half deck below. 'Top elevation, shoot for her rigging!' The command was confident, explicit and urgent.

'What the Devil…?' cried Captain Rodgers.

So expected was the order that the gun crew closest to the command instinctively touched off their cannon, and at the first detonation the others hurriedly followed suit, unfurling a wreath of gun smoke along of the deck.

Arthur followed the smoke, checking the elevation of each gun and shouting words of approval and advice above the roar of the cannonade. The battle they had so often rehearsed had been to repel pirates, to escape from them, not to batter them into surrender. The guns were loaded with bar shot, bags of scrap iron which split apart in flight to send hundreds of sharp-edged missiles through the enemy's sails and rigging.

'Now that battle has started, Captain Rodgers, you might as well take charge,' observed Kate. 'Unless you prefer that my servant carries on with it?'

Stephen Burroughs looked in dismay as chaos claimed the ordered decks of the *Edward*. He had known this would happen. Not that he had known the form in which it would happen, but he had known it would all end in disaster.

When Richard had left Kholmogory with half the *Edward*'s cannon Stephen had resolved to keep well out in the Dvina while he was away, to keep the Russians clear of the ship. If he had the chance to trade, he would take the woollens and other goods ashore by sleigh or boat and sell them on the quay. In this way, he would be free to leave as he wished when the thaw came, and to refuse any entanglement in the tsar's politics.

But the Dvina had not just thawed; it had become a raging torrent, swirling with icebergs, and Stephen had been forced to seek the shelter of the quay. The governor had promptly seized the ship, even as it moored, and six of the crew had been taken as hostages. The governor had lodged them hospitably in his kremlin, but hostages they remained. There would be no going home without Richard, even if they had to wait another winter.

Then frightened peasants began to bring news from across the Dvina that all was not well at Solovetsky. Finally came the incredible rumour that the Lapps had a battery of cannon – ten cannon – and were bombarding the monastery. The figure ten was suspicious. There were only ten cannon in the Northlands, apart from those on the *Edward*'s deck. In some way Richard's guns had fallen to the Lapps.

The governor had an idea. 'Stephen Robertski, I fear your commander is in danger. Some unfortunate happening must have delivered your cannon to the *Lappi*. An act of God, we must presume, for the *Lappi* have no military strength. The stories we have from the abbot's peasants are confused, but it seems that a group of our soldiers has arrived at the monastery and they are now invested by the savages. Our best hope is for you to go to Solovetsky with your ship and retake the guns.'

'The Lapps now have as many cannon as us,' pointed out Stephen.

'Ah, but they do not have the same skill to serve them. I will put some of my own men aboard your ship, to make up for those who left with your leader, and you can teach them to work your vessel. The six who are staying with me in my kremlin can stay a while longer.'

Stephen had waited two more weeks for the flood to abate, torn between anxiety about Richard and his men and reluctance to tangle further in an adventure already so ill-fortuned. At last, the day came when it was safe to move aside the log boom, which protected the ship from floating ice, and they dropped down the river with the current. They did not stop at St Nicholas but went straight to sea.

The moonlight encounter with the Lapp flotilla was a surprise. Not that at first it seemed a formidable armada. There were two larger boats of European design, with single sails, surrounded by a swarm of small, light craft. They must have come out to engage the *Edward*. Either they had hopelessly misjudged her size and strength, or they had planned an ambush in the mist further out to sea. As soon as the *Edward* appeared they sent up wild shouts and began beating their drums. Stephen answered with round shot.

It was pitiable to see the Lapp boats shatter so easily, for they had nothing with which to defend themselves. The small craft scattered for the shore, leaving the two less handy boats to fend for themselves. Stephen followed the small craft, aiming to sink as many as possible before getting too close to the land. He would then wear about and take on the two larger boats.

The *Edward* was a sharp black shape etched on a silver sea with the moon at her back. Ahead loomed the dark shore. The ship drifted closer, spitting fire, when to their amazement the darkness spat back. The Lapps had sprung an ambush.

At first Stephen thought the shot was coming from the land, but a lightening of the cloud showed the upper spars of a ship. An armed ocean-going vessel was lying in the shadows. Impossible! How could the Lapps have a ship? Had the Swedes arrived in some way to protect their claim to Lapland?

'Hard to port! Cut away the tackle there! Cease fire and attend to the ship.'

The *Edward* turned her head from the enemy. At best this would be a slow manoeuvre, and the other ship was denying Stephen the sea room he needed. He was now drifting sideways towards his opponent, exposing the masts and rigging more fully to the relentless cannonade. It was becoming difficult to co-ordinate the rudder and the sails and he dare not send any men aloft. They would have to anchor soon to avoid running ashore, or he could let the ship run right against the enemy and fight it out with pistol and pike. Stephen tried to calculate the odds, but they were incalculable. He had only half his complement of cannon and a mixed crew unused to working together. The strength of the enemy was unknown.

'Strike the flag,' ordered Stephen. They had been doomed to end like this from the moment Richard had taken the cannon. It was Richard's fault. 'Let's hope they can see we've struck. We've no quarrel with the Swedes.'

The other ship must have seen the flag being lowered, for there was a boat coming across.

'Cease fire, Captain!'

'Mistress Thomas, 'twas but moments since you told me to open fire.'

'Indeed, and now they have stopped shooting at us and are turning away. Stop the guns before there is any more killing.'

'Have you ever wondered why you hired a captain?'

'Often. But victory is not the moment to squabble. Stop this battle and send a boat to parley with them. Send Mistress Slant-Eyes, in case it truly is Mister Chancellor who has surrendered to us.'

'Cease fire!' roared the captain, but events still ran ahead of him. Most of the gun crews had already ceased fire and were pulling people on deck from the sea, strange little people bundled in leather. Arthur was leading one of them to the quarterdeck. He – or she – looked like a highly agitated, wet leather ball.

'Arthur, since you seem to have taken command of this vessel, perhaps you could explain to your admiral and your captain what is happening.'

Arthur knelt at her feet. 'M' lady, m' lady, do with me as you wish,' he sobbed. 'I had no choice. My people were crying to me from the sea, dying in the water while Mister Chancellor murdered them. How could I watch in silence?'

Before Kate could make sense of his outburst Tom Rodgers

had smothered her in a massive embrace. 'Look there! Look there! They've struck, my lady, they've struck! We've taken her in minutes. Did you see it, clear in the moonlight? What a victory! What a prize! What a crew we have, Kate!'

'Indeed, Tom. A wonderful crew and a worthy commander.' Kate caught her breath and freed herself. She had grown used to Tom's sudden shifts of sentiment, one moment a resentful rival and the next a warm comrade. 'Provided we have not mistakenly taken the *Edward*, we should have handsome booty. But I have business with my servant.'

'Your servant? Forgive a young man over-eager for the fray. He shares the temper of our brave crew.'

'You are a generous captain. But who are these strangers we are pulling aboard? Are they our late enemy?'

'This is Seena, my lady, who is now the *no'adi* of our *seta*,' said Arthur. 'She brought me to Wardhouse as I told you, and has since returned to Solovetsky to join the siege.'

'So we have chanced upon your Sami, at last? I am honoured to meet you, Mistress Seena,' said Kate, turning to the dumpling-shaped newcomer. 'Arthur has told me much about you. Captain Rodgers also extends his greetings, but as you see, he is occupied with a battle. Pray let us know if we can be of service to you. Now translate that to her, Arthur, and then kindly explain what all this means.'

Tom Cook spat into the water. It was still a novelty to see the spittle arc through the air without freezing.

'God damn their eyes, she's leaving us! Are they blind?'

'Mister Burroughs can save us best by worsting the savages first,' replied Richard. 'He'll be back to rescue us when he's put paid to them.'

'So long as he don't press too close to the shore. ''Twould be grievous bad luck if he ran aground.'

'There speaks a true mariner, always fearing the worst. I think we can trust Stephen not to risk his ship.'

They watched the silhouette of the *Edward* gliding away from them, the flashes of her cannon twinkling along the gunwales and the boom of artillery vibrating over the water. The fleeing Sami were barely visible; the *Philip and Mary* lay completely invisible against the shore.

A line of flashes split the darkness of the shoreline and the gunfire became a confused medley as cannon answered cannon.

'My God, Tom, we had it all wrong. It wasn't us the savages were hunting – they came out to lure the *Bonny Edward* onto a shore battery, and God's teeth, they've done it. Just as they lured our horsemen onto their cannon on the way to Solovetsky.'

The brief battle moved to its climax. 'They're striking,' gasped Tom. 'They've struck the English flag to a rabble of savages. We should never have taken so many of her guns.'

'Nay, Tom, 'tis a trick of the moonlight. That or the savages have shot away the halyard. See how the yard is swinging free? They're shooting at the rigging to make her unmanageable. They're more artful than most Christian gunners.'

'Nay, Richard, they're hauling in the ensign.'

The surrender was no longer in doubt. Not only had the flag been lowered from the masthead, but the big ensign which drooped over the *Edward*'s stern was also being hauled in.

'He doesn't understand,' said Richard, more to himself than to Tom. 'He doesn't understand what they'll do to him. They'll kill him, kill them all for what you and I did at the Lapp camp.'

The guns fell silent and for a while they drifted passively, watching the confusion of small boats milling around the ship.

'What d' we do now, Richard?'

'Do?' He seemed surprised at the question. 'We'll die fighting or they catch and kill us. They'll get us in the end.'

'But do we turn back to the island, press on to St Nicholas or drift ashore?'

'I think they may have forgotten us, Tom. They've got a greater prize. Let's be gone while we can. We'll try to get to St Nicholas. Better the mercy of the sea than the savages.'

23

Reunion

They were shouting at him again. Whenever he didn't understand them they shouted louder and then louder still, working themselves into a frenzy. One of the few words of Russian that Yelena had taught him was *nemsty*, meaning both 'foreigner' and 'deaf'. To Russians the two conditions were the same.

They were not the pair of guards who had been watching over him for the past week. That pair had never been impatient. They had shared his one-roomed *izba* in the governor's kremlin, sleeping on the other side of the stove and feeding the fire. A maidservant had brought the food and prepared it. He and the guards exercised together on silent walks around the great courtyard. They seldom spoke and, though he understood nothing of the little they did utter, they were never less than respectful.

The new guards had arrived early in the morning and after a lot of shouting Richard had grasped that they wanted him to go to the *banya*. Not the public bathhouse in Kholmogory, but to the *banya* in the kremlin used by the governor, his family, guards, servants and guests, and, from time to time, by his prisoners. It was in this *banya* that he had first seen Yelena naked. Where are you now, Yelena? Did you get through to Kholmogory? Were you on the *Edward* when she was captured by the savages? Why won't they tell me anything?

They spent over an hour in the *banya*, bathing, steaming, eating and drinking. Did they really need two guards, thought Richard, to stop him escaping naked into the morning chill, especially as the guards were themselves naked? It would have made an interesting chase around the fortress.

He supposed they were there to see that he was properly clean for whomever he was due to meet. Not that he was any longer the filthy, verminous creature who had arrived in Kholmogory after his boat journey across the White Sea, and his imprisonment at St Nicholas with his English and Tartar comrades. They were probably still at St Nicholas, but the governor had taken him away and brought him to Kholmogory and kept him alone ever since, alone except for the ever-present guards.

They brought him back to the *izba* and cut his hair and then began to dress him in new clothes. Perhaps they had spent too long in the *banya*, because they grew impatient and started shouting again.

Two days after his arrival in Kholmogory they had sent Brother Antonis to question him. He had seemed more interested in the fort they had erected on the Baltic than in the siege of Solovetsky, but he did half-explain why Richard was a prisoner.

The tsar's truce had failed to be renewed in Livonia. Ivan had a major war to face against the Baltic knights and the king of Poland, who was also king of Lithuania, and it was no longer wise to quarrel with the Swedes. A courier had been sent from Moscow along the flooded rivers to cancel the attack on Lapland, but he had taken over two months to reach the White Sea and had found the expedition long departed. Orders had been given to disarm the forces returning from Lapland, and to hold the leaders in solitary confinement until the tsar's officers could arrive to deal with them.

'So the Russians are going to blame it all on the English?' asked Richard.

'God moves in mysterious ways,' replied Antonis.

'None more mysterious than those of your emperor.'

It was no real mystery. He had seen it as a boy. Old King Harry had often sent ministers to the block to disavow out-dated policies, mariners caught by a change of wind.

Stephen had been right; he should have kept out of affairs

of state, but how could he have steered clear? The tsar had threatened to keep him in Moscow if he failed to join his Lapland adventure. Now they were coming to take him back to Moscow forever, to punish him publicly to appease the Swedes.

One evening by the campfire in Lapland Yelena had told him stories about Tsar Ivan, stories which she had never dared tell him on the journey to Moscow, of how Ivan personally beheaded and dismembered condemned prisoners on the scaffold in Red Square. Was this to be Richard's final royal audience?

So the waiting was nearly over. The person from Moscow had evidently arrived, or was close by, and the governor was grooming his prisoner for the handover. Out of habit, Richard felt for the silver brooch he had worn as a lucky charm, before remembering that he had lost it on the flight to Solovetsky. He wondered if he was the only English prisoner being sent to Moscow. What had become of the others?

More soldiers arrived at the *izba* and shouted at the two guards, and they all shouted at Richard. He was bundled hurriedly into his new clothes and marched briskly to the governor's residence. The governor was not there; he was presumably away meeting the person from Moscow. They sat Richard in the hall opposite the entrance. Almost at once there was bustle and confusion in the courtyard, the doors were flung open and the governor and his attendants surged into the room, stepping aside to bow in the emissary. The guards prodded Richard to his feet.

Richard looked around for an interpreter, probably a monk. There was nobody obviously occupying the role. Was he expected to bow or kneel? He decided to treat the emissary as a person of equal rank, meriting a brief, formal bow.

For no particular reason, Richard had expected the person from Moscow to be a large, majestic figure, similar to the tsar himself. He was surprised to find a slightly-built figure coming towards him with an outstretched hand.

'I've come to take you home, Richard,' said Kate Thomas, smiling.

*

The ice had melted, the Dvina had gathered back her floodwaters and become her stately summer self with the first hardy swimmers bathing and sunning themselves naked on Kholmogory beach, when the person from Moscow arrived with his convoy of one hundred barges. He was named Osip Nepa, a big man in a huge fur coat (now worn rather to show rank than to keep out the cold), and he found Kholmogory firmly in the hands of the English and the Lapps. They ruled through the muzzles of the cannon on the two ships moored in mid-stream.

As the barges rounded the bend in the river the ships welcomed them with a rousing salute from all their ordnance and the blue coats, cut to impress the khan of Cathay, were once again aired on deck. Kate was enjoying the taste of power.

When the two English ships had first reached Kholmogory from the relief of Solovetsky the governor had been welcoming enough, despite his shock at finding that the *Edward Bonaventura* had found a consort. The pawn he had sent away had returned a queen. He had willingly released the six men he had taken from the *Edward* before she sailed to the monastery, but said nothing of Richard and his men, who had arrived by boat from the White Sea a few days earlier. Instead, he kept them in a secret prison to deliver them to tsar. For three weeks Kate awaited the trade goods which the governor had said were arriving from Moscow, believing Richard had been lost at sea.

'To think, we followed him all around the top of Europe, Arthur, only to glimpse him for a moment in the moonlight.'

It was Brother Antonis who confessed to Stephen about Richard. Kate at once sent word ashore that Kholmogory would burn like Solovetsky unless the governor released Richard and his comrades at once. Hence the hasty visit to the *banya* and the new set of clothes.

'So you're England's ambassador once again, Richard,' said Kate. 'Assuming that our queen has now married her Spanish prince, you probably represent most of Europe. And this time it is we who hold the power, and they who must treat with us. If Mister Osip should forget himself we can gently remind him that he has moored his barges beneath our guns.'

There was no mention of Richard's imprisonment or the English occupation of Kholmogory when Richard, Kate and their retinue met the tsar's emissary at the governor's kremlin. Richard had requested the meeting on the pretext that the change of sovereign in England and the union with Spain required him to present a new set of credentials. Unusually for an ambassador, he insisted on providing his own guard of honour: fifty men and women from the Lapp war-band displaying the pikes and arquebuses they had taken at Solovetsky.

After Brother Antonis had translated Richard's speech from Greek into Russian, Kate spoke on behalf of Queen Mary to express her delight that Richard had established such cordial relations with the tsar, with such promise of trade and lasting friendship.

'Our gracious queen did not name Mister Chancellor in the proclamation I have brought, for she was unaware that he had reached Russia. She has, nonetheless, full confidence in him as her ambassador. However, it is meet that he should return to London this season to tell her more about the tsar's great empire, and to escort the tsar's ambassador to her court.'

Osip listened impassively to the hypocritical little ceremony and then rose to express the tsar's condolences on the death of King Edward, his congratulations on the accession of Queen Mary, and his felicitations on her marriage. He accepted Richard's new credentials on behalf of the tsar, rolling out the list of the tsar's titles which now paled in comparison with the list of exotic territories claimed by Philip and Mary. All this was patiently translated by Brother Antonis into Greek and paraphrased into English by Richard. Osip's next utterance took them by surprise.

'His Imperial Majesty has commanded me to present you with these gifts, to take to your king and queen as a poor token of his affection and respect.' He motioned to the back of the hall and four servants dragged forward a large bale and pushed it into the space between the two delegations. They cut away the cords and out spilled a glistening avalanche of furs: ermine and sable, fox and bear, wolf and marten. The servants gave Richard and Kate each a fur, black for Richard and white for Kate. Kate caressed the ermine. It tingled beneath her fingertips.

'The tsar promised a gift,' proclaimed Osip, 'and he keeps his promises. The tsar has also commanded that I, Osip Alexandrovich Nepa, be his ambassador at your court in London, and he asks that you give me passage to England as soon as you can sail.'

The Lapp and English guards patrolled the wooden parapet of the kremlin throughout the short night while their commanders and their Russian hosts feasted and drank in the hall.

In the early hours, shortly before dawn, Osip took his guests into a private room. He could speak enough Greek for a short conversation.

'When are you planning to sail?'

'Are you so anxious for us to leave? We will sail when I have sold our cargoes and loaded others.'

'The governor will take all your cargoes,' said Osip, 'and I have brought you goods from every province of our empire, as well as silks from Cathay brought across Tartary. If they are not enough, we can gather more for the next ship from England. It is important that you to send another ship before the winter -- or several if you wish.'

'There is the matter of Lapland.'

'Lapland is no matter,' declared Osip. 'The tsar knows about Solovetsky and Abbot Philip can treat with the Lapps himself and arrange suitable reparation. He has always wanted to build a new church and I am sure it will be magnificent.'

'There is the fort on the Baltic.'

'There is no fort on the Baltic. The tsar has sent an emissary to the Swedes to guide them to it and arrange for its destruction. The men will be brought to the Neva by sea to return to Russia. The war in Lapland never happened. Remember that, and never speak of it in London.' He saw Richard's mouth tighten and remembered that the tsar's writ did not run by the Thames. 'I mean, my friend, that I must attach one small condition to the tsar's friendship. The expedition to Lapland was a mistake – a sad mistake, best forgotten. Please do not speak of it in London or record it in your reports.'

Richard murmured noncommittally.

'You must understand,' pleaded Osip, 'the tsar has a war. A real war, not against northern savages or Tartars, but against his strongest and closest neighbour. You know that Lithuania and Poland now have one sovereign, a dominion that stretches from the Baltic to the Black Sea, over lands which were Russian before the Tartar conquest. King Augustus has failed to renew the truce in Livonia which has given us peace in the west for the past seven years. His frontiers are only three weeks' ride from Moscow and his armies are ordered in the modern manner, with munitions of war superior to ours. His cannon are much better and more numerous.'

'You mean you want more English cannon?'

'If I may recall the events in Lapland for one last time before they are wiped from memory, they showed that your English cannon was extremely reliable and hardwearing.'

'You want us to bring you cannon through the Frozen Ocean?'

'Exactly.'

The English had gathered at the quay to return to their ships. Kate was at Richard's side.

'Richard, do you remember when you entertained me aboard your ship the night you sailed for Cathay.'

'Could I forget it, Kate?'

'I was wondering if I could return the compliment, if you would care to join me on my vessel?'

24

Shipwreck

The clock showed almost midnight, but there was no night. The sun would not set for another six weeks, hanging low in the sky, scattering flecks of gold across the waters of the bay. Four ships sat in the bay, two of them with their masts standing tall and full-rigged with sails furled against their spars and the other two lying like hulks, their topmasts down and a litter of canvas and timber on their decks. The *Edward Bonaventura* and the *Philip and Mary* had found the Company's lost ships, the *Bona Esperanza* and the *Bona Confidenzia*.

'Why ever did Sir Hugh decide to winter here?' asked Kate. 'He could have reached Wardhouse in just a few days by following the coast to the west.'

'I don't think he was minded to meet Mr Chancellor, whom he thought awaited him there,' said Arthur.

One of the ship's boats pulled alongside the spot where Kate and Arthur waited, leaning over the gunwale of the *Philip and Mary*. The oarsmen grasped the ship's shrouds to steady the boat as the two of them climbed in.

'Help me down, Arthur. Shall we cross to the larger ship first? I may be a novice mariner, but from here they both look quite seaworthy.'

'I need tell you something about the ship, m' lady – the admiral's ship – before we step aboard. It will distress you but it is important that you know.'

'Let's get into the boat and you can tell me as we cross.'

'I need tell you now, m' lady, where none can hear us. I beg you, please.'

'I know your Sami pillaged the ships. You told me that. But there may still be cargo aboard worth salving.'

'There is more than cargo aboard, m' lady. Sir Hugh is still there, and so are his officers.'

'*Still there?* You mean the mutineers left them aboard ship? I understood that they had done away with them. You didn't explain but I thought it better not to ask. But surely they were not there when you came back for the guns?'

Arthur drew her back from the gunwale. 'We took care not disturb them, but so far as I know they were there then and may well still be there.'

'Arthur, you love enigmas. Just tell me.'

'They died in the stateroom, around the table. We left them in their seats. That was January and the cadavers would have been frozen until April.'

'Meaning that they are now well thawed. How did they die?'

'Slow gas from sea coals. We – I – banked up the fire and Jeremy and the others blocked the vent. They fell asleep drinking their wine and knew nothing amiss.'

'*You* did this? You led the mutiny?'

'I was the Devil's instrument. If I had died at Tyburn it would have been justice, but I had to reach you to help the Sami. I hated Sir Hugh. We all did, but he loved me and wanted me to be his consort in Cathay. The others wanted him dead so as not to dare the ice in the spring. They said I was saving their lives. I just wanted to escape – to escape going to Cathay...'

Arthur struggled to go on. Kate put her arm across his shoulder. It was an amazing act which astonished Kate even as she did it. Her servant had just confessed that he had murdered his previous master. How could she touch him without flinching? Yet she did.

'Tell me the rest later,' she whispered. 'What you did was a mortal sin but God has spared you. We all live by his grace. We will go to the other ship first and you need not come with me to the admiral's ship. Even if you do, 't'wd be better if you were not with me when I discover whatever may be in the stateroom. Let it surprise me. Richard is busy attending to Mr Lepa so I will be free to make my own report to the Company. Compose yourself now, and thank you for warning me.'

The door to the stateroom had been forced open and then jammed shut. There was no telling when this had last been done. Perhaps the Sami had visited the ship again. The door was difficult to reopen.

Even Kate had to stoop slightly to enter. Inside the room she straightened up, peered through the dim light and screamed. The two men behind her caught her before she hit the floor and pulled her into the open air.

She recovered quickly. 'I think we have found Sir Hugh. Go back and tell me what you find.'

That evening she recorded their findings in the log of the *Philip and Mary*.

> *Sir Hugh and six of his officers were found seated at table, struck dead by the wondrous cold 'twixt cup and lip. Others of the ships' companies were discovered on the shore, where their bones had been disturbed by wolves.*
>
> *I commanded that the bodies of Sir Hugh and the officers be sealed in casks of train oil for transport to England, and that the remains on the shore be given Christian burial by the rites of the Holy Catholic Church.*

The men and women of the Sami war-band were drawn up in two untidy ranks on the main deck of the *Philip and Mary*, dressed in a proud motley of red and blue garments, mostly cut from English cloth. They carried their traditional bows and spears in preference to the pikes and arquebuses taken at Solovetsky, which did not suit the Sami style of war or hunting.

This was a very special occasion, for parades and speeches were not part of Sami life.

'Friends, comrades, brothers and sisters,' announced Arthur, addressing them from the rail of the quarterdeck, 'the time has come for me to leave you, but only so that I can be your friend across the ocean in England. I will come back each year to trade with you, to take your train oil and furs in return for all the things you need, and which England can give.'

Arti and Seena stood at either side, ready to prompt or translate, but the three of them had rehearsed the speech together so well that for the moment Arthur needed no help.

'Soon it will be time for you too to return, each to his own *seta*, to tell your children and your elders how you carried the cannon across Sameatnum, how you brought down the towers of Solovetsky and how you mounted guard at the kremlin in Kholmogory. And you will show them your wounds and you will remember our brothers and sisters who were maimed and died, not for their own *seta* but for all the *seta* of Sameatnum. It was you – you, Seena, you, Arti and each and every one of you – who avenged the Sami people, who answered the strangers, gun for gun, so that our reindeer may graze in peace. When you go, take with you the cloth and the knives and the needles and the other good things that we could not take from the two ships in the spring, because we needed our strength for the cannon. In return I ask you to join the seal hunt, as you have always done at this season, and to render your train oil on the beach so that I can fill my casks with it and carry it to England, to teach my people how to use it. I know they will learn to value it and want more, and will send you more cloth and whatever you need in exchange, to enrich us all. Even when my body is away from you, my spirit will fly across the ocean to speak to you through the mouth of Seena. And when I die my spirit will join the spirits of the ancestors and dwell among your rocks and lakes and forests to guard and guide the Sami people forever.'

Arthur opened his mouth to carry on, but words no longer

came. What he wanted to say was both simple and difficult: that he loved them all and always would. He fought back tears. Unlike the Russians or the English, the Sami seldom cried. Seena took his arm and led him down the short set of steps to the main deck where the Sami threw down their weapons and crowded round, hugging and kissing. For all of them it was the end of a love affair, which hopefully none would ever experience again: the comradeship of warriors who had endured together, fought together, bled together and triumphed together.

The war-band broke into their *yoik* and passed around the jars of *juobmo*. The sailors of the *Philip and Mary*, who had been crowded on the upper decks to watch the ceremony, came down to join the celebration. Barrels of English beer had been brought on deck to serve them. In later years several Sami children claimed to have been conceived at the festivity.

'You are walking with danger, Yelena, meeting me like this.'

'I love it, Arthur, when you speak Russian. It is like listening to poetry.'

'Be serious, please. If you keep seeing me so often you will make Richard jealous.'

'Why should you care? You hate him.'

'I never said that.'

'Do you need to? He murdered your wife.'

Arthur stared at his fingers. 'I have done too much hating.'

'Some people deserve it.'

Arthur shivered. The Devil was speaking to him again through the mouth of Yelena, as he had spoken during the winter through the mouths of Jeremy, Martin and Stephen.

An unexpected lurch of the ship caught him unawares and he fell sideways against the bulkhead. The tankard he was sharing with Yelena clattered to the floor and the beer joined the slops on the cabin floor. The *Edward Bonaventura* was again in bad weather. She attracted storms like a magnet.

'But you don't hate Richard. You share his bed.'

'Sometimes. He only lies with me because that harlot is with her own ship and *Gospodin* Nepa wants me to travel with him in this vessel as his secretary. Otherwise Richard would have left me beside the Dvina. He's besotted with her. She believes she can do all that a man can do and yet still bewitch men like a courtesan with her ugly red hair.'

'My Lady Thomas is as capable as she is kind. She saved me from the gallows and brought me back to Lapland to avenge my people.'

'She knew Richard in England. It's obvious from the way she greeted him. She came to the Northlands looking for her lover to tell him his wife was dead. I used to believe that silver brooch he carried belonged to his wife, but it was hers. He seems to have given it back to her now. I've seen her with it. And why do you think Richard wanted you as his master gunner, when you had fought against him with the Lapps, rather than leave you to sail back with the *Philip and Mary* as her attendant?'

Kate had arranged for Arthur to travel in the other ship to save him sharing a vessel with the pickled remains of Sir Hugh and his officers, or so she had explained. She understood his nightmares; she understood everything. Some of the sailors had demurred at taking the corpses, but Kate had told them that the *Phil and Meg* was a lucky ship, which none could deny.

'I don't understand what you say. Richard needed me to replace Tom Lovelace. I may be young, but I am a good gunner and once gunned this very ship into surrender. I do my duty well and I think it time I checked that our ordnance is secure against the storm. You had best not call on me again.'

'You're angry because you don't want to hear the truth. Richard is keeping you away from her because he thinks she likes you too much, and he'll do away with you for good if he gets a chance. We're still some way from England.'

'Hold your tongue. The Devil has taken your tongue to spread poison. You're a witch.'

Arthur jumped from his bench, white with anger, and

Yelena retreated from the tiny cabin as hastily as the rolling ship would allow.

The *Edward Bonaventura* slammed into the oncoming wave and the massive yet familiar shock ran through her timbers. The return voyage had been every bit as tumultuous as the outward voyage – more so since they had been spared the weeks of idle calm which had wasted so much of their journey to the north. Wherever they were, they had made swift progress. Richard guessed that they were somewhere off the coast of southern Norway, but the incessant rain had given them no sight of the sun for several days, so he had been unable to reckon the latitude. They had not seen any of their three consorts since the third day out from Wardhouse.

The brave ship bit into the wave and threw her head back, as she always did in these terrible Atlantic gales, sloughing off the water and hauling herself up the long towering flank. She hung for a moment at the crest amid the spume, surveying the tortured sea. Ahead of her, almost at the limit of visibility, the white water gathered into a continuous line and another sound mingled with howl of the wind – the boom of surf on a shore. There was no lookout on the mast, for it was too exposed. Richard and Stephen on the quarterdeck were the first to see the danger.

'Dear God, it can't be! That can't be land ahead,' gasped Stephen. 'It can't be true. We're headed west. Norway is behind us.'

'Too far behind, perhaps,' Richard said. 'Maybe God has brought us to Scotland or the Northern Isles. The way the wind is blowing, I don't think He wants us to get away easily.'

The gale was set dead on shore. There could be no turning back. They could run before the wind and hope to find a break in the surf, and the shelter of an inlet or even a harbour. Failing that they could try to drive the ship up onto the beach, presuming there was a beach. If there was none, just cliffs and rocks, they were lost.

'Bring her round three points to larboard,' ordered Richard. 'It'll give more time to descry the land before we have to bring her in. And see to it that Mister Nepa and his Russians are readied for the boats.' Whatever his feelings towards the Russians, his first duty was to bring Osip and his entourage safe to land, before he could think of his own men.

The ship made a slight shift of course and climbed the next wave at a more oblique angle. At the crest two score pairs of eyes scanned the shoreline. It stretched the length of the horizon. This must be the east coast of Scotland, that sullen, hostile land at semi-constant war with the English. It would be better to be cast among savages.

They clawed southwards, gradually closing with the coast. Everybody gathered on deck and the Russians huddled alongside the pinnace, which was stowed upside-down behind the mainmast. They would be lucky to launch so large a craft in such a sea.

One moment they were flying before the wind and in the next it seemed as though a mighty hand had clutched at the underside of the ship and snatched her to a halt. The ship shuddered and a grinding, gnawing sound swelled from beneath the keel. Then, as if released from a bow, the ship sprang forward again on its headlong career. They had grounded on a bank and broken free. But where there had been one bank, there would be others.

'Head for the shore, Stephen. Take her into the beach as far as she'll live. Jettison cannon.'

The young master gunner supervised his first and only duty of the voyage. The cannon which had been the envy of an emperor and had ruled Kholmogory were lifted from their carriages and tumbled through the openings in the gunwales. It altered the trim of the heavily laden vessel, but did little to lighten the draught.

The beach came into view, a broad swathe of shingle beyond several lines of creamy surf. Closer they came, and then another check. The ship writhed and groaned and this time did not spring free. Instead she began to heel over, swinging slowly broadside to the wind. The slope of the deck and the shelter it gave against the wind made it easier than expected to slide the pinnace into the water. The Russians crowded aboard, diplomats, servants, secretaries and guards, together with as many English sailors as the craft could take. Osip's *streltski* bodyguard refused to be parted from their pikes and guns and the ambassador demanded that they load the tsar's gifts for the king and queen.

'The Devil you will, Mister Nepa. The treasure'll come ashore of its own, as will you unless you quit before the ship breaks.'

The pinnace pulled away into the shock of the wind and plunged into the lines of surf, its white stern bobbing in and out of the waves like the scut of a terrified rabbit. Freed from the weight of the pinnace and its passengers, the ship once more began to slide over the shingle. At the same time, she began to break apart. The main topmast and mizzen yard collapsed, cluttering the starboard sides with fallen rigging and spars and hazarding the launch of the two remaining boats.

'Time to go, Stephen. 'Tis a pity Sir Hugh is no longer with us to meet his old Scots enemies.'

25

Finale

Stephen Burroughs took command of the first boat and Richard the second. By the tradition of the sea, Richard was the last to leave.

Arthur found himself in Richard's boat. Had they waited longer it would have launched itself along with everything else on deck, which was rapidly being cleared to starboard in a seething jumble of flotsam. It reminded Arthur of the big cauldron in which they boiled the beef and fish in the days when he had fetched the rations for Jeremy and his other messmates.

The ship lay almost on its side, broadside to the waves, pointing the stubs of its shattered masts towards the beach. The waves breaking against the seaward side of the hull sent torrents of water over the gunwale to stream down the slanting deck and sweep it clean of deckhouses, gun carriages, and all that could be washed away, living and inanimate.

Getting the boat into the water was easy compared with getting clear of the tangled rigging and floating spars blocking its path and smashing against its sides. It was worse than the ice in Willoughby Land.

They pushed and fended themselves through with their oars and bare bleeding hands until at last they were out in the surf. Now there was neither need of oars nor any way to use them as the sea hurled them at the beach. The rain had stopped and a frail sunlight glistened on the surf. There was no way the boat could live all the way to the shore.

As they crashed through the first line of breakers the stern lifted high above the bow. Richard was at the tiller and Arthur near the bow, alongside Will Fletcher.

Richard screamed down to them. 'Arthur! Will! Hang yourselves over the bow as far as y' can go. Keep her head down as we hit the next one.'

He'll do away with you when he gets the chance. Yelena's words echoed in Arthur's head. He tried to push them away. Richard could so easily do away with him here.

It seemed like suicide to lean out over the bow as they hit the next line of surf, yet it was their only hope. They must keep the bow down as they hit the base of the wave in the hope that they would not be spun over backwards as the craft reared up, and then having crested the wave they would need to throw themselves to the stern to save being thrown over forwards.

Arthur and Will hung out over the bow, their shipmates clinging to their legs. The boat went into the wave with the bow well down. Arthur and Will were thrust into its heart, water forcing into their ears and noses, and then the pressure vanished and they were in daylight again. It had been in vain. The boat seemed to rise vertically and then it was flying, keel uppermost. The occupants dropped from it like coals tumbling from a sack.

Arthur dropped into the sea and went down, down, down...then a flash of sunlight and white water and then he was back under again. Sometimes he was drowning, sometimes swimming, and sometimes he seemed to be flying. He could see the beach and little dot-like people scurrying about on the shingle, and then he was flying over the ocean, far, far across the ocean until he saw Sameatnum and the high fells, the dark forest and the long winding lakes. He felt his knees hit the shingle and the vision disappeared. He was kneeling in shallow water with the waves breaking across him and the pebbles sucking back between his legs, pulling him into deeper water.

He struggled upright. He had lost his shoes, which was to the good. He had been barefoot most of his life and was more surefooted without them. Another figure was lying in the surf a few yards away. He was not trying to rise. He saw Arthur and stretched out his arms, screaming over the sound of the waves. It was Richard.

The next wave knocked Arthur back to his knees. He struggled upright as it passed and waded over to Richard.

'My leg, my leg! I hit it on the boat.' Richard reached out again.

Arthur looked down on him. The man who had turned his cannon on Leeuna was helpless at his feet – the man they had hunted across Sameatnum, and who had slipped away from them at Solovetsky. The man who was Kate's lover – dear, kind Kate – the man who might even marry her and become Arthur's master. He could leave him, turn away and let him drag himself ashore as best he could, hoping that God would see to it that he failed, or he could finish with him here himself. He still had his knife at his belt.

Richard looked up as if reading his mind. How much did he know of Arthur's history? How much had Kate told him? He must know that Arthur had fought for the Sami.

Arthur could almost hear the excuses going through Richard's head – I had to, I did it for the Company, to get back to England, I had no choice – the same excuses Arthur used to cleanse his soul.

We all live and die by God's grace. Kate spoke inside his head, and Arthur reached out and pulled Richard upright. Richard screamed as his leg took the weight.

'You'll have to walk, damn you! Keep walking or I'll leave you here, like you left Tom Lovelace.'

They sloshed towards the beach, Richard hanging on Arthur's shoulder, growing heavier at every pace as though Arthur were a modern-day St Christopher.

A dragonfly settled on Richard's tunic. At second glance it was a feathered crossbow bolt, its flight so nearly spent that it did no more than snag the wool. The archer had shot into the wind and perhaps misjudged the range.

For the first time Arthur looked aside from the beach directly ahead to scan it on either side. The crossbowman – assuming it was a man – was about 200 yards to the right. Behind him a group of people was pulling at something on the shingle. They could be either men or women, their loose, dark clothes streaming in the wind. Arthur knew what they were: wreckers, villagers drawn to the stormy beach to scavenge and murder.

Arthur changed direction, aiming for the beach as far from the wreckers as possible. To the left a tumble of rocks divided one reach of shingle from the next, with maybe a hiding place for them.

'Hurry, hurry! Damn your eyes, or I'll leave you to be gutted by a Scots fishwife!'

He dragged and kicked Richard over the slippery rocks. The wreckers had seen them and were hurrying towards them.

Richard had fainted. Arthur hauled him over the last of the rocks and faced the next stretch of beach. A line of men was spread across it, advancing towards them. They halted, and Arthur saw the glint of steel.

He caught his breath and let Richard's body slide onto the shingle. 'This is the end for both of us, Richard. This is where we die.'

'They're the *streltski*, you blind fool,' hissed Yelena. 'Run to meet them!'

The voice came not from inside his head, but from his ear.

'God's truth! Why are you here, Yelena?'

'I came to meet you. I hoped you'd be pleased to see me. And drop that old fool. Leave him for the Scots.'

'I can't leave him, Yelena.'

'Now you can,' she replied. She took the knife from Arthur's waistband and slid it into Richard's throat as calmly as a butcher in a meat market. He did not even shudder and there was no immediate gush of blood.

Arthur gaped incredulously.

'An old Tartar custom. Never leave the wounded for the enemy. Now leave him and run. I'll occupy them a while.'

'But you, Yelena?'

'I am a slave. Now run!'

'Yelena!'

'See you in Paradise.'

She climbed up onto the rocks and stood in full view of the advancing wreckers, glaring at them defiantly, her black hair streaming in the wind. Raising her arms, she began to chant, stepping down towards them over the wet granite.

The mob halted in amazement and then began to shrink back.

'She's nae witch, y' fools,' called one of them. 'She's nae more than a crazed wench.' Still they shrank back, and then one of them hurled a beach stone. It caught Yelena on the side of the head and she went down. It broke the spell, and the mob were onto her.

Arthur had to choose quickly between joining Yelena in Paradise or letting her buy him a few moments more to get within closer range of the *streltski*.

He ran towards the *streltski*, heedless of the sharp stones under his bare toes. Ahead of him the arquebusiers deployed with the same unhurried formality they had shown on the Arctic ice. Despite the wind and wet the sergeant had his pot of fire, patrolling the line to light each man's matchcord and tap the levelled firearm to ensure that it aimed off for the breeze. Arthur remembered that this time he must throw himself flat as soon as he saw the flash.

Oh, how he had hated the Russians, even before he knew they were Russians! How he had hated their lances and pikes and arquebuses and their borrowed cannon. Now he was in a race between the screaming murderers at his back and the shelter of a line of Russian steel.

A gust of flame belched from the levelled handguns.

'I owe you my life yet again, m' lady.'

'I doubt the queen of Scotland wanted another war with England just for the sake of hanging you and your friends,

Arthur,' laughed Kate. 'She has problems enough of her own. Besides, I enjoy freeing prisoners. 'Tis more exciting than selling kerseys.'

Not that I am very good at selling kerseys, she thought. Arthur would probably do it far better. She had found it easier to save London and conquer a Russian province than to give her household a livelihood. And now she had helped to hold Scotland to ransom and release three score prisoners, including an ambassador.

How strange that they had so mocked Sir Hugh for his exploits in Scotland at that meeting two years ago at Penshurst, only to end the Cathay voyage with an expedition to Edinburgh to force the Scots to hand over the men and treasure the Company had lost on Peterhead beach.

Kate had not been as confident or carefree over the past few weeks as she now pretended. The *Philip and Mary* had been as lucky as ever and had reached the Thames without incident four weeks after leaving Wardhouse. The cargo had sold well, especially the train oil, but for several weeks nothing was heard of the other three ships. Kate was sleepless with dread and her gossiping servants diagnosed lovesickness for the missing pilot general. Then word came from the English embassy in Scotland that Osip Nepa and his staff had been brought to Edinburgh by one of the Scots nobles from somewhere north of Aberdeen, where their ship had been wrecked. There was also an unknown number of English survivors, some of whom had been brought to the capital.

The Scottish court was strangely silent. They did not try to hide the Russian presence in the city, but there was no communication with England. Mary of Scotland might be more beautiful than her namesake in London but her hold on government was much less sure; the Scots were divided on how to handle their unexpected visitors.

Kate went straight to the queen at Whitehall. This was a matter of state that went beyond affairs of commerce. Mary responded with her usual resolution. A commission was appointed to go into Scotland to trace the survivors and retrieve the gifts from the tsar. It was given a strong military escort and a fleet of five heavily armed ships, ready, if need be, to take Edinburgh once again and teach the Scots how to behave towards an ambassador.

As soon as the English appeared in the Firth of Forth the Scots had sent out a messenger to assure them that the Muscovy ambassador (as they called him) and his entourage were safe and well and had been held in custody only for their protection. He promised they would be handed over, along with the English sailors who had been brought to Edinburgh, and that the English Commissioners would be allowed to visit the scene of the wreck where they could trace any other survivors and search for the tsar's treasure (of which the Scots denied any knowledge). The only condition was that the English should not enter Edinburgh.

The English disembarked at Leith and parked their cannon overlooking the Scots capital. The Scots brought their Russian prisoner-guests down to the port in great state. Osip Nepa was mounted on a fine white horse and he and his compatriots all had handsome new coats. The English sailors trudged behind in the clothes in which they had been washed ashore. The sun glittered on the waters of the Firth and the air was so clear that the hills of Fife looked close enough to touch.

Kate met Arthur on the quay. She seemed almost lightheaded with joy and embraced him eagerly with no thought for the onlookers. Not that some mistresses were not prodigal with kisses among their household, but kisses from a fair lady always attract more comment. Arthur was confused and embarrassed. It was wonderful to see her so happy, but she did not yet know about Richard.

'It pains me to tell you this, m' lady, but we lost our captain. Mister Chancellor is dead.'

'Dear Arthur, it is too soon to bury hope. You say you joined with the Russians and stayed with them on the beach until the Earl of Mar's men arrived and took charge of you. Perhaps others came ashore elsewhere and are still in the countryside.'

Arthur was puzzled that she seemed to be consoling him for the loss, despite the fact that while he had lost an enemy, she had lost a lover. To have saved Richard would have cleansed his soul and spared Kate, but his loss spared Arthur from having to serve the man he still thought of as Leeuna's murderer.

'My lady, the villagers of this country do not shelter distressed seamen – at least, not strangers. It breaks my heart to tell you, but I saw him die. I was with him. He was murdered by the wreckers. I brought him ashore but he was too hurt to run from them. Yelena stayed with him to defend him and cover my escape. She wanted to be with him to the end.'

'I think she died to save you, Arthur. She was an ill-formed creature but she was brave and loyal, and I think more than a little in love with you.'

Arthur blushed. 'You flatter me, m' lady, but her attachment was only to Mister Chancellor, though I am sure that he thought of her merely as a servant and took her as a consort in Russia solely after the custom of the country.'

'I am sorry to hear that our pilot general is dead – it is a great loss to the Company – but you need not strain to defend his private life.' She paused, as if debating what to say next. 'At one time I had hoped that Richard might ask me to marry him – perhaps you guessed as much – for I need a man to run my enterprise. I am not a good merchant. I became a heroine in the late rebellion mainly because I valued my life and fortune less than most Londoners. Richard was well thought of as a trader.'

'I am sorry to have had to bear such bad news.'

'I need no pity. I was trying to save myself and my enterprise by giving myself to a wealthy and well-connected man. It is something that good-looking women often do. I have few other assets and my face will not be comely forever.'

'My lady, I would happily serve you all my life, comely or no.'

'Arthur, let us find somewhere where we cannot be observed so easily.'

'That may advertise us more than staying with the crowd.'

'I don't care.' Her effervescent joy had vanished, and she was flushed and distraught. 'I don't care. I am beyond caring. Arthur, dear Arthur, I have been in Purgatory waiting for your ship to arrive, and then knowing you were a prisoner of the Scots.' She paused and fought for words. ''Tis proper that we each remember our station but sometimes...'

She began to sob, and shook so heavily that Arthur was frightened she would slip on the slabs of the quay or topple into the dock. He put his arms around her to steady her. He wanted to kiss away her tears and tell her that he was there to comfort her.

'Arthur,' she said, clinging to him with surprising vigour, 'it is most improper of you to behave like this in front of the assembled dignitaries of three nations. You have ruined my reputation. Do you think you could now make an honest woman of me?'

Author's Note

The idea for this book was born over twenty-five years ago, not by the White Sea but the Black Sea. I was sitting in a restaurant overlooking the Black Sea with a group of tourists visiting what was then the Soviet Union. The room was lined with stained glass panels illustrating great scenes from Russian history. One panel showed a group of men in Tudor dress standing before a tall bearded figure in a long robe. It was England's first ambassador to Russia, Richard Chancellor, meeting Ivan the Terrible. In later years I was to see the same picture in many other places, in Russian schoolbooks and in mosaics on the ceilings of the Moscow underground. The picture and the episode it portrays are familiar to the Russians, although none of our English tour group could identify it.

For nearly a century English and Russian history were intertwined. There is more English Elizabethan and early Stuart silverware in the Kremlin than in England. The silverware in England was mostly melted down in the Civil War; the English silver pieces in the Kremlin are the Russia Company's annual gifts to the tsar. Russia's first bank was formed to trade with England, and collapsed when the price of honey fell on the London market. The inn where Richard Chancellor stayed in Moscow is still called the English House, although it is now a museum stranded in the car park of the vast Rossaya Hotel.

This book is an attempt to recover this episode for an English-speaking audience, for it was significant for England too. It was England's first venture into the Age of Discovery, and although Richard Chancellor turned back at Moscow, other 'adventurers' for the company reached the Caspian, Persia and Central Asia, and brought silk to London via the Arctic. Many of them were also later prominent in colonising North America.

This book is, however, primarily an entertainment. It is historical fiction, fantasy woven on a framework of fact. Richard Chancellor really did reach Russia by accident while trying to sail across the Pole to China, he did become the confidant of the tsar, and he was finally murdered on a Scottish beach. The Kentish rebels really did loot Knightsbridge, Sir Hugh Willoughby really did sail his two ships to Nova Zemlya and try to winter in Lapland, and he and his officers really were found (according to the contemporary historian Hakluyt) seated around the table in the admiral's cabin, frozen dead 'twixt cup and lip'.

Sir Henry Sydney, John Dee, Sebastian Cabot, Stephen Burroughs, Ivan the Terrible, Tsarina Anastasia Romanova, the monk Sylvester, Metropolitan Makary, Abbot Philip, and many other of my more colourful characters really lived and acted in this drama but the cabin boy, Arthur Petty, and the young widow, Kate Thomas, are products of my imagination, as is most of the action in Lapland.

However, the Lapp war (or guerrilla skirmish) has a historical context and my account of Lapp life is based (if freely) on contemporary sources. The Russians and Swedes had rival claims to Lapland and Ivan did send an expedition across the country to set up a fort on the Baltic. The confrontation was abandoned when the Livonian War broke out further south. If the English had been involved they would have had cause not to record it. They were certainly no strangers to the Lapps, and brought their seal oil to England to light London streets.

Kate is fictional, but there were five women among the founder shareholders of the Russia Company, all widows (i.e. heads of household). Elizabeth and Mary were not the only women to play a part in public life in the 16th century England. My own college in Oxford was founded by a rich widow only fifty years after the events in this book. All such women owed their place to inherited wealth and status, but so too did most of the men.

The Tartar princess Yelena is also an invention, but who is to say that Richard did not have a mistress in Russia?

The English dialogue is not written in 16th century English, any more than the Lapp conversations are written in Sami. However, some fragments of the beautiful Tudor English of the Company's Articles are included in Chapter Three so that I can share the delight with my readers.

My main source is Richard Hakluyt's *Principal Navigations Voyages Traffiques and Discoveries of the English Nation* (1589). The Cathay voyage is the main substance of Volume 1. Hakluyt shared rooms at Oxford with Philip Sydney, Sir Henry's son, so he had privileged access to the family traditions. For the life of the Lapps I have used Olaus Magnus' *A Description of the Northern Peoples* (1555) and Ernst Manker's *People of Eight Seasons* (1963). The Russian material is largely drawn from Benson Bobrick's *Ivan the Terrible* (1987), and for the Wyatt rebellion I have used *Tudor Rebellions* by Anthony Fletcher and Diarmaid MacCulloch (1997).

Since I first wrote this story there has been a revived interest in the Muscovy voyages. In 2005 Kit Meyers published *North-East Passage to Muscovy: Stephen Burrough and the First Tudor Explorations*, (Sutton Publishing). As the title states this is mainly about Stephen Burroughs, and describes his later attempts to sail beyond the White Sea to Cathay. In 2013 James Evans published *Merchant Adventurers: the Voyage of Discovery that Transformed Tudor England* (Weidenfeld and Nicolson). This covers the same ground as my fictional account, based on the most recent research. He, too, distrusts the story that Willoughby and his officers died by being flash-frozen during the course of a meal, and supports my view that they probably died of carbon monoxide poisoning. He presumes this was accidental but I do not think it at all impossible that it was engineered by the crew. On at least one polar expedition in the 19th century the crew poisoned the captain so as to turn back.

Hakluyt collected over a hundred sea stories which he first published in 1589 and republished in 1600. A new scholarly edition is currently being prepared by a consortium, including the Greenwich Maritime Museum. I have used another of his stories to write *Freedom's Pilgrim* (Amazon Kindle, 2014) about an English boy who survived the battle of San Juan d'Ulloa, when John Hawkins and his slave trading fleet were ambushed by the Spaniards (1568), and who was marooned in Mexico, to reach England seventeen years later after an amazing series of adventures in America and Spain.

If you wish to know more about me and what I have written please go to my blog: busywords.wordpress.com.